THE SECRET KING

C.J. Miller

HARLEQUIN® ROMANTIC SUSPENSE

If you purchased this book without a cover you should be aware that this book is stolen property. It was reported as "unsold and destroyed" to the publisher, and neither the author nor the publisher has received any payment for this "stripped book."

Recycling programs
for this product may
not exist in your area.

ISBN-13: 978-0-373-27936-4

The Secret King

Copyright © 2015 by C.J. Miller

All rights reserved. Except for use in any review, the reproduction or utilization of this work in whole or in part in any form by any electronic, mechanical or other means, now known or hereinafter invented, including xerography, photocopying and recording, or in any information storage or retrieval system, is forbidden without the written permission of the publisher, Harlequin Enterprises Limited, 225 Duncan Mill Road, Don Mills, Ontario M3B 3K9, Canada.

This is a work of fiction. Names, characters, places and incidents are either the product of the author's imagination or are used fictitiously, and any resemblance to actual persons, living or dead, business establishments, events or locales is entirely coincidental.

This edition published by arrangement with Harlequin Books S.A.

For questions and comments about the quality of this book, please contact us at CustomerService@Harlequin.com.

® and TM are trademarks of Harlequin Enterprises Limited or its corporate affiliates. Trademarks indicated with ® are registered in the United States Patent and Trademark Office, the Canadian Intellectual Property Office and in other countries.

Printed in U.S.A.

www.Harlequin.com

C.J. Miller loves to hear from her readers and can be contacted through her website, cj-miller.com. She lives in Maryland with her husband, son and daughter. C.J. believes in first loves, second chances and happily-ever-after.

Books by C.J. Miller

Harlequin Romantic Suspense

Hiding His Witness
Shielding the Suspect
Protecting His Princess
Traitorous Attraction
Under the Sheik's Protection
Colton Holiday Lockdown
Taken by the Con
Capturing the Huntsman

Conspiracy Against the Crown

The Secret King

Visit C.J.'s Author Profile page at Harlequin.com, or cj-miller.com, for more titles.

To my brother, Dr. Andy. Your sense of humor cheers me on my darkest days, your love of adventure inspires me and your unending support means the world. Love you, buddy.

Chapter 1

Casimir felt the pulse of power in the ballroom of the Acacian castle. Three influential leaders, each with their axes to grind, were setting problems aside tonight in a public display of unity that hadn't been witnessed in the past twenty years. The king of Acacia was turning sixty and the night was meant for frivolity.

Too bad one of the kings would die tonight by Casimir's hand. He hated to ruin the party for the king of Acacia, but attacking the king of Rizari away from his palace made the logistics much simpler.

With the president of Icarus's help, Casimir had smuggled his weapons into the room. He was ready. He had mentally run the plan dozens of times. He had trained. He would do what needed to be done, shed his fake identity for good and he would disappear, taking asylum in Icarus.

Casimir was careful not to touch the gun at his side, a habit he'd formed in the military to ensure it was in place. The knife in its sheath at his hip brushed against his pants. He did nothing to call attention to himself. In addition to the three leaders, the room was filled with security—each of the king's guards and the president's servicemen, all armed to the teeth.

Danae, the eldest princess of Acacia had her guards close as well. She was the heir to the throne, and watching her, Casimir understood why she was being courted by the king of Rizari. Princess Danae looked like a woman who liked to have fun, but who couldn't organize her closet, much less a country. Her brunette curls bounced as she laughed and threw her head back in delight.

The younger princess of Acacia, Serena, was standing alone on the perimeter of the party. Unlike her sister's vibrant, fanciful energy, Serena had a quiet, serious beauty about her. Her blond hair hung around her shoulders and she looked almost ethereal in a light blue gown. She sipped her glass of wine and watched the party with little change in her expression. No one spoke to her. She had to be bored. Casimir had been studying King Warrington's social circles, and he found her behavior curious, very different from what he had experienced in Rizari. To blend in to the royal social circle, extraversion was critical.

Why was the princess so removed? He knew little about the king and princesses of Acacia. They didn't factor into his plan, except that he was using their castle to exact his revenge. He would send an anonymous note of apology once he'd returned to Icarus and was safe in his new life, revenge complete. Perhaps then his soul would be quiet and peaceful.

"She is beautiful, no?" Demetrius DeSante said. The president of Icarus, and his good friend, spoke softly. Though DeSante and Casimir were careful not to give away how close they were, especially in regard to this conspiracy, DeSante had been making the rounds through the ballroom, talking to everyone with a title or a fortune. Casimir was pretending to have the latter.

Though DeSante had been accused of many bad things, he was a good leader and one of his best qualities was his charisma. He could talk anyone into doing what he wanted. It was another way he was dangerous.

The lights flickered and then went out.

"Is this your plan? You're doing this now?" De-Sante's voice in his ear.

The blackout was not part of his plan. Casimir was nowhere near King Warrington of Rizari. Casimir could only see by candlelight in the darkened room. Acacia was plagued by energy distribution problems. "Not my plan. Rolling blackouts—"

The sentence died in his mouth. At the sound of gun-fire, Casimir dove for the floor, instinctively dragging President DeSante with him. The ceramic tile was cold against his hands, but his body broke out into a sweat and adrenaline charged through him. Gunfire had that effect on him. He had already been keyed up, waiting for his chance to kill Warrington and now, he was all systems go and on full alert.

The music died. More gunfire and the room was filled with screaming and shouting. Glass was break-ing and objects hit the floor. A woman's heel pierced his hand. Damn stiletto shoes. Shaking off the pain,

Casimir belly crawled toward the darkness, away from the windows. If an active gunman was peppering the area with shots, he was safer in the darkest corner of the room. Once there, he would take stock of his position and kill whomever had decided to ruin his revenge.

Casimir assessed the area. Though his eyesight was compromised, his hearing was sharp and his nose searching. As if his senses had been attuned to violence, he peered through the candlelit glow of the room. The king of Acacia was slumped on the floor, the older princess next to him. In the dimness, it was impossible to know if the king was dead or injured. The sound of gunfire was elsewhere in the castle. Seeing no one guarding the king, Casimir filled in the blanks. Security had fled in the direction of the shooting, leaving the bodies of the king and princess alone. Were they already dead?

Dread consumed him when Princess Serena's face came into view. She was moving toward her father and sister. Was she trying to get herself killed? Wasn't she aware she should run away from bullets, not toward them?

Forgetting his own safety, Casimir rose to his feet and sprinted toward her. Princess Serena was pulling her father behind a table. For protection? Her face was grief-stricken and her eyes met his. They screamed for help, pleaded with someone to come to her aid.

Women in need were a soft spot for him. He could have used the darkness to search for King Warrington and kill him. But the probability of finding him unguarded was slim. More pressing was the beautiful woman who needed his help.

Serena shouldn't have come to the capital tonight. She had decided at the last minute to forgo her usual excuses and instead had driven to the castle for her father's birthday.

Serena's face felt sticky and her feet slid on the floor. She had to drag her father and sister to safety. Someone was shooting into the ballroom. No answers came to mind as to why.

She couldn't find her father's security. She had commanded her cousin and personal secretary Iliana to hide in the coat closet. But Serena couldn't leave her father and sister exposed. She had no medical training, but she could be with them until help arrived.

Pulling her father's weight was nearly impossible. Why was the floor so slippery? Her shoes slid out from under her again. Her dress tangled around her ankles as she fought to stand. A shadow blotted out the little light shining in her direction. Help had arrived! She lifted her head to welcome whomever had come to assist her.

Instead, she came face to face with the muzzle of a gun.

Before she could scream, not that screaming would have made a difference in the current environment, a hot and wet liquid hit her face. She closed her eyes and when she opened them, the lights were on again. She blinked as her eyes adjusted to the scene.

The man who'd been holding a gun at her was slumped in the arms of a stranger. A very dashing stranger, with reddish-brown hair, hazel eyes, a mustache and goatee, pronounced cheekbones and a perfectly straight nose. Serena was sure she had never met this man before and yet he seemed so familiar.

He threw the body to the side. She winced at the sound it made hitting the porcelain tile. The man slid his knife into a sheath beneath his black suit coat. A knife-wielding stranger had saved her life.

He extended his arms to her. On the heels of a violent attack, she should be more wary of him, but her instincts told her he wouldn't harm her. He had saved her life. If he wanted her dead, he could have allowed the gunman to kill her.

She took his hand. Her feet slid beneath her. Blood. It was blood she'd been slipping in. In stark contrast to the gruesome scene, the stranger was watching her with the kindest eyes she had ever known. She turned her head to look at her father and sister, to see what help they needed.

The man put his hand on her cheek. "Do not look, Princess. This is not what you should remember." He took a white handkerchief from his pants pocket and wiped her face. Blood smeared the material.

He began to escort her away. Suddenly, her father's guards flew in her direction, ripping her from the man's arms and slamming him against the wall.

"Release the princess!" More shouting and commands.

Serena held out her hands toward the stranger this time. "Please stop. Stop! I command you to stop! This man saved my life." Now the guards appeared again? In the chaos, they had left her and her family unprotected. Hysteria threatened to consume her. She stared at the stranger. If she looked away from him, she would look back at her father and her sister.

"Come, Princess, you need to be taken to the safe room."

The stranger looked over his shoulder at her. Her guards released him and he turned toward her, bowing slightly. "You will call on me again if I am needed."

He fled the ballroom, toward the sound of sirens. He was gone before she realized she didn't know his name.

President DeSante pulled Casimir away from the crowd. Everyone was being questioned by the police. In the circle of DeSante's guards, they could speak freely.

"Was this your plan?" DeSante asked.

"I already told you it was not." Casimir threw off his fury and focused. Someone had beaten him to the punch, but the assassins had killed the wrong king, at least in his thinking. "I had nothing to do with this." His plan had been to kill King Warrington of Rizari only. His revenge did not include a massacre.

"This was chaos. This was reckless." DeSante's fingers bit into Casimir's arm and his eyes were blazing with intensity. "This was not the revenge you had planned, but this is an opportunity. Don't squander it."

An opportunity?

DeSante spoke quietly. "Think like a king. Who is next to inherit the throne in Acacia?"

"The princess. Princess Serena." It had been difficult to walk away from her. But he couldn't stay. He had no reason to remain with her and if he did, too many questions would be asked.

"That's right. The princess, the woman whose life you saved."

Casimir mustered control of his anger over his lost chance. He focused on what his old friend was saying. They were not blood relatives, but they were brothers on the battlefield and DeSante owed Casimir a debt. A debt that would not be paid until Casimir'd had his revenge.

"I killed one of the assassins." Casimir had slit the throat of the man who had planned to kill the princess at point-blank range. The assassin had gotten what was coming to him and Casimir felt no regret for his actions.

"That you did. I promised you revenge and asylum from the fallout of that revenge, but this is more than I could have given you. Use her."

Use her for what? DeSante was a chess master, seeing many moves ahead in the game and in life. For Casimir, his anger often drove him harder than reason. He shook off his anger and took a cleansing breath. "You said she is to inherit the throne. Are the king and Princess Danae dead?" From what he had seen, it didn't look as if they had much chance of survival, but doctors could sometimes perform miracles.

DeSante inclined his head toward the ambulances. "An official announcement has not been made, but I would assume that yes, they are dead."

The ground had been covered in blood. The assassins had worked quickly.

True peace in the Mediterranean between Icarus, Acacia and Rizari had never been achieved. After tonight, Casimir guessed it would be impossible. Accusations would be made and blame would be spread around enough for everyone to be hit with some.

But perhaps DeSante was right and this was an opportunity for Casimir to achieve a goal he had never believed possible. As a royal, Princess Serena would be part of King Warrington's social circle. After all, he had been planning to marry Serena's sister. Casimir could use contact with Serena to keep the king close while Casimir planned his next move. If he was lucky and played his cards right, instead of killing King Warrington outright as he had intended tonight, perhaps he could clear his mother's name. Casimir could make a play for the crown and the throne of Rizari. The crown that rightfully belonged to him.

King Warrington would pay for what he had done to Casimir and his mother, but not with his life. Instead he would lose everything that mattered to him.

"Do you think that President DeSante is responsible for the bloodshed?" Iliana asked. She set a cup of coffee next to Serena's easel.

Serena didn't look away from her canvas. She had been painting since midday. Painting and thinking. Her long-term therapist, Dr. Shaw, had helped, but she'd had only a couple weeks to process what had happened the night her father, sister and fifteen others had been killed in a massacre the media had dubbed the Birthday Bloodbath.

Serena found the name distasteful, but she found everything about the situation distasteful and almost too painful to bear. "He denies it. The investigation hasn't uncovered who hired the assassins to murder my father."

According to the one killer who had been apprehended by the police, the deaths of her sister and the others had been collateral damage. As if they hadn't considered that firing bullets into a crowd in the dark would result in deaths. Serena wasn't surprised to learn the ME had found amphetamines in the assassins' bloodstreams. Their behavior had been aggressive and erratic.

Serena had never planned to be queen, and yet she would be Acacia's queen in a few weeks' time. She hadn't had a boyfriend, and yet negotiations were in progress for her to marry the king of Rizari. Samuel

Warrington had been courting Danae, and now, as if the two sisters were interchangeable, he planned to pursue Serena.

Serena had asked for a fortnight to grieve away from the public eye in the seclusion of her beach house, knowing that being granted that amount of time was a boon. Her personal feelings didn't matter. Her country needed a strong alliance with King Warrington and Rizari, the closest country to the east, to keep the dictator of Icarus on their western shores from attacking during a time of weakness. Acacia's Assembly would keep the country running while she grieved, but the country needed their princess.

King Warrington would provide military protection in exchange for uniting their countries and placing his own advisers in positions of influence in Acacia's Assembly. He had agreed to respect her country's culture and traditions and give Serena a certain amount of independence. It was the best and only offer she'd had. Her advisers were discreetly inquiring about other arrangements, but Icarus, through that detestable Demetrius DeSante, was rattling its saber, letting it be known that the death of the king of Acacia had presented them with an opportunity to strike. Rizari and Icarus had long been enemies and Acacia, being geographically in between them, was subjected to the fallout of that long-standing feud.

Serena's solitary time was up and she would need to paste on a brave face and pretend as if she could be a competent and strong queen. Danae had been the perfect princess and would have been the perfect queen, the perfect bride and the perfect wife. Serena would be none of those things. Her formal training was untried and she hadn't been blessed with the grace and elegance her sister had had.

Serena had much to do, much to plan, yet she was spending an inordinate amount of time thinking about the stranger who had saved her life. No one could give her his name. Witnesses who had seen him save her life provided varying accounts of the incident. He had been described as brown-haired and blond, tall and short, overweight and slender.

Someone recalled seeing him speaking to President DeSante, but when questioned, that loathsome man had claimed to know nothing about Serena's protector. Serena knew how to tell when DeSante was lying: his mouth was moving.

Serena wouldn't give up looking for the man with the kind eyes. Though her country didn't have the resources to launch a national manhunt, especially for a man who was a hero, Serena had a few private investigators searching for him. The birthday guest list was being reviewed to see if someone could discover his identity. Whoever brought her information would be handsomely rewarded.

Serena wondered about the man with the gentle, compassionate eyes. Could he have been from Icarus? From Rizari? That would explain why no one seemed to know him. He had been granted entrance to her father's birthday, meaning he was either invited or had attended as someone's guest.

Her emotions were volatile, grief amplifying every feeling, and Serena tried not to become frustrated with her inability to find him.

Serena heard tires spinning on gravel. Looking out her second-story window, she saw her uncle Santino driving to her beach house, his off-road vehicle kicking up dirt. Her guards stopped him for a moment and then waved him through. After parking in front of her house, he climbed out of his car, limping as he walked. Though he had a cane, he hated using it, believing it made him appear weak. Uncle Santino had a scar that intersected his right eye and as a child, Serena had called him a pirate. The scar was a result of a tragic boating accident that had killed his wife soon after they were married.

Serena set down her paintbrush. She met her uncle on the wraparound porch, holding up her hands. "I would hug you, but I need to wash up first."

"Painting again?" he asked.

"Yes." Art calmed her and the past two weeks had given her many reasons to need serenity.

Iliana poked her head out on to the porch, her long red hair swinging around her shoulder. "Why don't I prepare tea for everyone?" Iliana was her cousin on her mother's side and officially Serena's personal secretary. But their relationship went far deeper than boss and subordinate.

Serena and her uncle had met several times since the massacre. Sometimes they spoke about her father and sister, sometimes about the kingdom and sometimes about nothing of importance.

Santino sat at the kitchen table. With the curtain open, Serena counted four guards at the back of her house. With her being a potential target for yet unknown reasons, her security team wasn't taking chances.

"When are you meeting with King Samuel?" her uncle asked.

King Samuel had been her sister's boyfriend and according to Danae, he had been smitten with her. How could Serena put her heart into a relationship that should have been her sister's? It felt twisted. "He wants to meet tomorrow evening for a dinner party."

It was her understanding that others would be in attendance, which should make it less awkward in some ways, more stressful in others. Serena would need to behave and speak in a certain manner. Her every action would be scrutinized and criticized. The media would pick apart her clothing, hairstyle and how she accessorized. Serena dreaded it and promised herself she wouldn't read their articles, which would undoubtedly accent her every inadequacy and include a snarky review of her love life or lack thereof.

"You look tired. Are you getting enough sleep?" her uncle asked.

"Not really." Thoughts of her sister and father kept her awake and on particularly bad nights, she lay in her bed and waited for morning to come.

Nightmares about the night her family had died, nightmares about the mother she hadn't had in years and nightmares about her future haunted the little sleep she did have.

"Still thinking about the man who saved your life?" her uncle asked.

Sometimes. Often. "Now and then." Why was she so obsessed with someone she had met once, for no more than a few minutes? If he wanted to be found, he would be.

What if there was a compelling reason he wanted to remain anonymous to her? He might fear the media response. He might not enjoy the idea of his rescue story being printed in the papers. It was another reason she had to keep her search quiet.

"Let it go, Serena. You don't know what you saw. You'll go crazy if you let this consume you," her uncle said.

He had urged her to forget everything she could about that night. Serena wasn't in any hurry to relive it, although occasionally brief flashes from that night interrupted her thoughts. "I know someone saved me."

"And then disappeared. He could have been working with the assassins."

"Yet he chose to kill one of them to save me?" It didn't make sense. Unless her instincts were totally skewed, her protector wasn't involved in the plot to kill her father.

"Please let this go, Serena. You will only be hurt again. I can't stand to see you in more pain. You have enough grief to manage without adding to it. This fixation with him is unhealthy."

Maybe she was thinking about her protector because it was easier and far more pleasant to think about him than to think about her father's and sister's deaths or how much she missed them. Though she had not lived in the castle and had been happy to have some independence, knowing she could reach out at any time was a comfort. Now, she felt alone.

Serena's uncle wished to protect her. But he didn't need to protect her from the man who'd saved her. Iliana returned to serve the tea and Serena changed the subject. No point in upsetting her uncle who was wrestling with his own grief over losing his older brother and his niece.

Her uncle left around nine that evening.

"You're not giving up on finding the mystery man, are you?" Iliana asked.

"Not a chance," Serena said.

"Why don't you let me fly to Icarus and speak to DeSante? He knows something about everything and his spies are everywhere. Give me a few minutes alone with him and I can force the information out of him." She lifted her knee mimicking hitting the dictator in the crotch.

Serena cracked a smile, rare for her these days. "I don't think that's advisable. He has big, scary guards and you're topping out at five foot two."

Iliana set her hands on her hips. "For you, I'd kick his butt. You know I could. I'm pretty mean when I'm angry."

Serena loved that about her cousin. She was loyal and spunky and feared nothing. Her business phone rang and Iliana frowned and answered it, her tone professional and cool. "Princess Serena's office. Iliana speaking. How may I help you?"

Iliana swore under her breath. "He's a real piece of work. Hold on." She pressed a button on her phone.

Dread coiled inside Serena. "What now? What's happened?" Was her uncle okay? He had only left a few moments earlier.

"The coast guard is on the phone. The Icarus navy is preventing ships from entering our waters."

Icarus's navy, one of the fastest, biggest military operations in the region, boasted hi-tech equipment and sailors who came from generations of sailors. They were experts on the water. "What did you say?" Serena asked.

Iliana repeated her statement, this time slower. Serena had heard her the first time, but she hadn't fully processed the information. Was DeSante planning to attack? Serena had no military experience. How should she maneuver in this situation? Who should she call? Though she had the ear of the head of the Assembly and she was supposed to wield influence, she was green and DeSante knew it.

It was dark, but that wouldn't matter to the experienced Icarus navy. Was DeSante hoping to catch her off guard, ill equipped and scared? The idea incensed her. She might be weak now, but she wouldn't be for long.

"Has the coast guard made contact with DeSante? What does he want?" Serena asked.

"I don't know, hold on." After a few moments, she said, "They say they want your confirmation that it's okay to let boats through."

Her confirmation? That made no sense. Icarus wasn't in charge of screening what boats entered and exited through their waters. Acacia and Icarus had no such arrangement. "What do they really want?"

Iliana repeated the question into the phone. "He wants to speak to you. He being DeSante, the warlord."

DeSante wasn't exactly a warlord, but he wasn't a peaceable man either. He had come to be president of his country during a violent coup.

This was a warning, then, from Icarus. If she refused to speak to him, DeSante would place an embargo on Acacia.

The dictator of Icarus was playing a dangerous game, mostly dangerous to Acacia with its weaker navy and dependency on imports. If DeSante refused to allow boats into their ports, Acacians would starve. "Put Demetrius DeSante on the line." She sounded stronger than she felt. She had been avoiding the dictator's requests for an audience and instead had allowed Iliana to put him off and explain that she'd needed time to grieve. Apparently, that time was over.

Iliana handed Serena the phone.

"Good evening," Serena said, keeping her voice cool and polite.

"Finally, I have the pleasure of speaking with you," DeSante said.

She wasn't in the mood for a conversation with DeSante. "Let the boats through."

"I would be glad to. I am an ally who can secure your western waters from enemies."

What a load of crap. Her enemies consisted of him and whomever had killed her family, although Serena still suspected they were one in the same. "Let them through."

"As you command. I expect a meeting with you shortly or my navy may again feel the need to question boats coming close to your shores."

"You'll have your meeting," she said. She hung up the phone with a quaking hand.

Iliana grabbed her arm. "You did good, Serena. It's okay. You sounded strong and the right amount of pissed off and polite."

It wasn't okay. The sharks were circling because they smelled blood in the water.

"She's looking for you," DeSante said.

Casimir knew it. He needed to play it cool. If he came on too strong, Serena would be suspicious. Casimir needed to approach her in the right manner with his plan in place.

When he was ready, he would allow himself to be found. Or perhaps he would show up at her castle and catch her off guard. The biggest downside to his plan was living with his fake persona a little longer. Being a wealthy heir who liked to party didn't suit him, but it had been his cover to infiltrate King Warrington's social circles. Though he had never breached the inner circle, he'd gotten to know enough royals and hangers-on that he couldn't change his identity now.

"Someone may recognize me and tell her who I am," Casimir said.

"As long as they give her the cover story and do not reveal who you actually are, you can handle it," DeSante said.

Casimir could handle anything. He would leak the story that he had been the man who'd saved the princess's life. It might keep him interesting to the royalty of Acacia and Rizari. Staying close gave him leverage to manipulate the situation to his benefit. "I'm not worried." Yet. Living a lie every day was almost as hard as harboring the rage he felt toward Samuel Warrington.

"Call me after you make your move," DeSante said.

"Will do."

Casimir hung up the phone and slid it into his pocket. Few people trusted the president of Icarus, but Casimir did without question. Not only did DeSante owe him, DeSante had a vested interest in Casimir taking control of Rizari. Having allies in the region and preventing Rizari from interfering with Icarus had long been DeSante's goal. With Casimir assuming the throne, DeSante would have the freedom to do as he wished.

Casimir entered his mother's house. His weekly meetings with her were difficult to press through, and grew worse with each visit. Casimir hated the stink of booze and cigarettes. "Hey, Mom."

His mother, Anna, rarely greeted him. She was sitting in the dark in her living room, like she often did. She had the television on, but seemed to be staring blankly at it. Casimir muted it. His mother hadn't always been this way. Every year, she grew noticeably more withdrawn, tired and depressed. Now, he couldn't convince her to sit outside on a nice day. She was a recluse and if he didn't do something, she would die in this dark, dank house.

"He's still alive," his mother said. She was looking haggard, having lost weight, and her skin appeared sallow.

Samuel Warrington was still alive. Casimir hadn't killed him. He had told his mother he would take care of it, but he had failed. The knowledge burned him. But he wouldn't give up on his new plan. "There were other assassins in the room. They killed the Acacian king and his daughter Danae."

His mother lit another cigarette. "What's that have to do with anything?"

Casimir hid his frustration. His mother's sole focus was revenge. "I couldn't get to Warrington in the confusion."

His mother said nothing and her silence reeked of censure. Her history with the king and his family was a bitter one.

One year into her marriage to King Constantine Warrington, he had falsely accused her of having an affair with his brother, Charles, and had exiled her. Anna had blamed Charles's jealous wife, Katarina, for manufacturing stories about her. She had fled to Icarus with a new identity. Fearing for her life and the life of her unborn child, she hadn't told the king that she had been pregnant with his baby. She had lived in Icarus and raised her son with her eyes on one goal: for Casimir to return to Rizari in glory and take his crown when he was of age.

But when Constantine and his brother were killed ten years ago, Casimir knew presenting himself as the rightful heir would earn him a knife in his back as well. He needed to be more careful, more crafty. Martyrdom wasn't the goal. Making things right for his family and Rizari was.

Casimir's existence and true parentage was a secret from everyone in the world, except his mother and DeSante, whom Casimir had allowed into his confidence when he was fifteen.

When his father had died, so had his mother's chance of revealing to her ex-husband his true heir. With false accusations about her participation in his and his brother's murders and her conviction without a trial, her life had spiraled further into darkness. Anna had sworn to Casimir all his life that she still loved his father. His death had robbed her of the family reunion she had not-so-secretly wished for. Anna had believed that Constantine would see that she had been loyal and that Katarina would be revealed as a liar.

That hadn't happened.

When Anna had heard rumors that Constantine and Charles had been killed by Charles's son, Samuel, in an effort to usurp the throne, she had made Casimir swear he would avenge his father's death by killing the king who had stolen his life.

Chapter 2

Iliana recognized the country calling code for Icarus and felt a jolt of adrenaline. She had arrived at the castle early that morning to start work and she was eager for a tussle with DeSante's goons.

They thought they could push Serena around because she was young and had been distant from her father for some years. There had been no bad blood between Serena and her father, but Serena preferred the quiet of her beach house and the private pursuit of her interests. She hadn't been idle. She had painted a number of amazing landscapes and was making a name for herself—at least, under her alias—in the international art community. Iliana had brokered deals for her in the United States, Canada, Italy and France as well as throughout the Mediterranean. Iliana's law degree had some use after all, which was a mild salve on her ego, considering she'd failed the bar exam three times.

"Princess Serena's office. How may I help you?"

"Iliana."

One word and Iliana knew instantly she was speaking with Demetrius DeSante, Serena's enemy and the biggest bully in the Mediterranean. He thought he could push around smaller countries like Acacia. Maybe he had the stronger navy and maybe his economy was larger, but he wouldn't push Serena around and he wouldn't push Iliana around either.

"This is she. Who is calling, please?" Pretending she was unaware would knock his ego down a peg.

He had the gall to laugh. Pompous jerk. "This is President DeSante. Iliana, I enjoy our talks so much. But please, call me Demetrius."

They had spoken twice before. Iliana had been openly hostile both times and she didn't regret it. "President? Is that your official title? I mostly hear you referred to as a dictator."

He was quiet for a beat and she wondered if she'd gone too far. Her mouth had gotten her in trouble before.

"I will take great delight in winning you over and hearing you call me by my given name."

A little shiver of relief mixed with pleasure danced over her. "I wouldn't hold your breath on that."

"Such hostility from someone I barely know. Of course, I would like to know you better. You've proven to be quite spirited. I like that in a companion."

Companion? What did that mean? Like a friend or a prostitute? She would be neither to him. Her heart raced and it was not because she found his confidence appealing. He was appalling. She would be wise to remember that. "What is it that you want? The princess is not available right now."

"Such a shame. I was hoping to speak with her this morning about several pressing matters."

"If you tell me what they are, I will relate them to the princess." She wondered if he would tell her anything. In the past, he had refused to give her details of why he was anxious to meet in person and speak with Serena.

"Her father kept the peace between Icarus and Rizari. I need to know the princess's stance on that."

Was DeSante interested in peace in the region or did he want to stir up trouble? "I can assure you the princess wants no bloodshed." Iliana shuddered, remembering the night of the king and Princess Danae's murder. Serena had commanded her to hide in a closet and then had run off to aid her father and sister. Risky and bold, it was the side of Serena that came roaring to life in defense of the people she loved. When Iliana had left the closet where she'd hidden with several other women, the ballroom had looked like a slaughterhouse. Even now, the ballroom had not been reopened. Iliana wondered if it ever would be.

"What do you want, Iliana? Because you sound like you want to wrap your hands around my throat and throttle me, which wouldn't be keeping with the princess's desire for peace."

She scoffed. "I don't want to wrap my hands around your anything." Why did that image elicit a strange stirring in her stomach?

"Perhaps you're attracted to me and you hate that, so you're lashing out."

"I am not attracted to you." Except it was a lie. The first time she had met him in person, she had had no defense against the rush of sensations. Her body had tingled and though he had been professional with her,

she'd harbored some decidedly nonprofessional thoughts
about him, his mouth, his body. She chalked it up to
hormones. Her attraction to the dictator meant nothing.
Handsome on the outside, he was a troll on the inside.
Handsome could trick her hormones. Mean would prevent her from doing anything about it.

"What is it that bothers you most about me?" De-
Sante asked.

Listing his deficiencies could get her killed. At least,
if rumors were true. "I do not feel safe enough to hon-
estly answer that question."

"You are afraid of me?" He sounded surprised.
Wasn't he accustomed to fear from his countrymen?

"I am afraid of nothing. I just don't want to disappear." Or be murdered in her bed.

"You have nothing to fear from me. I will not hurt
you. Not today and not ever. If I found out that you had
been harmed, I would seek vengeance for that atroc-
ity. A lady should never be on the receiving end of violence."

Why did he seem sincere? Why should she believe
that? Even more, why did he sound as if he were ear-
nestly trying to convince her? "How many people have
died at your hands, believing that same thing?"

"What I have done for my country is not something
I am ashamed of. I have spilled soldiers' blood, but I
have done so for the greater good."

The greater good, which had fortuitously brought
him into power.

"What is most difficult is accepting that you believe
I am a monster."

He was a monster. "Do you deny subjugating your
people?"

DeSante made a sound of disgust. "I deny it emphatically. If you are asking if my methods of leadership are harsh, then yes, they are. But I am not ashamed that every Icarus family has food on their table and important work that contributes to our economy."

Iliana had heard that conditions had improved in Icarus since DeSante had come into power. She couldn't quite accept how he had come to power, but she felt a chink in her armor.

"I want you to come to Icarus as my guest. I will show you. I will let you see with your own eyes."

His guest? Nothing in those words was sexual and yet her heart was doing somersaults. He had been secretive with the media and yet he wanted her to visit? "No." Her reasons for saying no were complex. She couldn't leave Serena now. She would feel like a traitor traveling to Icarus to spend time with DeSante. Spending time with DeSante under certain conditions could bring up some emotions she didn't want to confront.

Iliana did not have a good track record with men. She was easily seduced. DeSante could break down her defenses. Iliana knew it. She was loyal to Serena and she would remain that way.

"Perhaps you will be persuaded in the future."

To sleep with him? She smothered her outrage, realizing he'd meant changing her mind about traveling to Icarus. Iliana pulled her emotions under control. What about this man riled her so deeply? "We will see."

"I believed you to be an open-minded woman. Did I misjudge you?"

"Of course I'm open-minded. But I cannot travel to Icarus unless Princess Serena decides she wishes it.

Did you have anything else you wanted to talk to the princess about?"

"Tell her she is contemplating marrying a cad."

She hadn't heard that term in years. "A cad?"

"King Warrington will not make her happy."

"And you would?" Iliana asked, feeling a stab of jealousy at the idea of Serena dating President DeSante.

"Not at all. I am not interested in marrying the princess. My interests in her are political and professional."

Right. Though Serena hadn't had many boyfriends, mostly as a result of her avoiding crowds and staying away from being the center of attention, she was a beautiful, voluptuous woman. "I'm writing this down. You're not interested in war, you don't want Serena to marry the king and you're interested in her. Professionally."

"Don't forget that last word. My personal interests lie elsewhere. Until we speak again, and I do hope that is soon, be well. Good day, Iliana."

She hung up the phone being more turned on from one phone conversation than she had by her last boyfriend in the year they'd been together. President DeSante was the trifecta of attraction: bad boy, bad ass and far too handsome for his own good.

Serena took her guard's hand and stepped out of the town car to catch her balance and not trip over her gown. A plane flight and a long car ride had brought her to the palace of Rizari, King Warrington's home.

She smoothed her green dress, hoping it was appropriate for the evening's events. Iliana had helped her select it and yet Serena was a bundle of nerves about the entire visit, including what she was wearing. This was not where she shone. She was not great at small talk and mingling, and preferred to stay on the outskirts of a crowd and watch. Or better yet, to sketch or paint from a safe distance. Even hiding behind a camera had a certain appeal.

Before her father's birthday party, Serena had not been to a formal occasion in years, avoiding them with carefully constructed excuses. Grief knotted in her stomach and she blinked away tears. How she wished her father and her sister were still alive!

"Your Grace?" her guard asked.

Serena realized she had been standing rooted in the same place, looking up at the palace. It was a breathtaking display of architecture and design. When Samuel had inherited the throne after the untimely death of his uncle, he had put energy and resources into renovating the two-hundred-year-old structure. The effort showed.

"I'm fine." Her guards flanked her and she took the stairs to the front door. It opened and she was escorted inside.

She had always believed her castle to be ornate, but the palace of Rizari made Acacia's royal home look like a straw hut.

This was her first date with King Warrington, although she wasn't sure if he would consider it a date. Officially, it was a dinner party with members of the royal social circle, some whom she knew by name and others not at all.

Her heels clicked against the floor as she was escorted by King Warrington's butler and her guards into the dining room. She was almost used to having her guards so close, but in her home, they didn't hover over her as they did in public.

Serena scanned the room for an inconspicuous place

to sit or stand, as was her usual technique when being in an unfamiliar place. Her eyes landed on a man across the room and her breath caught in her throat.

"Your Grace, may I offer you a drink?"

She held up her hand to decline, vaguely aware that she may have been rude, but she was impossibly fixated on one person. The man who had saved her life. As she crossed the room, she realized she could be mistaken. She could be imagining him. Thinking of him so often had a strange effect on her. She found herself almost subconsciously looking for him everywhere she traveled.

When she was a few feet from him, he took a sip of his drink and then turned his head toward her. Their eyes connected. She remembered those kind eyes, eyes of strength and compassion.

"Is it you?" she asked.

"Your Grace." He bowed to her.

"What is your name?" She had to know before he disappeared again. A swell of emotion and questions rose up inside her.

"Casimir Cullen."

Casimir. A regal name. His voice set off a sensation in her stomach, and excitement spiraled throughout her body. "Do you remember…" She didn't know how to finish her thought. He had to remember that night. Anyone who had lived through it would have it seared into their memory.

She had thought, upon their reunion, her protector would grab her, hug her to him, and now she realized, she had pictured him kissing her, banding his arms around her and making her feel safe for the first time in weeks.

"I remember."

She would have to settle for being the target of his warm, intense gaze. But the effect was much the same. "I've been trying to find you."

He inclined his head and Serena glanced at the person he had been speaking to. More specifically, the woman he had been speaking to. This was the king's dinner party. Was Casimir here with his wife? Why did that thought devastate her? Her entire being should be focused on grieving for her father and sister, and trying to wrap her arms around the tremendous tasks ahead of her. Yet part of her clung to Casimir as being something bright and good in her future. It was presumptuous of her to think they had a future.

"That night was difficult. I have been traveling, trying to clear my head," he said.

"With your wife?" she asked, gesturing to the woman standing across from him.

The woman smiled. "Cas and I aren't married." The look she gave him implied she would like to change that at some point.

Cas. The nickname suggested familiarity and Serena was confused. Was this his girlfriend? Suddenly, her mind was reeling from a barrage of thoughts. What was he doing here? How did he know King Warrington?

The king of Rizari. Serena's heart dropped and she felt sickened. She was at the palace to spend time with King Warrington and she was fixating on Casimir. She glanced around the room. As if reading her thoughts, Casimir spoke.

"The king has not yet arrived."

The woman giggled. "He tends to be late. You know the type."

Serena didn't know the type or understand the reason for the laughter, and while his tardiness might have been rude, she was grateful he had not yet arrived. It had given her this moment with Casimir. "Casimir, could I speak with you alone for a minute?"

The woman frowned but stepped away. Serena walked toward the double-wide glass patio doors. Casimir followed her, as did her guards. Casimir opened the doors and led her outside.

"I have so many questions," Serena said.

"Please ask them. I told you I was yours to call upon."

He had said those words and yet he had disappeared without giving his name. "Do you live in Rizari?" she asked.

"I do not. I live in Icarus, but I travel frequently throughout the Mediterranean."

Many follow-up questions came to mind. "What were you doing in Acacia?" Serena asked. She wanted to know everything about this man. Everything.

"Acacia is known for their world-class boat making and I am having one built. My friend Fiona," he gestured inside to the woman he'd been speaking with, "knew I was in town and invited me to your father's birthday party as her guest."

His story made sense. Acacia's boat-building history dated back a thousand years. Most of the royal naval fleet had been assembled in Acacia. To hear him refer to his companion as a friend soothed some of her worry. "I am pleased you recognize quality."

He glanced at her lips and then his gaze skimmed down her body. "I recognize it." His meaning was decidedly sensual.

"I have wanted to thank you for what you did that night. I don't recall if I did at the time."

She didn't want the conversation to circle around the worst night of her life. Serena struggled with her grief and anger over what had happened. Yet, she felt it was important to acknowledge what he had done and express her gratitude.

"I did what any man would have."

Except that he had done what no one else had. "My guards had left me." Before becoming the heir apparent to the throne she had only traveled with one guard. That night she'd had two, but they had been trying to stop the gunfire and in the chaos, they lacked the training to execute the proper response.

"Their mistake," Casimir said.

A mistake that could have cost her her life. Her uncle was reviewing and changing security measures to ensure nothing like it happened again. "You owe me nothing. But I want to know more about you."

"Your Grace, you may ask me anything you wish," Casimir said.

It was a cool evening and Serena noticed she could not see or smell the sea from the palace. "What do you do? I mean, besides saving the lives of princesses?"

He grinned. "My father owns a financial services company. He and I recently parted ways. A life of numbers and spreadsheets bored me. Until I figure out what I want to do next, I've been traveling, studying and having fun."

She didn't want to ask, but she needed to know about his relationship with King Warrington. She was aware, of course, that nothing could come of her attraction to Casimir. The king was courting her. This could be the

only night she had with Casimir. The idea was beyond
depressing. "How do you know King Warrington?"

"He and I have been traveling in the same social circles for years. Fiona invited me here tonight. I didn't
realize you'd be in attendance."

Serena felt a mix of emotions about Casimir's connection to King Warrington. She almost wished no one
in Rizari had known Casimir, that he could exist in
some space with her where they would be free to have a
friendship without the interference of others. A strange
notion, since she was not a possessive woman. Casimir had saved her life. She owed him, not the other
way around.

"Are you pleased to see me?" she asked, trying to
understand if he reciprocated any of her feelings.

Casimir looked over her shoulder and then returned
his gaze to meet hers. "Yes. I should not say things like
that to the princess, and to King Warrington's future
bride, but yes, I am pleased to see you."

Though two of her guards were standing inside the
door and another two were on the patio with them, Serena felt the space surrounding her and Casimir closing in on them. "I've thought of you often." An honest
admission that could cost her.

"I have wondered how you were coping. I read that
your father and sister's send-offs were touching. Many
people have had nice memories to share about your
father."

A water burial, as was tradition in her country, had
taken place for both the king and the princess. "I am
glad to hear it. I've distanced myself from politics and
the day-to-day duties of the royal family in recent years.

But I'll be forced into the center of the arena now and I have big shoes to fill."

"Why haven't you been involved in politics recently? I thought that was mandatory for a princess," he said. He took a seat on a concrete bench with birds carved across the back of it.

Serena sat next to him, thinking how to frame her answer and not give away what she had been doing while at her beach house. No one except Iliana knew she had been selling her artwork and building her career as a painter. "My sister was to be the queen. I didn't think my future entailed a throne, so I found other interests to pursue."

"Tell me about them."

Casimir hadn't asked about her art directly, but she wanted to tell him. They had shared an experience that had changed her life and now she wanted to share this piece of her life with him. "I like to paint. And do yoga." She spoke quickly, feeling strangely vulnerable.

"What do you like to paint?" He sounded both calm and interested without censure in his voice.

"The sea." The beautiful sea, a source of calm and joy for her.

"I've never had much success with art. Or yoga. But I'd like to try it."

"I could teach you to paint." She offered quickly, without checking the words before she spoke them. It wasn't like her to talk without thinking. She wanted a connection with Casimir, something to keep him in her life.

"Then it's date. I'll be in Acacia tomorrow to meet with my boat builder. Do you have time tomorrow?"

Tomorrow was Boat Day, a national holiday celebrating the water, and her schedule was full, but she would make time. She agreed, both nervous and excited about seeing Casimir again. Though this couldn't end in a friendship—or something deeper—perhaps another day with her rescuer would satisfy her curiosity and she would stop thinking about him.

But looking at his handsome face in the soft lights of the patio, she had the impression it would be hard to forget a man like Casimir.

Casimir was glad he'd arranged an excuse to be in Acacia before tonight's dinner party. His plan was unfolding as he had wanted, without as much manipulation as he'd expected. Tonight was about keeping the door open to his connection with Serena.

Convincing Fiona, the Countess of Provence in Rizari, to attend this party and bring him along had been easy. Making it clear that their relationship was platonic was trickier. He had been careful to keep their association on neutral ground. It worked out better for his plans for Serena. The princess had to see him as available.

Going through a traumatic experience, Serena's heart would be guarded. Casimir would have to be diligent to breech those shields.

He had learned through a friend that King Warrington had been with his mistress that afternoon. Based on the king's tardiness at tonight's dinner party, he may still be with her. The idea disgusted him. Had Warrington considered Serena's feelings before inviting her tonight and booking time with his lover earlier in the day?

The silver lining was that, for once, the situation was progressing to Casimir's benefit. The king was missing in action and Serena had been drawn to Casimir immediately.

Casimir had to help her see that she would be miserable married to King Warrington. Though Warrington could give her some freedom, mostly because he cared only for her position and not for her, she would be bound by her marriage vows. Casimir sensed she was a woman who would keep those vows sacred. She would be loyal and true and consequently, she would be lonely and disappointed. The king would see no reason to stop seeing his mistresses on the side.

He wouldn't treat Serena as an equal; he would devour her. He would exploit her, sleep with her, marry her and then keep her in his life in some superficial manner, maybe use her to give him legitimate heirs. He wouldn't give her the respect and love she deserved. It incensed Casimir to think about it.

Granted, almost everything King Warrington did or said fueled Casimir's anger. He wanted the man to suffer for what he had done. Killing his father, and dooming his mother to a life of misery, came at a heavy price and Samuel would pay it. That Samuel had killed, or arranged to have killed, his own father as well, spoke to the depths that Warrington would descend for power.

The doors to the patio opened and Samuel's mother exited the dining room. Katarina strode toward Serena, looking regal in a red dress. Her dark hair bounced as she walked. Casimir recognized the glint in her eyes. She, like her son, was hungry for power and she would do anything necessary to secure an alliance with Acacia.

Underestimating Katarina's ruthlessness would be a mistake. She held sway over her son and according to Casimir's mother and rumors, she was vicious. Casimir wasn't sure what role she played in the king's and her husband's deaths, but he guessed she was at least aware that her son had been responsible for it.

"Princess Serena, what are you doing out here?"

Serena blinked in the dark and rose from the bench. "Hello."

"I was concerned when I saw you exit the dining room." She glanced at Casimir and narrowed her eyes. "Do I know you?"

Casimir had been introduced to her twice before. Nice of her to remember. "I'm a friend of your son's. My name is Casimir Cullen." The word *friend* burned his tongue.

Katarina narrowed her eyes. Did she see the resemblance to his father? That resemblance had been difficult for his mother and she had made no secret of it. "Please excuse us. I would like to speak to the princess alone."

Serena held out her hand. "If you think something improper was occurring, I must correct you. My guards are with me," she gestured over her shoulders, "and Casimir saved my life."

"Did he now? And how is that?" Katarina looked irritated.

Serena swallowed heavily and Casimir detected a tremor in her lips. She blinked and Casimir saw the tears shining in her eyes. Speaking about the night her father and sister had died was difficult for her.

"I was close to the princess during the massacre at her castle. I prevented one of the assassins from attacking her." Short and to the point. No use drudging up the gruesome details of that night or saying "killing her." Hearing him mention the tragedy had to be hard enough for Serena.

Serena looked at the ground and Casimir knew she was trying to compose herself. Grief was a brutal, unrelenting animal. He would have done anything in that moment to take away some of Serena's pain.

Katarina folded her hands in front of her. "I see. Then allow me to thank you on behalf of my son for saving his bride's life."

Serena's chest lifted and lowered as she took a deep breath. She seemed to be pulling herself together and when she lifted her head, her expression was calm. "Has His Highness arrived?"

"Not yet. Please, Serena, let's have a little girl talk. What do you say?"

Before she could answer, Katarina turned to Serena's guards. "You may wait inside."

Serena straightened. "My guards stay with me."

"The king has guards to protect his palace. You are not in danger while you are on the premises."

"As you can imagine, after what I have been through over the past several weeks, I would feel better if my guards remained close." Serena's voice was saccharine sweet but there was no mistaking the edge in it.

"Very well."

Casimir bowed to the women and strolled inside. Serena was timid in some ways, but when pushed, she wouldn't hold back defending herself. He had thought Serena would be easy to manipulate, but seeing her strength in action was impressive. Made his plan harder, but notched up his respect for her.

Serena would not be shoved around by her future mother-in-law. Starting the relationship on that note would doom her marriage and Serena already had doubts about its future happiness.

"I know you are adjusting to your new position, but I should warn you, being alone with a man who is not my son is asking for trouble."

It annoyed Serena to be spoken to condescendingly as if she were a teenager and the implication, that she had been doing something wrong by talking to Casimir, pissed her off. Her emotions were on a hair trigger, admittedly, but she thought Katarina had crossed a line. "Casimir is a man of honor. I am not ashamed to be seen with him in any context." Maybe not naked with him in bed, which would certainly be inappropriate, but she was dressed and in view of her guards and the guests at the dinner party. But now that she was thinking about being naked with Casimir, she had trouble putting it out of her mind. Despite the coolness of the night air, heat flamed up her back and a new tide of arousal washed over her. Utterly distracting.

"I don't say these things to chastise you, but if you read up on the history of the royal family of Rizari, you will find the implication of any disloyalty is not taken lightly."

How would King Warrington react if she spoke to or flirted with another man? Behead her? "I will look into that."

Katarina lowered her head, but Serena did not mistake the gesture for subservience. She would need to watch her back when it came to Katarina. Serena hadn't planned to make an enemy of the king's mother, but if she felt attacked, she would defend herself. She wished her sister was around to ask about the queen. The thought brought another wave of loss crashing over her.

"I will have my son send over some literature."

"Speaking of your son, do you know where the king is?" Serena asked. Why invite her to a dinner party and then stand her up? He had to know she'd traveled a distance to be in attendance.

Katarina looked into the dining room. Stalling for time to manufacture a lie? "I know he had an important meeting this afternoon. Perhaps he lost track of time."

"I see. That does not bode well for our relationship."

"You cannot expect the king to be someone he is not."

What did that mean? Expecting him to show up for plans he'd made wasn't expecting too much. She was the princess and she had cleared her schedule. Serena had been second all her life. Everyone whom she'd loved had put her behind something or someone else more important. She could not live with being her husband's second, at least not in his heart.

"I will keep that in mind in the future." Serena walked away from Katarina, feeling daggers being shot at her back.

When Serena reentered the dining room, the same sense of dread and anxiety volleyed through her. Relying on her coping mechanisms, she found a chair in the corner of the room and sat, watching. Her gaze was drawn to Casimir. He was the most handsome man in the room. Apparently, the other women thought so as well. They fawned over him, touching the sleeve of his suit coat, practically stroking him to win his attention.

After several moments, he glanced toward the patio. Her heart thumped hard. Was he looking for her? Checking on her? He looked around the room and when he saw her, he said something to the woman he was speaking to and strode to Serena.

"Pleasant conversation with the king's mother?" he asked.

"I've been warned that you could sully my reputation."

"She said that?" He sounded incredulous.

"Not in those words. But apparently, I should have eyes and words only for women friends and the king. The king who is not yet here."

Casimir's eyes darted left and right. "Is this your first time in the palace?"

She must have made him nervous with her negative observation about the king. She had been thinking about Casimir so much, building him up in her head, she'd forgotten that she didn't really know him. He had no reason to trust that she would not relate anything negative he said back to the king. She felt embarrassed for putting him in that position. "It is my first time in the palace. It is beautiful. My one complaint is that I can't hear the sea."

"The sea is a distance from the palace."

"I won't live here," she said, thinking of the future.

"The king might be surprised when his bride moves to the beach," Casimir said.

She hurried to explain, trying not to make him think less of her. "I used to fish and swim laps in the Mediterranean Sea and walk along the shore where the waves met the sand, letting the water cool my feet. I can't give that up." Not forever. She wished she were in her beach house now, listening to the water with Casimir.

"Marriage in any context is a negotiation."

Except that in her case, she had none of the power

and it entailed a lot of personal sacrifice with little personal gain in return. Acacia needed Rizari far more than the other way around.

On their first meeting as intended fiancés, the king was late. Was this an indication of how she would be treated during their marriage? Serena had a sense of foreboding. On the heels of that emotion was anger that the king thought so little of her. Would he have been late if he were meeting with Danae? Or perhaps the king was dreading this marriage as much as Serena was and looking for a way out. But if he offered an alliance without marriage, she would be turning Acacia over to King Warrington without any legal protection. That didn't sit right with her.

Her father had always told Serena that she should not accept subpar treatment from anyone. She had tried to be pleasant and accommodating, despite the challenges she was facing. But the well of pleasantness was about to run dry. The last several weeks had depleted it.

A woman stumbled over to them and slid her arm around Casimir. She kissed the underside of his jaw. "I am so glad to see you. You make these dull parties fun."

The woman took a big swallow from her glass of wine and glared at Serena. "Who are you?" The question sounded borderline hostile.

Casimir took a step away from the woman. "This is Princess Serena Alagona of Acacia."

"Nice to meet you. Are you the one who'll marry Samuel?"

Casimir shifted on his feet, clearly uncomfortable, but Serena was intrigued by this intoxicated woman and what she had to say. "Nothing has been decided, but our countries are negotiating."

The woman leaned forward and giggled. "I could tell you some hot stuff about Samuel. Most of the women in this room can. We've all slept with him."

Serena hid her disgust and pretended she wasn't repulsed by the idea of a slutty king who had invited his conquests to a dinner party with his future fiancée. "That's a lot of women."

Another giggle. "Not all at once. I mean, not usually more than one at a time. But sometimes."

Serena's hopes for a monogamous and meaningful relationship drifted further out of reach. King Warrington had been engaged to her sister. Was this woman speaking of the distant past? Could the king have been wild in his youth? Serena desperately wanted something to explain his behavior so she wouldn't be doomed to a life of unhappiness. "The king enjoys spending time with a lot of women?"

"Sure. Of course. You'll see. I'm sure you'll receive the royal treatment, you know, one-on-one with him. But maybe not every night. He is easily bored."

Was this a palace or a house of ill repute? "I see."

She had been thinking that perhaps she could make this arrangement work, and maybe it was this woman's intention to run her off, but after an altercation with the king's mother and now this, Serena wanted more than ever to be home.

"That's enough sharing. We can swap stories some other time," Casimir said, leading the other woman away.

Everyone in this room must think Serena was an ignorant moron. If the women had slept with the king, were they laughing at her? The king might be tied to her in marriage, but would that mean anything to him?

She turned to her guards. "I'd like to leave now."

They would not question her. As she moved toward the door, she tried not to think about what a spectacular failure this evening had been for her and her future with King Warrington. She had not made a connection with him. If anything, the experience had driven spikes between them.

She was on the front steps of the palace when she heard Casimir's voice. "Your Grace, please wait!"

Her guards stepped between her and Casimir. "It's okay." She wasn't mad at Casimir. Embarrassed by the king's behavior and feeling like a fool, yes.

"Serena, those are wild tales about the king. He likes to have a good time. Don't let a little provocation from his friends upset you. They are probably just having some fun at your expense."

"He didn't show up tonight." Even if the stories the woman had related about Warrington's bedroom behavior weren't true, his absence couldn't be disputed.

"He is being a fool," Casimir said quietly.

"Seeing you again was the only thing that salvaged the night."

She shivered and Casimir removed his jacket and draped it over her shoulders.

"I hate seeing you upset," Casimir said. "And yet every time I am near you, you seem to be in that state. Let me do something that will make you happy."

Serena felt the air sucked from her lungs. Was he planning to kiss her in front of the palace of Rizari? With her bodyguards standing around her?

"I will meet you in Acacia tomorrow," Casimir said. "And I will bring a surprise."

Not a kiss, but a promise of tomorrow. "Okay, tomorrow, then."

* * *

Serena was too warm. She had her windows opened and the overhead fan running, but heat seemed to pour from her. Anger for one man and desire for another made her blood run hot.

King Warrington had humiliated her. She hadn't been looking forward to the evening, but it had turned out worse than expected. With as much anxiety as she had about her social awkwardness and lack of finesse, her usually low expectations of social gatherings hadn't been met.

Serena would rather focus on Casimir. When she thought of him, she felt white-hot desire. The emotion could be completely inappropriate given the recent deaths in her family, but it persisted. Having located Casimir, she'd thought thanking him for what he'd done for her would give her some closure about that night. But instead, she found herself longing for him more intensely. He had slipped his suit jacket over her shoulders and she had forgotten to return it to him. It was hanging on her bed post, which felt wild and forbidden. The pockets were empty, but the jacket smelled of him, like sandalwood and spices.

She rolled to her side, adjusting her sheets. Closing her eyes, images of her father and her sister's bodies on the floor of the ballroom struck her. Nausea rolled over her. She opened her eyes. Maybe television would lull her into a mindless state.

She heard music as if caught on the wind, the light strumming of a guitar and the melodic sound of a man's voice. Casimir's strong, yet soft voice. Where was that coming from? Was she hallucinating at this hour? It was 1:15 a.m.

Looking out her bedroom window, she saw one of her guards patrolling her front yard. She knew at least two others were on the premises. Tugging a short robe around herself, she took the stairs to the main floor. On her wraparound porch stood Casimir, playing an acoustic guitar and singing quietly. She watched him for a moment, taking in how gorgeous he was. His dark silhouette was framed against the moon and the sea.

She memorized the image, thinking she could sketch it later.

Her heart was thumping as she walked outside. He continued playing, but had stopped singing.

"What are you doing here?" she asked. The wind blew and she shivered.

"We made plans to see each other today. Since it's past midnight, this counts," Casimir said. "I couldn't wait longer. I needed to see you now. I was serenading you."

Her knees felt weak. She had never had a man anxious to see her. She held on to the back of one of her porch chairs.

She glanced at her guard, surprised he had allowed Casimir onto her porch.

Her guard's shoulders tightened. "Do you wish to be alone, Your Grace? I overheard you agree to see him at the palace."

She had agreed to meeting Casimir and she was happy he was here, at her beach house. Though they were not lovers, this had the makings of a secret rendezvous. She shivered at the thought. "Let me get dressed." It wasn't as if she had been sleeping anyway.

"You don't need to change. You look good to me," Casimir said.

Her legs were bare and her nipples were pebbled against the cotton of her tank top and robe. It was hard to believe he was actually here. "Want to come inside? I can show you where I paint."

He shook his head and set his guitar on the porch, leaning it against her wooden chair. "No, we'll save my first painting lesson for another day. Being in the princess's house without a chaperone could be trouble."

"My guards can be trusted," she said.

"Perhaps I do not trust myself," Casimir said. "Let's go for a walk. You said you loved the sea."

They started down the stairs and her bare feet sank into the cool sand. Her guard followed at a distance. As they walked along the water's edge, Casimir didn't touch her, didn't hold her hand. His hands were tucked into his pockets in a boyishly charming manner. He had changed out of his suit and was wearing a pair of khaki shorts and a navy T-shirt. She could make out the muscles of his shoulders, arms and chest. She suppressed the urge to run her fingers down the hard planes of his body.

"I'm glad you came to see me tonight," she said.

"I'm sorry if I woke you."

"I wasn't sleeping."

Concern dotted his face. "I imagine you've had a hard time sleeping since that night."

He bent to pick something up.

"I miss them. I go over the sequence of events and try to think if there was more I could have done. I try to remember the last thing I said to each of them. I don't even understand why it happened." Who had wanted her family dead? Why that night? The questions yielded no answers, only more frustrating questions.

Grief made her throat tight and she went still, closing her eyes and gathering her strength.

"You don't have to be strong in front of me. Cry if you need to. I'll be strong enough for the both of us. For you."

A great heaving sob shuddered over her.

"I want to hold you. Let me hold you. Is that okay?"

She answered by stepping into his arms.

Casimir gathered her against him, his powerful arms clutching her to his muscular frame.

He held her while she cried. The water lapped over her feet at uneven intervals, the cool sensation soothing the burn of grief. The wind blew and the quiet of the night made her feel as if she and Casimir were hidden from the rest of the world.

When the tears stopped, only deep unrelenting sadness remained, heavy in her heart. Taking a deep breath, she rested her head on his chest. "A queen shouldn't cry."

"Where did you hear that? That's nonsense."

"My country needs me to be strong."

"Crying and showing emotion doesn't make you weak. It takes real strength to open up about how you're feeling," he said.

She broke away and sat on the sand. He sat next to her. He had his elbows propped on his bent knees. "You can say anything to me, Serena. I won't sell you out."

"I hardly know you," she said. Yet she trusted him more than a princess should.

"When two people have been through something like we have, there's a bond. It's hard to ignore that connection. You can trust it. If you listen to your instincts, you'll know I'm right."

Then he had felt it, too. She would be careful what she said to him, knowing a woman in her position should be, but she had someone to talk to and that was what she needed most. "I was humiliated tonight. The king never showed and he never called."

"It was a jerk move," Casimir said.

Then she wasn't the only one who thought so. "Why plan a party and invite me if he had no intention of coming?"

"I am not sure that he had no intention."

"He could have called. Texted. Had someone else call or text."

"That's true."

"I didn't want to see him tonight."

"Then why were you at the palace?" Casimir asked.

A complicated situation made more complicated by the day. "I don't know how much you follow politics, but my country needs me to marry the king."

"Why?"

"We're in a difficult location being between two life-long enemies. If Icarus decides to take a shot at Rizari, we're in the way. Therefore, Icarus may want to use us or invade to have easier access to Rizari."

"The president of Icarus told you this?"

She had yet to have a reasonable conversation with the president on the matter. "No, but Danae was planning to marry King Warrington to form a strong alliance with Rizari. Rizari's military presence can prevent Icarus from seeing us as an easy mark and attacking. The Assembly believes it's inevitable for Icarus to make a play for more power and more land."

"I see," Casimir said. He didn't seem eager to share his thoughts on the matter.

"What would you do?" Serena asked.

"That's not for me to say."

She wanted to know. "I asked your opinion."

Casimir glanced at her, amusement on his face. "Is that a royal request?"

"It is," she said with a smile.

"I would hate to belong to someone in marriage who I could not tolerate as a person and who did not respect me."

"I belong to no one," she said. Yet even the denial was a lie and she knew it. From the weaker position, she would be forced to agree to Warrington's terms. He would own her.

Serena watched the endless waves and thought about running away, just getting in a boat and sailing off. "I was never meant to be queen."

"Life has its own sense of humor. Perhaps you never believed you would be, but you have what it takes."

She scoffed. "If you knew me better, you would not say that." He didn't know about her social anxiety, the complete lack of experience and the fact that she had zero desire to be the figurehead of a nation.

"What I know tells me you are strong, faithful and loyal. What better qualities to have in a queen?" He handed her a piece of green sea glass.

She held it up in the moonlight.

"A broken shard of glass, someone's trash. It's been tumbled by the water and smashed by the rocks and the sand until it's beautiful and shiny."

"What it's gone through is what makes it beautiful," Serena said. She held the sea glass in her palm.

Casimir had the soul of a poet, the strength of a fighter and the bravery of an explorer. Everything she had been looking for in one man and had never found. Her heart clamored at her to crawl into his lap. But she couldn't.

She belonged to another man.

Chapter 3

Serena picked up the small globe from her therapist's desk. Dr. Albert Shaw had been her therapist for five years and she had seen him more frequently in the past several weeks. He had been helping her with her social anxiety and more recently, with her grief. He asked her prying questions, he was perceptive and she wanted to convince him she was fine and healed, as if that would actually prove she was better.

She had to fight through this period of her life and be strong, not break down into tears and sob about her father and sister—which had happened twice in this office—and remain calm. Immediately after the morning's session, she would be heading to the Spear's Point Marina to give a speech for the start of the boat-racing season, locally and affectionately known as Boat Day.

Water and related sports and hobbies were integral to Acacia's culture. Almost every child she knew—herself included—learned to swim at a young age, learned to captain a water vessel as a teenager and learned to fish somewhere in between.

Serena thrived when she was on the water. She hoped to hang on to those feelings while giving her speech and not let the stage fright that plagued her consume her. Stage fright was not a good quality in a queen. She knew it and her father had known it. To a large degree, he had tried to help her through it. Speech tutors and public-speaking lessons hadn't worked. When she'd turned twenty, he'd given up and switched to helping her avoid the limelight. It was one of the reasons it had been easy for her to stay out of politics.

Serena had instead focused her time and energy on her artwork, a fine hobby for a princess. Serena had crossed a line when she'd asked Iliana to help her sell her work. Yet those sales had meant something to her. She had felt as if she had worth beyond her title and breeding.

Dr. Shaw entered his office, his gait implying he was in no hurry. He had a full beard, a warm smile and rosy cheeks, making him look a little like Santa Claus. But his leisurely movements, advanced age and jovial appearance were misleading. His mind was sharp. He missed nothing and he saw through lies. Serena didn't bother lying to him. Lying to herself, however, could still be a problem in tough situations.

Serena sat on the same chair she always did during her sessions.

"Have you had an easier time sleeping?" Dr. Shaw asked, taking his seat.

Serena had declined a prescription for sleeping pills, but had agreed to try lavender oil and some calming breathing exercises before bed. She'd tried to cover the dark circles under her eyes with makeup, but Dr. Shaw had a way of seeing through smoke and mirrors.

"A little."

"What's helped? What hasn't helped?"

Though she hadn't slept long, after Casimir had left her on the porch of her beach house, she had found the deep sleep she'd craved but that had been out of reach. "I found the man who saved my life." Saying the words made her feel breathless and excited.

Dr. Shaw shifted in his chair, dragging his hand over his beard. "Tell me about that."

Serena related the situation. She left out how attracted she was to Casimir, how much she wished she could have a relationship with him.

"What did you feel when you had to part ways?" Dr. Shaw asked.

A combination of emotions, sadness and loss, but also hope and excitement. "The same grief I've been carrying around, but I felt better."

"Sounds like he's a good man to have around."

That was putting it mildly. He had been helpful to her in every situation they'd been in together. But she had to be realistic about her boundaries and accept her new life and responsibilities and that meant she had to let him go. "He and I can't have a relationship and we both know that. It wouldn't be appropriate."

"Inappropriate to have a friend?"

The way Dr. Shaw posed the question, he had picked up on the fact that Serena was attracted to Casimir. They weren't simply friends and to pretend so was to lie to herself, to Casimir and to Dr. Shaw. "I'm attracted to him."

"Grateful for what he has done or attracted to him?"

"Both."

"What does he feel about you?"

Serena didn't know. He had been courageous for her, attentive to her and had made her feel desired and wanted. But he hadn't made any advances toward her. Could he want to be friends? What reason did he have to pursue a friendship with her? "I don't know. I assume he likes me. He acts like he does. But maybe he's just using me." Being a royal hanger-on was a full-time occupation for some.

"Nothing you've told me would suggest he is using you, but I would be cautious about requests in the future. When there's an emotional debt, it can be exploited."

Serena heard a commotion outside the office. Dr. Shaw rose to his feet. The door banged open and a man in a ski mask entered. He fired his gun at the window and it shattered.

Fear torqued through her. Immediately, the night her father and sister had been killed snapped to mind. Not again. This couldn't be happening again.

Casimir wasn't here to save her and she would have to save herself. She leapt to her feet, diving behind the couch.

One of her guards burst into the room, weapon drawn, and fired at the masked man. Two. Three. Four shots.

The man fell to the ground.

Serena climbed to her feet. Her guard rushed to her. She was fine. Rattled, but physically okay.

But Dr. Shaw was not moving. He was lying on the ground, blood pouring from his shoulder. A scream died in Serena's throat. She peeled off her sweater and hurried to him, pressing it to his wound.

"Help me!" Serena shouted to her guard.

He rushed to her side, taking over trying to stop the doctor's blood loss, and Serena fumbled for the phone on the doctor's desk to call for an ambulance.

Two of her guards had been killed by the masked men who had stormed the therapist's office. Her security had killed one of the men outside the private office and the other had been gunned down in front of her.

With those images pulsing in her brain, Serena changed her clothes. Iliana was helping her and for that Serena was deeply grateful. She couldn't think of anything except Dr. Shaw. He was in the ICU at Thorntree General and his fate was in his doctors' hands. When he was more stable, he would be helicoptered to a larger hospital in Rizari with better equipment.

The media was reporting on the incident as another failed attempt on the princess's life.

"Serena, are you sure you want to do this?" Iliana asked, sitting next to her and putting her arm around her shoulders. "Because if it's too much, we can come up with an excuse and you can go home."

Serena would have critics no matter what she planned today. In the past, she had been blasted for being too shy and too quiet. She had been called slow, although testing proved what she had tried to tell her father and her doctors. Her mind was fine. It was her mouth that didn't want to work. Even when she tried to say the words that came to mind, they sounded garbled when they left her lips. And worse still, she hated the look on people's faces after she spoke. They'd look confused or bored. She had a unique talent of making awkward silences fall over a conversation. It was her superpower.

Her sister had known what to say, even in tense situations. Her sister had charmed men into doing what she wanted. But Serena was not her sister.

Serena wouldn't go down this dark road, especially not now when she was rattled, her emotions in tatters. Her public failings were in the past. She had a new life path and she had to get on board and give it everything she had. Serena took a deep breath. "I want to do this. I want to show whoever is targeting me and my family that I won't be intimidated by threats and violence."

Iliana's eyes were deep pools of worry. "If you're sure…"

"I am sure."

The Spear's Point Marina had been decorated in Acacian colors: red and gold. Flags were posted at the ends of the docks and boats were likewise decorated. Citizens wore red and yellow T-shirts. Bands played patriotic songs. Over five thousand people were expected to attend this year's Boat Day celebration.

Iliana left Serena alone for a few minutes inside the marina's private suite. Serena looked out at the water and tried to center herself and her thoughts. She needed to appear strong and in control. While she did not want to look hard and distant, she had to keep her emotions on a short leash.

Iliana returned, looking excited. "The king is here!"

For a brief moment, Serena thought she could mean her father, but Serena then remembered it couldn't be so. Iliana meant King Warrington.

King Warrington had been scheduled to be part of the day, but had not committed to specifics. Serena's feelings about him were mixed, at best. They hadn't spoken since he had stood her up the night before. No calls or text messages with an explanation.

"Are you excited?" Iliana asked.

Serena hadn't told Iliana about what had happened with King Warrington or about Casimir's late night visit. She didn't have time to discuss the details now.

"Of course," she said.

Iliana narrowed her eyes. "You sound just the opposite. Did something happen with him last night?"

"Nothing happened and that's why I'm anxious. He didn't show up."

Iliana winced. "That bad? You should have called me. We could have commiserated over glasses of wine."

"It was late when I arrived home. I didn't want to bother you."

"You are never bothering me. You can call me anytime you need to. I'm not saying that as an employee. I'm saying that as a friend."

Iliana was loyal and steadfast. Serena would be lost without her. "Was the king headed in this direction?" Serena asked.

"I don't know. I didn't see him myself. Your uncle told me he was here. Speaking of…"

Her uncle entered the tent. Worry etched his face. He hugged Serena. "Are you okay? I heard about what happened this morning."

Serena blew out her breath. "I survived."

"And I am grateful. Do you need anything?"

She considered asking him to give the speech, but she wanted to honor her father and sister's memories. She wanted her father's legacy as a good and strong leader to continue with her. "I have the speech written.

I'll be okay." Her uncle didn't know the full scope of her public-speaking anxiety. Her family had concealed it even from him.

"That's my girl," her uncle said and kissed her cheek.

"Ready?" Iliana asked.

Serena stood on shaky legs, but at least she was standing. Heat flamed up her back. Her chest felt tight and she couldn't pull enough air into her lungs. This couldn't happen now. She had four minutes until she was scheduled to speak. A panic attack was unacceptable.

She had practiced her speech a number of times, but she couldn't recall how it started. Then, somehow, she was standing on the platform overlooking the crowd. Balloons blew in the wind, streamers whipped in the air and every eye was on her.

The head of the Assembly was making his opening comments and introducing her. She stepped forward, scanning the crowd for King Warrington. When she reached the podium, she opened her mouth to speak. Her tongue was impossibly dry. She took the water cup from the hidden ledge inside the podium and drank.

"Hot day," the head of the Assembly commented.

Uneasy laughter rolled over the crowd. Serena started again.

Her tongue felt heavy. Her hands felt sweaty and she was clammy and hot. She glanced at Iliana. She appeared concerned, but smiled encouragingly. How much time had passed? Seconds? One minute?

Serena tried again to read the words of her speech, but they were blurry on her notecards. She hadn't had time to memorize it. That could have helped.

Then King Warrington was at her side, moving her

away from the podium. "Good thing I'm here to save the day. Please allow me to welcome you to this Boat Day celebration."

Serena felt dismissed and overshadowed. She had flailed, but she would have pulled it together. She hid her frustration and pretended to gaze on King Warrington with affection.

She had to give him credit. The man had presence. In seconds, he had the crowd laughing and hanging on his every word. Serena couldn't track what he was saying. She could hardly define how she felt, a combination of annoyed and embarrassed.

It was the second time in two days that the king had made her feel that way.

"As for Princess Serena, I will be taking her to my palace in Rizari for a few days. She can relax under the constant vigilance of my guards and then I'll return her to you."

Serena felt a jolt of outrage. He hadn't consulted her about taking her away from Acacia. He was likely trying to imply they were closer than they were or to start planting the idea of a union between their countries. Either way, she was furious.

With that, Warrington led her away from the podium. He more than led. He practically carried her. Her legs were weak and her stomach roiled.

When they were back inside the marina suite, King Warrington poured himself a scotch from the bar in the room.

"What happened out there?" he asked. His dark brown hair was perfectly styled and his brown eyes were cold. Why had she never noticed how much he looked like a boy bander before?

Serena felt as if she were slipping into misery, deep and dark and all-consuming. This was her first private conversation with her future husband? What a nightmare. "I've had some anxiety since my father and sister were killed." Add to it what had happened that morning and she thought flubbing the speech was understandable.

"You'll need to pull it together. I can't have that kind of crap happening on a regular basis."

Serena had been this way since childhood. When she and Danae had played with their friends, Serena had been teased and mocked. Her sister would stand up for her, but it had still hurt. Now her sister was gone. She didn't have anyone to protect her in that same way and Serena felt resolute in protecting herself and making Danae proud.

Iliana entered the room and rushed to Serena, taking her hands. "Are you okay?" She glared at King Warrington. "What happened?"

"I just felt hot. And overwhelmed."

Iliana gave her a sympathetic smile. "It's been a very bad month."

"I am not leaving Acacia. I am fine here," Serena said.

"Your recent history proves otherwise," King Warrington said. He took a swig of his drink and stared at her, looking bored.

As if she didn't have enough to deal with, her uncle entered the room.

How could she explain it? She had taken on more than she could handle. She had screwed up. She had pretended she could make it through a short statement and keep her cool, but under the circumstances, the task was beyond her.

"Serena, I have tried to be patient with you. I have tried to give you space. But a stunt like that will make everyone in the country think you're on the verge of a nervous breakdown. Do you know how this will look for the royal family? Do you realize how weak we seem? President DeSante could attack and take over our country. Is that what you want?" her uncle asked. He seemed at his wit's end.

Serena didn't feel on the edge of losing her mind. She had a lot to learn and an overwhelming number of tasks ahead of her, but she was prepared to tackle them and work until she had the country's problems under control and they were united with Rizari. "I am not having a breakdown. I do not wish to turn our country over to a dictator. I've had a bad day."

Her uncle threw his hands in the air. "This is too much for you, Serena. I hate seeing you struggle this way."

Serena glanced over her shoulder at Iliana and Warrington. "Could you give us a few minutes?"

Iliana and Warrington left the room.

"I need time," Serena said.

"To do what? Leaders of countries do not have the luxury of time. You don't get to recover in your remote beach house and ponder the meaning of life and death. When your mother died, do you think your father took a vacation from his responsibilities?"

Her father had not taken vacations. It was a harsh truth she was well aware of. No family trips out of the country for pleasure, only the mandatory appearances at social functions. "He didn't. I remember."

"The media will be asking for a statement. What should I tell them?"

"Don't tell them anything. Give me a few minutes and I'll walk through the crowd, just as I planned. I will say I've had a tough day, but I'm fine. We don't need to overreact." Her words sounded stronger than she felt.

Her uncle sniffed. "Now you're decisive. Do what you must." He turned on his heels and stopped once to look over his shoulder. "Just remember that your weakness reflects on the entire country. Your unwillingness to be the princess you were raised to be leaves us vulnerable to attack by our enemies. Unless you want a hostile takeover by a dictator, you had better marry King Warrington and do it soon."

Serena was pinned between four bodyguards. Her security team was controlling the scene the best they could, under the circumstances. Boat Day was a huge holiday for Acacia. Docks were full, the marinas were crowded and banks and schools were closed.

Serena couldn't enclose herself in her beach house and sulk about her embarrassment or worry about Dr. Shaw. Especially after what had happened during her speech, she needed to save face and inject some confidence into her countrymen. She focused on the task at hand: shaking hands, posing for pictures and smiling. The crowd was stifling and after an hour, Serena needed a break. She was dizzy and tired and her brain felt foggy. She was wearing a bulletproof vest under her dress and it felt hot and heavy.

"Could we grab some lunch?" she asked the guard closest to her.

She was scheduled to have lunch at one of her favorite restaurants in the area and now was a good time for it.

Her guard nodded, said something into his wrist-watch communication device and she was led in a different direction.

Then, she saw him. As if a shot of adrenaline had hit her system, the fog lifted and her senses were completely focused. Casimir was speaking to a boat vendor, perhaps the vendor who was selling him the boat he'd mentioned.

"I see a friend. I'd like to say hello." Before her guards could stop her or warn her about the security risks of deviating from the planned path, she moved through the crowd toward Casimir.

She knew the moment Casimir had spotted her.

He had stopped talking and was staring in her direction, his lips slightly parted. Her guards held the crowd at some distance. The boat vendor bowed to her and moved away, giving her and Casimir a few feet of privacy.

"Casimir, hello." She wished she had said something more clever to him. She wanted to hug him in greeting, but knew the crowd was watching her and cameras were snapping pictures.

"Your Grace," he said, bowing to her. His body language was formal and he did not touch her, but his eyes conveyed heat and desire. Would the crowd pick up on that? Did she care?

"I didn't realize you would be here today," she said.

"I mentioned I was planning to buy a boat. And so I am. Best day of the year to get one. Fire sales, I tell you."

It was a big week for the boat trade. Serena had

bought her first boat around Boat Day when she was sixteen. "I am happy to see you."

"I am happy to see you as well. I heard you had trouble this morning." Lines formed around his eyes as his expression shifted to concern.

"I'm surprised you heard," she said. "I thought the police wanted to keep it under wraps."

"Most of the island heard about what happened through unofficial channels. I tried to call you." The second sentence was spoken so softly, it was almost impossible for her to hear.

She was pleased he had been concerned about her. That might be the only good thing that came from the attack that morning. Nothing like finding the bright side. "I haven't been near my phone."

"That wasn't an accusation. Just expressing concern."

"Could you meet me somewhere for lunch?" she asked quietly. They couldn't leave together or rumors would run rampant, but she could meet him.

Casimir straightened. "I could. Where?"

"The Steel Anchor Lounge? Now?" she asked. Her guards had reserved the top deck for her to have a lunch in a safe place away from the crowds. The restaurant also happened to serve the best lobster bisque.

"Sure. I am almost finished here. Are you sure I'll be allowed past security?"

She could have stayed with Casimir all afternoon. She wanted to know more about his boat, to see it, to find out if he had enjoyed their time together on the beach as much as she had. "I will make it so," she said.

Every moment with Casimir felt like borrowed time, but Serena would take what she could until she belonged to King Warrington.

* * *

Casimir had known that Serena would walk near this location. DeSante had a source on Serena's staff. Casimir didn't know the details. Either DeSante was paying for information or he had positioned one of his spies close to her. DeSante played his cards close to the vest, even with Casimir.

The situation with Serena had played out how Casimir had hoped, except for one small problem. He had expected to look at her and see a potential ally, one he could easily negotiate with once he inevitably won his throne in Rizari. But those thoughts were far from his mind.

He looked at her and he saw a woman whom he wanted to sleep with. He struggled to control his emotions when she was near. The relief that had consumed him at seeing that she was safe after this morning's attack was a clear sign that she wasn't another political tool to use. Then he had been concerned watching her on the podium giving—or rather not giving—her speech. It had taken speaking to her personally for him to feel that she really was okay. Physically at least, and that she wasn't so far down that she wouldn't rebound. She was stronger than she gave herself credit for. Some people who had experienced what she had wouldn't yet be out of bed.

Among his emotions was jealousy, jealousy that Serena belonged to another man. A competitive spirit urged him to pursue her regardless of her ties to the false king of Rizari. A bone-deep desire commanded him to throw her over his shoulder and carry her to bed. King Warrington had announced Serena would be coming to Rizari with him and it had angered him. Though it had been brief, her reaction told Casimir she hadn't known of the plan before Warrington had publicly announced it. That had shifted Casimir's anger into fury.

He didn't want Serena pushed around because she was inexperienced and in the weaker political position.

But overthinking her relationship with Warrington and being consumed with thoughts of her meant his goals were becoming muddled. Serena wasn't supposed to be his concern. Her well-being was her and her administration's problem. She had her uses and those should not extend into any real concern for her. Revenge against Warrington was his primary objective. When Samuel was no longer king, Casimir's mother could stop harboring anger and hurt. And he could take his rightful place on the throne.

But Casimir was troubled by how much he felt for Princess Serena. He was preoccupied with her and was spending more time than he needed to in order to accomplish his goal. Time he didn't have to waste. His plans with DeSante were complex and involved many moving pieces.

At the close of his negotiations for the boat, the boat vendor sized him up. "You and the princess seem close."

It was best to deny it. "Not really. I'm friends with King Warrington," Casimir said. The words tasted dirty in his mouth. He would never consider that liar, thief and murderer a friend.

"I see. I thought I caught something else between you two. Must have been my imagination."

The man walked off and Casimir didn't pursue the comment. To go out of his way to explain things would only make him seem as if he was covering up the truth.

He wasn't sure where the truth lay and he didn't want to look too deeply into how he felt about that.

On his way to the Steel Anchor, he resolved to stay the course. This meant winning Serena over, making her an ally and keeping her out of King Warrington's despicable, lying hands.

At the restaurant, Casimir was hustled through security and then he took the wooden stairs to the upper deck.

Serena was alone, save for three of her guards. She smiled at him and gestured to the seat across from her. To his left was a gorgeous view of the sea.

Casimir sat at a red linen–topped table. "I didn't realize this would be a private lunch." He assumed she only took audiences with groups during this highly anticipated and well-publicized event.

"The only way I can recover from a huge crowd is to have some time to myself."

"But I am here."

She smiled. "That's true. But you don't exhaust me."

He was glad to hear it. "If I may speak freely, I need to tell you that I was troubled to hear rumors about what happened to you this morning. I didn't want to ask you about it earlier when others could overhear."

She took a sip of her water. "I don't know what you've heard, but let me clarify. I was at a regularly scheduled meeting with my therapist, and two masked assailants broke into his office and attacked us. Dr. Shaw was gravely injured."

"I am sorry to hear that," he said. A second failed assassination attempt. Either these assassins were completely inept or they had another motive. Was it to scare her? Force her into some agreement?

Her hands trembled. "I care a great deal about Dr. Shaw. I heard from his doctors a few minutes ago. He is stable, but time will tell if he'll fully recover."

"Any news about the men who attacked you?"

DeSante had hired a few investigators, some of a violent persuasion, to obtain answers about who was targeting the Acacian royal family. Whatever information Casimir could feed him from Serena would help narrow the search.

"Nothing yet. Or if the police have discovered anything, I haven't been kept abreast of that part of the investigation," Serena said.

She had removed her sweater and it was draped over the back of her chair. The dress she was wearing fit tightly at the top and when she leaned forward in her chair to set her hands on the table, he had the most enticing view of her cleavage.

He tried not to focus his attention there, but rather on her.

He had to get his attraction to her under control, or better yet, stamp it out completely. He had allowed emotion to rule his thinking in the past and that never turned out well.

"I plan to sail my boat to Rizari later today," he said.

Serena lifted her brow. "Did you hear the announcement King Warrington made? Apparently, I am headed there myself."

"I would be happy to escort you," Casimir said. Not a smart offer. Being with her in the small confines of a boat wasn't a way to put distance between them.

Serena drummed her fingers on the table. "I was planning to tell Warrington that I wouldn't go, but being in Rizari will give Samuel and me a chance to talk and see if we can come to an understanding. Our relationship is off to a strange start and I don't want it to become hostile. To make matters more awkward, I know he's dealing with his own grief over Danae's death."

The idea of Serena alone with Warrington, a perpetual philanderer, was enough to drive Casimir insane. He needed to find a reason to be around the palace. Warrington regularly invited his social circle to the palace for a large number of events. Casimir would need to contact the Countess of Provence again and use her to get inside the palace. It was a tricky proposition. Fiona had seemed annoyed at him for leaving in a hurry the night before. No good-night kiss and no plans made for the future. Casimir hadn't even promised to call.

His hurry had been spurred by his anxiety to see Serena again. As much as Fiona claimed she understood that they were friends, Casimir sensed she had hopes of being something else in the future.

He would work his contacts, make excuses or lie. He couldn't leave Serena alone with Warrington. The man had proven he was capable of anything.

"If you had something to do with the attack on Serena this morning, I will gut you," Iliana said. She was gripping her phone so hard, she was afraid she would crack it. But the more she thought about Serena and how close she had come to being hurt again, the more intense her anger had become. She was almost blackout angry. All she could see and taste was her fury.

"Are you aware that threats against the president of Icarus are grounds for an investigation and jail time?" DeSante asked.

He sounded entertained, as if he was toying with

her, which set her temper on edge. "Don't make light of this. Serena was almost killed."

"*Almost* being the operative word. If I had set out to kill her, she would be dead."

"Are you threatening her?"

"Not at all. Just pointing out a simple fact. When I choose to do something, I do it. I don't bungle it repeatedly." He had the nerve to sound calm and unconcerned.

"You are deplorable!" Iliana said.

"You are the one who called me and made an unfair accusation based on emotion. Tell me, do you always make decisions based on how you feel in the heat of the moment?"

Iliana felt an emotion akin to desire ripple over her, dimming some of her rage. But she did not feel desire for the dictator. She hated him. *Hated.* He was pushy and rude and thought his title and position meant he could do whatever he wanted. In his country, maybe he could. But she was an Acacian citizen. He had no hold over her.

"I was hoping you were calling to tell me you had reconsidered my offer to visit," he said.

That wouldn't happen in her lifetime. "I am calling to make sure you know that if Serena is hurt, I'm looking in your direction."

"As much as I would enjoy you looking at me, I must tell you that you are looking in the wrong direction. I have no reason to harm the princess."

Iliana despised how smooth his voice was and how composed his tone. "I can think of a few reasons. It would clear your path to taking over Acacia."

"That is factually untrue. Someone else would be crowned king or queen and then I would be forced to negotiate with that person. As it stands, I don't have enough information about the princess to say whether or not I will find her to be a hindrance or an asset. All I really know about her is that she keeps a pit bull for an assistant and a rather fearless one at that. If she prefers strong people around her, then I imagine she is a smart woman and will be reasonable to deal with. As was her father."

Iliana was disarmed by his words. Serena's father had been key to keeping the peace in the region. He had often served in an unofficial capacity as mediator of disputes between Rizari and Icarus. Without him, Iliana was concerned how long peace would remain in place.

Iliana kept her tone sharp. She'd show no weakness. "I am worried about Serena and I wanted to make sure you were clear that you are not to harm her."

"It's rare to have a friend so loyal that she is willing to directly threaten the leader of a nation."

Iliana would do more than threaten DeSante if he attacked Serena. "Serena is my boss, but she's also my friend. We're family." Their mothers had been sisters, close until Serena's mother died when Serena was a child. Then both of Iliana's parents died in a car accident while Iliana was at university. She was no stranger to grief and that experience made her ache that much more for Serena.

"You're doing what any blood relative would do. Setting the expectations and making sure I don't cross them. Tell me though, what would you do to me if I did cross them, by say, showing up at the castle in Thorntree?"

His voice had taken on a dangerous tone, but she didn't feel afraid. She felt turned on. Iliana wasn't certain how to respond to him. Flirting was unacceptable, wasn't it? And what if she was wrong? What if he wasn't flirting, but rather using her to dig for information about Serena? Her temper flared anew. "You are not welcome here. Good luck getting past our security." Although the words were bluster. The Acacian military was weak. It was the main reason that Serena had to marry King Warrington and form a strong alliance with Rizari.

"Loyal and patriotic. I like that."

She felt as if she was a mouse and DeSante was a cat, watching her, deciding when to strike with his enormous claws. "I've made my position clear. Don't hurt the princess and don't send any of your goons after her. If you do, I promise, I will make you regret it."

"I suppose it's too late to tell you that you have nothing to fear from me. If you do not get in my way, I will not hurt you or the princess. I will only do what is necessary to protect Icarus."

Chapter 4

Spending time on the water had put Serena in a better mood. She was smiling and laughing, sitting close to Casimir as he steered his new boat toward Rizari. Casimir was pleased with *The Buccaneer*'s inaugural trip on the Mediterranean Sea. The water surrounding Acacia was blue and tranquil. The sun was high in the sky and the clouds blocked some of the light, providing relief from the heat.

Serena was wearing a pair of red pants that fell midcalf, showing off her shapely legs, and a sleeveless red-and-white-striped shirt. The pants emphasized her hips and rear, and Casimir had a thing for women with curves.

"Have you been boating long?" Serena asked.

"Since I was a boy." He had liked being on the water, whether it was kayaking or canoeing or taking out the fishing boat he had found and refurbished to be seaworthy.

"Me, too."

Casimir glanced at his GPS. Two boats were moving in his direction. His instincts put him on guard and he reduced his speed. From what Serena had related, Samuel Warrington had not been thrilled about her arranging her own transportation to Rizari. Though he doubted Warrington would aggressively intercept his boat, other dangers lurked. These waters were not controlled or policed by anyone and pirates took advantage of that.

Casimir had a sidearm within reach. Was it enough to protect her?

"What's the matter? Why did you slow down?" Serena asked. She was too experienced of a boater not to recognize the change in their speed.

"Two boats are moving in my direction."

Serena stood behind him and set her hand on his shoulder. She looked at the GPS. Her guards were on board and she called to them. They arrived on deck, guns drawn, Iliana behind them.

"We may have a problem," Serena said.

It was too early to call the situation a full-fledged emergency. He could be overreacting, though his instincts had served him well and he did best when he followed them.

When the boats turned in their direction, Casimir knew his concern wasn't an overreaction.

As the boats came into view, Casimir felt simultaneously relieved and worried.

Both boats belonged to DeSante. The Icarus flag was stamped on the side, identifying the boats as vessels of the navy of Icarus. Demetrius wasn't in stealth mode, meaning he intended the boats to be seen.

The vessels pulled closer and slowed almost to a stop. Casimir's radio beeped and he answered.

"Good afternoon crew of *The Buccaneer.* This is the president of Icarus. Who do I have the pleasure of speaking with today?"

Serena's eyes were wide. Casimir didn't like Demetrius strong-arming Serena into speaking with him, but it was his style to get in Serena's face and force her to deal with him. Demetrius had been keeping tabs on Casimir while he was in Acacia, but had said nothing about forcing a confrontation today.

"This is Casimir Cullen, the boat's captain. This is my vessel."

"Your guest is the princess of Acacia. Don't deny it. I can see her."

"She is my guest and I will protect her as such."

DeSante laughed. "I mean her no harm. May I come aboard? Or perhaps I can send a dinghy and we can speak aboard one of my boats?"

Casimir released the radio so DeSante couldn't hear them.

"He is very insistent, isn't he?" Serena asked. She swallowed hard.

"I would suggest allowing him onboard. We can't outrun the boats and we're outnumbered."

Serena extended her hand for the radio. Impressed with her nerve, Casimir set the radio in her palm. "President DeSante, how interesting that we should meet on the open water. Tell me how I had this good fortune today."

"Your beloved alerted me to your travel plans hours

ago, as he did the entire country. So much for security protocols," DeSante said.

"Then you were lying in wait," she said. She released the radio button and added, "Like a snake."

Iliana had pushed to stand next to Serena and set her hand on her cousin's back protectively.

"I'd hoped to meet you. Decide, princess. We will have a conversation today."

She glanced at her guards. "You may come aboard. Just you. No one else."

"I agree to your terms and I will warn you that I will come armed."

Casimir wouldn't let this situation escalate to the point of using guns. He needed to maintain everyone's emotional calm. Usually he was on the other side of that arrangement, with DeSante asking him to stay in control. Though DeSante wasn't the type to shoot at Serena, her guards seemed twitchy. That could escalate the situation and DeSante would return fire. He always did.

DeSante sped to their vessel in a small powerboat. He threw Casimir his line and Casimir drew him close and then helped him aboard.

"You could have warned me," Casimir said under his breath.

DeSante ignored him. "Good afternoon, Princess. And Iliana, it is a pleasure to see you."

Iliana's expression could have iced over the sun. "President DeSante, I thought I made myself clear."

Serena glanced at Iliana. Casimir was equally confused. Was Iliana in private communication with DeSante? He had not said anything. DeSante did nothing without intent and Casimir wondered what his intention was with Iliana.

"I am a man of my word. I have no plans to harm the princess."

Was it Casimir's imagination or did DeSante look at Iliana with interest? His gaze seemed to linger longer than it should.

DeSante turned his attention to Serena. "You have been a difficult woman to reach."

"I have a country to run," Serena said.

"As do I. But I find time to speak to my neighbors and make sure we don't have any misunderstandings," DeSante said.

"What misunderstanding are you concerned we've had?" Her voice was arctic. She was holding her own and DeSante would respect that.

"Your father had been keeping the peace in our corner of the Mediterranean. With his untimely passing, you can understand that I have misgivings."

Casimir caught the first crack in Serena's composure at the mention of her father. Casimir moved closer to her. He would step in if needed. He didn't know what DeSante had planned here and he wouldn't allow the other man to bully Serena.

"This is a wonderful opportunity. You've refused my other requests for a meeting and now we are together."

"You have my attention. Please speak plainly," Serena said.

"I wish for our countries to unite. I won't be so crass as to require you marry me."

A dig at King Warrington and Serena's arrangement. Casimir hid his amusement.

"You may pass me control of your islands and I will make sure you live comfortably for the rest of your days," DeSante said.

Serena looked at him as if he was insane. "Give you Acacia in exchange for a comfortable retirement? Surely, you don't think so low of me that you expect I would sell out my entire nation for myself."

"Not for yourself. An alliance with Icarus is the better option. Our military strength and our protection are incomparable and unbeatable."

"Who is it that you would be protecting us from?"

The implication being that Serena wanted to be protected from Icarus. DeSante caught her meaning. "With the shift in power, Acacia is weak. Others may choose to strike."

"A threat?"

"An assessment," DeSante said. "And if protection does not appeal to you, we are a profitable trading partner and I can help build the infrastructure to boost tourism in your country."

Serena shook her head. "I must decline your offer. You are aware of my plans to marry King Warrington."

Casimir felt a jolt of surprise. She spoke as if it were a done deal. He had hoped he had sowed enough seeds of doubt on that matter.

DeSante didn't like being refused and he wouldn't view this as a final negotiation. Casimir recognized the glint in his eyes. He was just getting started. "King Warrington is a fool. He will run your treasuries into debt, probably planning parties. You will be totally dependent on foreign aid to feed your children."

Serena's eyes flashed with indignation. "As yet, I require no such aid to feed my countrymen and women."

DeSante looked at Casimir. "Who are you exactly to the princess? Her lover? I find it strange that she tells me her plans to marry one man while sailing on a private boat with another."

Though Serena seemed shocked, Casimir didn't let his old friend rattle him. "I am a friend."

"That's all? She looks at you as if you are more."

"I have earned the princess's trust," Casimir said.

"Then maybe I should be speaking to you, learning what it is that I need to win her over."

"I am not a person to be won," she said, sounding angry.

"You control access to something I want. That means I will not stop pursuing you. Say it however you wish. Winning you over or buying you out, but I will have my way."

"Bullying me won't get you far," she said.

DeSante came closer, but Casimir put up a hand to stop him. "Don't touch the princess or I will be forced to restrain you."

"Even knowing my reputation and that I am armed, you make a threat against me?" DeSante asked.

It was his opportunity to show Serena he would stand with her. "I would sacrifice my life for the princess's safety and well-being."

The president smiled between them and then looked at Serena. "If you negotiate with me, you could run away with your friend and live the life you want."

"That is a ridiculous statement. Casimir and I are not planning to run away from anything. Not bullies. Not assassins. Not responsibilities."

DeSante was planting ideas. He wanted Serena to think about having a relationship with Casimir. Casimir had considered it from a purely lust-fuelled perspective. He wanted to get Serena in bed, but he thought it better to keep those desires buried. Why did DeSante want to force this line of thinking? To keep Warrington further out of Serena's thoughts?

"Tell me what it will take and I will give it you," DeSante said.

"There is nothing you have that I want."

DeSante looked away. "I ask that you reconsider. Think carefully about the future you want. This is not the end of our negotiation." He looked at Iliana. "I hope to see you again soon."

Iliana shot daggers at him. "I hope that you slink back to Icarus and stay there, quietly."

Casimir gave both women points for boldness. Not many people had the courage to stand up to Demetrius DeSante.

As they docked *The Buccaneer* in Rizari, Serena composed herself. The altercation with DeSante had left her shaking and concerned. The Assembly and her uncle had warned her that President DeSante was a threat and he had made that clear today. He wanted Acacia and he would stop at nothing to have it.

Casimir drew her into a hug. "It's okay. I promise that you're safe with me. I will not let him harm you."

"He trapped me like a rat," she said.

"His tactics lack finesse," Casimir said.

Iliana approached, typing on her phone with her thumbs. "Serena, I need to talk to you about something."

From her tone, it was more bad news or more problems. "Is it Dr. Shaw? Is he okay?" Serena asked.

"Nothing about Dr. Shaw, but I will call the hospital again and request an update. This is about King Warrington. I heard something that might be a rumor and could hurt you for no reason, but I need you to know. I've always been honest with you."

Her cousin was reluctant to cause her pain unnecessarily and she understood. "Just tell me, Iliana." Even if it stung, how bad could it be?

"The night that Warrington stood you up, the night of the dinner party, he was with his mistress." Iliana's breath left in a rush.

Serena felt as if the air had been sucked from her lungs. She was so angry and frustrated, she wanted to demand that Casimir return her to Acacia. Or if he wouldn't, she would take the next flight home.

Iliana touched her forearm. "Did you hear me? Serena, are you okay?"

"I'm fine."

Warrington's mother, Katarina, was strolling down the dock toward her and on the heels of this news, Serena was spoiling for a fight. She felt embarrassed and angry at both DeSante and Warrington, and while it was juvenile, they weren't around and she wanted to unload on someone. "Say nothing of this to anyone. We will discuss it later."

Casimir glanced down the dock. "That looks like an *un*welcoming party. I'll see you around the palace?"

"I hope so," she said.

Serena didn't know Warrington's plans for her stay. She hoped her time in Rizari included face time with him so they could talk, but given their history, she didn't expect it. King Warrington seemed keen on presenting a certain front to the people of their countries, but behind closed doors, he was dismissive to her at best.

Serena climbed onto the dock. Katarina had reached *The Buccaneer* and was frowning at her. "I see that you didn't take my advice regarding the company you keep." She pointed to Casimir's retreating back.

She had been holding her tongue and that comment sent her over the edge. "Casimir is my friend. I don't think you need to be worried about where I spend my time. Perhaps you should speak to your son about where he spends his."

To Katarina's credit, she appeared unfazed. "I do not tell my son what to do."

Serena wasn't ready to back down. "Someone needs to. Because I won't be second to someone's mistress."

"The king will do as he pleases."

"So will the queen." With that, Serena brushed past her. Her guards and Iliana stayed close. Serena might have burst into tears if not for their support.

It wasn't in her character to mouth off to someone. She was accustomed to being polite and quiet. But polite and quiet wasn't cutting it in these situations. These circumstances called for boldness she didn't know she had.

"Was that Warrington's mother?" Iliana asked when they were out of earshot.

"Sure was."

"She's a real biddy, isn't she?"

"Every time I have spoken to her, which is twice, she's been like that to me."

Iliana made a noise of disgust. "What is in the water today? Everyone is acting crazy."

"Let's hope the day turns around," Serena said, but had no reason to believe that it would.

Serena's guards escorted her and Iliana to the palace. Serena was ushered to a room that was beautiful and the view, while not of the sea, was spectacular. Iliana was given a room nearby.

When she was alone in her room, feeling audacious, Serena sent a message to Warrington, asking when she could see him. She waited a full five minutes. No reply.

She sent a message to Casimir. He responded in less than five seconds with a phone call.

"Is your stay everything you hoped it would be?" Casimir asked.

Since she'd had low expectations, she supposed it was. "I haven't seen King Warrington. His butler mentioned he may join me for dinner."

"That's kind of him," he said dryly.

She snorted inelegantly. "Instead of waiting around for him, can you meet me here?"

"In the palace?"

"If you suggest somewhere else, I'd be happy to meet you. But that will mean my guards will have to join us." She wanted to be alone with Casimir so they could talk. Though her guards had sworn their allegiance to her, she was still unsure if they could keep secrets.

"I'll meet you in the king's library," Casimir said.

Serena agreed. It took her a few tries to find the library. It was on the main floor in the east wing. The mahogany double doors leading into the room were beautifully carved into an ornate design. She entered. Casimir was waiting.

How he managed to arrive before her, she didn't question. He was making her feel what she needed in that moment: wanted and worth his time.

They walked down the aisles of books and turned out of view of anyone who might enter the library.

"Does it shock you that the king could have been meeting with his mistress the night of the dinner party?" It hurt her more than she would ever admit.

"You can't ask me to speak ill of him here. That's treason."

She rolled her eyes. "The king's bedroom proclivities are hardly a matter for the court system."

"You may be surprised what's prohibited in Rizari," Casimir said.

Casimir socialized with King Warrington. Did he know more? "Tell me what you've heard about the king and his affairs."

"It's a story for another day."

"Then tell me what's the story for today," Serena said.

Casimir stopped so abruptly and spun, trapping her between his arms against one of the tall stacks of books. "I think the story for today is that the princess of Acacia is acting more like a royal and playing a dangerous game." His tone was downright flirtatious.

"I don't play games."

"Asking me to meet you here? If I weren't more trusting of you, I would think this was a trap."

"How could this possibly be a trap?"

"I think you know how the king and his mother would respond to finding us alone in the palace. It would call your pending engagement into question."

"We haven't done anything wrong."

"Katarina seems to believe my very presence is wrong," Casimir said.

"She knows her son and I don't have a relationship. Any male is a threat to the little that we do have."

Casimir's eyes traced from her eyes to her lips. "Do you want to make me a real threat to him?"

His meaning was clear. Did she have the courage to nod her head or say the word yes? She wanted him to kiss her. Desperately. Everything that had happened lately had been emotionally brutal and physically draining. Was it wrong to want something purely for herself even if it was for a brief period of time? Just to feel good for a few seconds?

She lifted her mouth. "Casimir."

His name communicated what she wanted. He reached for her, aligning their bodies, and his mouth came down on hers in a gentle kiss. She parted her lips and nipped at his, and a growl sounded in his throat. He deepened the kiss and she returned it with shameless abandon.

Putting her hand around the back of his neck to anchor herself, she gave herself over to him. His tongue left a tantalizing imprint and she felt simultaneously restless and excited. She lifted her leg and ran her foot over the back of his calf.

She knocked into books on the shelves, sending them to the floor in loud thumps. She would clean up the mess later.

The sound of an opening door had them both going still.

She moved her arm and another book landed with the others on the hardwood floor.

"Is someone here?"

Serena's eyes went wide. It was Warrington's butler. She gestured to Casimir to move deeper into the stacks. She snatched a book off the shelves and held it up as she exited the row of books. "Just me. Looking for a book."

Warrington's butler frowned. "You are certainly welcome to borrow any book you'd like. I didn't realize you were interested in weapons of the fifteen hundreds."

Serena glanced at the book in her hand. She wasn't

interested in weapons of any time period, but she smiled. "I enjoy reading about history when I have the time."

"Very well." The butler bowed to her. "Unless you need anything, I am here to retrieve a book as well."

Serena hoped that Casimir was finding his way out of the library. "I'll be returning to my room to read and work."

As she hurried out, relief tore over her. To invite Casimir into the king's library and then kiss him was dangerous. If anyone had seen them, the repercussions would be disastrous.

In her room, Serena checked her phone messages and, having none from Warrington, she attacked her email queue. The task was boring and her thoughts wandered. She steered them away from her father and sister and they landed in a curious place, or rather, on a curious person.

Curiosity got the better of her and Serena typed Casimir's name into an internet search engine.

His name popped up in connection with a financial-services firm, as he had told her. She found no social media accounts or personal websites. Was he an intensely private person? She didn't post information about herself online either. The media took care of that for her.

Though it was a mistake, she typed her name into an internet search. The first results were about her father's death and her sister's funeral. The further she scrolled, the more upset she became. Though she didn't click through to the articles, the headings were disparaging enough.

Speculation about her screw-up during her speech,

stating she could have a drug problem or that she was not mentally fit to handle the position, were the most popular posts. The accusations incensed her. She did not have a drug problem. She hadn't taken an illicit drug in her life. She was barely even a social drinker.

The drug accusations were blatant lies and easier to dismiss as ludicrous, but attacks on her character cut to the core. Was she strong enough to lead a country? She wasn't certain. Her sister had been fierce and brave. Her father had been driven and focused. But Serena wasn't bent on wielding power. She didn't have a strong vision for the country. She didn't have items on her political agenda. She wasn't even sure she had a personal agenda that she planned to use her position to achieve.

Should she address the media about the incident? She had thought it would blow over, but it seemed that hope was naive.

She typed a response, all the things she wished she could say, and saved it to her drafts. She would not send it. She wouldn't even know where to send it. But the more she stewed on it, the angrier she became. Her birthright was to be queen of Acacia and she would prove she could handle the task. After rereading her response several more times, she grabbed her phone and sent a message to Casimir. She could trust him. He wouldn't go to the press about anything they discussed.

What was it about Casimir that made him easy to talk to? He was a strange combination of genteel and strong, like a wealthy heir who had been raised to street fight.

A light tap on the door. Serena expected Warrington's butler. It was Casimir.

"You got here fast," she said.

"I never left. I ran into a few friends in the garden and I was chatting with them when I received your message."

She nodded toward her guards standing post on either side of the door. "Could we talk privately?" She stepped back and allowed him inside the room.

Casimir's hair was askew, poking up on one side, but he was otherwise perfect. Handsome and charming. Why couldn't she feel this way about King Warrington? Because the king was no Casimir. When she thought of Casimir, lust and desire radiated through her.

Was he flexing his muscles or was she turned on and looking for ways to satisfy her lust? Just like that, her worries about the media's vicious speculation about her took a backseat to her far more powerful feelings for Casimir.

"I've never been allowed to have a relationship that I've chosen," Serena said.

"That can't be true."

"It's very true. The only boyfriend I've ever had was paid off by my father to stay away from me."

Casimir winced. "That's pretty rough. What made your father hate him so much?"

"My father didn't hate him. He just wasn't the right man, at least, in my father's eyes. He wasn't rich and he didn't bring anything to the table that our family needed. No political connections, no military experience and no favorable trade arrangements. After it was over, I didn't have an interest in getting close to another man because I figured it wasn't worth it. I planned to wait for my father to pick someone and then I would marry that person."

"Then marrying King Warrington is exactly what you expected."

Not precisely. She found it hard to imagine her father forcing a relationship that was obviously a poor match. "I don't want to spend my life being unhappy." Marrying King Warrington would make it difficult to find happiness. He may allow her some freedom, like returning to her beach house and spending her life painting. But she would be alone, without a real partner in the truest sense of the word.

Casimir circled her room, looking at the artwork on the walls. "You have another option."

She inclined her head. "What option?"

"You could marry the president of Icarus."

The dictator? She laughed. "Demetrius DeSante is a tyrant and he would ruin our country. He stole power from the last ruler of Icarus and forced changes on his people. Besides that, he explicitly stated that he wanted Acacia, but without the marriage. He would take over and shut me out. I'd have no recourse to protect my people." In short, Demetrius DeSante was not to be trusted. Acacia was a monarchy, but they had the Assembly, a legislative group that was representative of the people and their wishes. The president of Icarus didn't believe in representation by the people or input from the public. He ran his country on his terms. He made unilateral decisions and showed no mercy.

"His coup was backed by a number of constituents and many in the country are faring better since he has been in power," Casimir said.

Sounded like political spin. "It's a firm no. I want happiness, remember? Not another relationship wreck."

"Then you are left with one remaining option. Stand alone and make it work. Your father did. You can, too."

She blinked at him. Her father had known keeping the peace was a tenuous balance. Icarus and Rizari were old enemies with a bitter past and a long list of reasons to attack each other. If they went to war, Acacia would be torn apart in the crossfire. "My father knew the time for peace was ending. He wanted my sister to marry the king of Rizari." And now tensions were escalating beyond the point of discussion.

"You have choices, Serena."

Did she? Why did everything feel decided for her? Every choice put her in a scenario where she was unhappy. "It doesn't seem that way."

"Then you don't see what I do. I've seen you be quiet and passive, but I've also seen you be bold. Tell me what's brought out the passive side of you. Tell me why you doubt your abilities."

"The media is questioning me as a leader." Questioning her in the same way she questioned herself at the darkest times.

He looked at her computer screen. "Do not read that gossip. Don't put any stock in a story in a tabloid. You will lose your mind. One minute, they will call you weak and useless, and the next, a power-hungry despot." He closed her laptop. "Forget about this trash. What do you want, Serena? Go after that."

She hadn't realized that she'd been walking toward him until the scent of him hit her and she extended her hand to touch him. He smelled great. The heat of his body beckoned and the power of the moment wasn't lost on her. He didn't move and she wasn't sure what to do next.

There were rules about what was and was not proper and what had happened in the library was decidedly not appropriate. That didn't stop her from wanting more or wanting him.

"I know what I want," she said.

"Then take it," he said.

Touching him was living a fantasy. His maleness was almost overpowering. His eyes were bright, greenish in some light, and other times, more brown. His hair was dark with flecks of copper. She wasn't usually a fan of facial hair, but his goatee was neat and well kept, framing his mouth.

She touched his chin and he remained still, but concern appeared in the corners of his eyes.

She drew away. "Is this too much?"

He laughed. An outright bark of laughter. "With you, it is never enough. I want this to happen. I'm letting you show me what you want. I know what's at stake. I will let you decide how this plays out."

Serena pushed on his shoulders to get him into her desk chair. The bed was far too…intimate. She wasn't ready to go there with him.

His eyes blazed with sex. She climbed into his lap, facing him, letting her legs dangle over the sides of the chair. What they were doing took on epic possibilities. Serena kissed him, soft, gentle and slow. She wanted him to take control. If she kissed him long enough, he would take over. It was in his nature.

She ran her hands over his shoulders and down his arms, relishing the feeling of his muscled arms. His goatee tickled her face and she smiled when he deepened the kiss.

In one smooth motion, he stood and she wrapped

her legs around his waist. He hit the light switch on the wall, plunging the room into darkness. Was he taking her to the bed? She made the decision in that moment to let this happen, to experience real passion and heat with a man who desired her.

Casimir carried her to the balcony, holding her with one arm and opening the door with his free hand. Outside, he laid her on the lounge chair and lay on his side next to her. It was almost completely dark, the last of the pink and purple of the sky disappearing into the deep blue of night.

"Why outside?" she asked. Not what she had expected and not what her hormones wanted.

"If you are quiet, you may hear the sea."

He had remembered that the water was a source of joy for her.

He half covered her body with his and returned to kissing her. He moved his mouth from her lips to her cheek and she angled her head to give him access to the spot on her neck where she loved to be kissed.

As her eyes adjusted to the dark, she could make out the features of his handsome face.

The man was masterful with his mouth. The right pressure and speed and she was melting in his hands. He moved his body down hers, stopping at her clavicle. "Tell me when to stop."

The words *no* and *stop* were light-years from her brain. "You don't have to do anything you don't want to," she said.

His eyes danced with merriment. "I never do."

He didn't continue down her body, a disappointment to her aching breasts and trembling thighs. Instead, he gathered her against him, shifting her to be close and held her in the nook of his arms. "Tell me why you're worried about what the mudslingers are writing about you."

Her stomach knotted. "It's not easy to read criticism, but it reminds me of my dad's disapproval. He didn't think I was smart enough or quick enough."

"Why's that?"

She'd given her father plenty of reasons to be disappointed. She wasn't an athlete or an academic. She didn't have many friends or a suitable boyfriend. People didn't like her. Her social awkwardness made them uncomfortable. "I am more introverted than my sister. After my mother died and my sister was of age, she took over as hostess for events. It was seamless for her to slip into the tasks that my mother used to handle." Their father had relied on Danae to deal with parties and the staff and the thousand other details that were involved in running and maintaining the castle.

"Your sister was organized and good at planning events. You have your own strengths."

Their father hadn't seen it that way and after Serena had moved to the beach house, she'd stopped caring. The tranquility of her home had provided more contentment than attempting to win her father's approval ever would. "I prefer the company of my art to people and I would rather have an intimate sit-down dinner than throw a splashy party."

"Nothing wrong with that."

"Everything is wrong with that when you're royalty and you need to cater to a country of people who want to see you and talk to you."

He kissed the tip of her nose. "You'll come into your

own. You'll let people see your strengths and they'll love you for it."

"A public figure who hates being in public?" It was a disaster.

"You don't need to be a political monster with a big mouth to get ahead."

It felt as if she needed a toolbox of skills she didn't have. "I guess we'll see. The next few weeks will provide plenty of tests."

"Don't worry about that now. Just think about you and me and this beautiful night."

Serena snuggled close to him and closed her eyes. Her problems would be waiting for her in the morning.

Serena's eyes popped open to the sound of knocking. It took her a moment to place where she was and what she was doing. Casimir was sleeping beside her on the lounge chair. She shook him. "Cas, you have to hide. Someone's at the door."

Another knock. This time sharper. "Princess Serena? You have not answered your phone and the king is concerned."

Serena had left her phone in the bedroom. She hadn't heard it ringing from the balcony. Serena gestured to Casimir, who ducked into the closet.

Adjusting the comforter and sheets on the bed to make it appear as if she had been sleeping, she cracked the door open. "My apologies. I turned off my phone. I was sleeping."

King Warrington's butler straightened. "The king requests an audience with you for breakfast."

Her stomach growled at the mention of food. She

had skipped dinner. "I'll need a few minutes. I'll meet the king at the top of the hour."

She closed the door and locked it. Casimir stepped out of the closet looking as handsome as ever. His hair was mussed, but it was a look that worked on him.

"That was close. I must apologize to you, Your Grace. I didn't mean to spend the night here."

Time with Casimir rejuvenated her spirit. She looked forward to spending time with him and every hour they spent together made her long for more. More days, more kisses, more Casimir. "I slept well for the first time in a long time. Thank you for staying with me."

"Sounds like you have plans with the king."

The king's expectation she appear at a meal with no warning annoyed her. She was a guest in his home, but he hadn't made much of an effort with her and that bothered her. Why should she center her schedule around King Warrington if he would not do the same for her? "I need to make myself presentable."

"You could meet with him looking like you do just now. You have no idea how beautiful you are."

Wrecked hair and everything? "You make me feel beautiful."

"Your beauty has nothing to do with me. I'm just a man who gets to enjoy it."

She looked down at her rumpled clothes. "I think the king expects something different."

"The king expects a lot from you, it seems."

It was true. "You'll need to be careful. If someone sees you leaving my room, it won't look good for either of us. I'm not sure how easily we could explain what happened last night." The circumstances were compromising. She had enough problems with King Warrington's philandering. If she opened the door to the concept of spending the night with anyone, things could only go downhill.

"I know how to go unnoticed," Casimir said.

Should she hug him goodbye? Kiss his cheek? Shake his hand? Spending the night with someone felt intimate. She decided to let it be his call. She waited and he leaned forward. He set his hands lightly on her waist and kissed her cheek.

His eyes indicated he would have liked for it to be more. But she didn't have time to dally. She couldn't risk Casimir being discovered in her room.

She stretched on her tiptoes to hug him, lingered and then drew away. "I hope I will see you soon."

"Same goes," he said.

Knowing she could have talked with him for hours more, she fled to the bathroom to get ready.

Forty minutes later, she was running at least ten minutes late for her breakfast with King Warrington. Perhaps he had invited a large group of people and wouldn't notice her tardiness. Perhaps he wouldn't show up at all.

She smelled fresh coffee, bacon and bread. As she entered the dining room, her heart dropped.

King Warrington was seated at the head of the table. He was alone.

Serena pasted a smile on her face and entered. "Good morning, Your Highness."

"Good morning, Serena. I trust you slept well."

Did he know she had spent the night with Casimir? "I did. Very well. Thank you for your hospitality."

"I have invited your guest to eat with us."

Casimir? A flare of panic hit her, but then Iliana

entered the dining room. She was all perky smiles and excitement. "Good morning."

Iliana sat next to Serena. "Sorry I'm running late. I've been awake for less than two hours and already half the country is demanding a statement about your relationship with the king." Iliana seemed comfortable with King Warrington, and Serena wished she had that same ease with him.

"What did you tell them?" Serena asked.

"That a statement was forthcoming. I wanted to talk with you first."

Serena didn't want to make a statement about her relationship with Warrington. Things were rocky between them at best. But being part of the Acacian royal family meant personal lives were not private and everyone wanted updates and explanations, even though Serena didn't have any.

The king's waiter brought her coffee with a small pitcher of creamer and a sugar bowl. As Serena made her coffee, she struggled to find words to break the silence.

Conversation with Casimir flowed without effort. She said what came to mind, but sitting across from King Warrington, Serena felt awkward and unsure.

A man hurried into the room. "Excuse me for interrupting, but the king is needed."

King Warrington appeared relieved. "Please pardon the interruption." With that, he fled the room.

"Thank God I can talk to you now," Iliana said.

"Tell me," Serena said, taking her phone from her handbag and looking at the emails Iliana had sent to her.

"A road washed out on the north side of the island.

Traffic is being diverted, but the highway administration is holding an emergency meeting to discuss repairs and how they'll acquire the money to fix it," Iliana said.

Serena typed notes into her phone as Iliana spoke.

"Cyrus Angelo is in the hospital. Heart attack."

Cyrus Angelo was one of the more outspoken members of the Assembly. His father and grandfather had been elected members and Cyrus wanted to make his own mark by being one of the biggest mouths in politics. Cyrus had been supportive of Serena's father. Serena didn't know where she stood with him. "Please arrange for flowers to be sent to him. How is Dr. Shaw?" Serena asked.

"I called the hospital this morning. No change in his condition."

"Please send flowers to his wife as well as a meal from the kitchen," Serena said.

Iliana nodded. As she continued to review the issues that had cropped up overnight, Serena grew increasingly frustrated. She didn't belong in Rizari. She belonged in Acacia. Why was she here? She had allowed herself to be persuaded. She needed to show more strength.

Serena had come to Rizari in good faith, hoping that she and King Warrington would have time together to talk. Publicly declining his invitation would have been seen as rude and hostile. But she needed to return to Acacia. She had made no progress here. "Please arrange for transport to the airport. I'm flying home immediately," Serena said.

Serena sent the king a text, brief and to the point. She was needed at home. She couldn't live this sham, not when her country needed her.

She sent a message to Casimir as well. He agreed to meet her in her bedroom before she left.

When she entered, he was pacing. "That was a quick meal."

Serena wished she could have had breakfast with Casimir, or that he had been in attendance. "The king had other priorities that required he leave after a few minutes. I have pressing matters to address as well. I am flying home in an hour."

Casimir drew her close to him. "Staying close to you is becoming a full-time job."

When he was near, she felt safer, more confident and more relaxed. "Is that what you've been doing? Staying close to me?"

He nodded. "I suppose it is. I find myself pursuing you back and forth across the Mediterranean Sea."

A thrill raced over her that he was making time for her. "When will I see you again?"

"I plan to sail my boat to Icarus. I have matters to attend to at home. I promise it won't be long."

She wished he had made firm plans with her, but Casimir seemed to show up when she didn't expect it. When she needed him. And she had a feeling that would be soon.

"Is something on your mind?" Iliana asked, as she entered Serena's office later in the day.

"Lots. Why do you ask?"

Iliana sat across from Serena. She set her tablet on Serena's desk. "You're brooding."

"Thinking," Serena said.

"About Casimir?"

How had she known? "Sometimes." Could she tell

Iliana she had spent the night with him? "He came to see me in Rizari yesterday."

"You mean after the boat ride?"

Serena nodded. "We fell asleep on the balcony of my room."

"You slept with him?"

Serena felt her face growing hot. The door to her office was closed, but she couldn't risk someone overhearing and misinterpreting. "Just slept. Nothing happened."

"Wow. Then he's more than a friend."

"I didn't say that."

Iliana rolled her eyes. "Were you touching when you slept with him?"

They had been curled on the same lounge chair, sharing their body heat. Her mouth went dry at the memory. "Yes."

"QED. Thus it is proved. You are more than friends."

Serena rubbed her face. She felt more for Casimir than just friendship. But she couldn't act on those feelings. It was a complication neither of them needed. "I don't know what to do."

"What do you want to do?"

See Casimir again. Spend time with him. Walk on the beach with him. Talk to him. "I miss him."

Iliana frowned. "What about King Warrington?"

What about him? Every time they were together, it was uncomfortable and obvious that neither of them wanted to be there. "Among other things, he's a big reason I should keep my distance from Casimir."

Iliana's phone rang and she answered it. "I am with the princess. I will be right out." She ended the call. "Flower delivery. Wonder who they're from?"

She left Serena's office door open, retrieved the flowers and brought them to her. Serena hoped they were from Casimir.

They were from King Warrington, and the attached card stated he apologized again for his abrupt departure at breakfast.

"Please send a thank-you note to the king for the beautiful flowers." She would feign that she was pleased by his empty gesture.

Serena carried the flowers to Iliana's desk and set them down. Iliana looked at her in surprise. "You want the king's flowers on my desk?"

She would prefer to shove them in the trash, but that could start a rumor. Besides, the flowers were lovely. "More people will see them on your desk. Their beauty should be enjoyed."

Iliana's phone rang again and this time, she sat at her computer while she spoke. From the sound of it, it could be a lengthy conversation.

Serena returned to her office and shut the door. She had tried to organize the dozens of tasks she had to complete and yet she felt out of control. Countless staff members, politicians and business leaders were waiting to talk to her and she needed time to process their requests.

At two in the afternoon, Iliana buzzed her to let her know that the police chief had arrived. They had a scheduled meeting to discuss the investigation into her father's and sister's deaths. She was simultaneously dreading this meeting and anxious for a culprit to be named.

Serena opened her office door and gestured for the police chief to enter. Perseus Valente was soft-spoken but commanding. He was young to be the head of the local police, but he had made a name for himself early in his career. From what Serena knew, he was above reproach. "Please, Chief, sit down. May I offer you a drink?"

He shook his head. "No, thank you, Your Grace."

She sat behind her desk and, based on his expression, braced herself for what would be an unpleasant conversation. "I hope you have good news to share with me."

"I am sorry to report that we've encountered a setback. The man we had in custody from the shooting at your father's birthday party was stabbed to death last night during a prison fight."

That man was the best lead they had and now he was gone. "Did you learn anything from him?"

Perseus shook his head. "He said nothing to his cellmates about who hired him or how much he was paid or even how he was paid. What we've uncovered about his life revealed a very isolated man who had no ties to the community. He had no personal effects in the hotel where he was staying week to week. He spoke to almost no one. I should warn you that we're looking at the possibility of someone on the inside being involved in the assassination."

A ball of dread formed in the pit of her stomach. "In what way?" Someone who worked for the royal family was working with the assassins?

"The assassins had a detailed list of who was scheduled to attend your father's party and an outline of the security protocols the royal guards followed. They exploited the vulnerabilities to smuggle their weapons inside the castle. I'm sharing our suspicions on that matter with few people. We don't know who we can trust. Until we find a mole, if there is one, we need to be on guard."

Serena felt sick. Feeling safe was nearly impossible, but she hadn't considered someone close to her being involved with the murderers. "I will be careful. Is there anything else?"

"I will keep you apprised of the investigation as it unfolds."

Serena stood. If the chief had no further information to share, their meeting was over. She didn't want to discuss her family's deaths any longer than was needed. Marshalling her emotions during those conversations was grueling and her objective was to appear in control. "Thank you for making the trip to the castle."

Perseus stood. "We haven't given up. We won't give up."

Neither would Serena. After the chief left, Iliana entered and handed Serena a dark brown folder. "One of the PIs you hired dropped this off. He has been following Casimir."

Serena had hired a few PIs to find Casimir and she had forgotten to call them immediately and inform them that their services were no longer needed. An oversight on her part and now curiosity got the better of her. She took the folder and opened it. Inside were photographs of Casimir, at least a dozen of them. The PI had tailed Casimir for the past several days, taking candid shots of him and noting what he did, where he went and whom he spoke with. Many of the photos had her in them. One picture in particular gave her pause. In the snapshot, she was looking at Casimir. The expression on her face was a mix of lust, admiration and intimacy.

Perhaps that expression was what Demetrius De-Sante had seen when he'd commented on their relationship. She searched the pictures for an expression revealing Casimir's feelings for her, but she saw only his stoic, unreadable look. Except when they were alone in private, his expression revealed nothing.

One photo had him looking serious, his hair wind-blown, and his eyes alive and taking in every detail. She hadn't missed that he was a handsome man. Turn-her-head-around handsome.

The office line rang and Iliana rushed to answer it. When Serena's phone beeped a few moments later, she remembered she had a scheduled conference call with the country's technology adviser. She lifted the receiver.

Forty minutes later, she was hanging up, her head aching with confusion. Too much jargon and new tech-nology and catchphrases she didn't understand.

The door opened again and Iliana entered her office, her expression troubled. Serena's guard went up imme-diately. "What's happened?"

"I have some bad news. We—you—received a death threat."

Serena's heart raced. "Tell me what it said."

"It said, 'Fear not, darling princess, you will join your father and sister soon.' I contacted Perseus Va-lente immediately. He's called in his best detectives to investigate."

"I want to see it," Serena said.

"The card? Why? It's really creepy," Iliana said.

It was creepy and sick and twisted. The killer who had targeted her father was now targeting her. Why? Serena wouldn't cower in fear. "Maybe the handwrit-ing is familiar. Maybe something about the card is fa-miliar. I want to see it."

Iliana blew out her breath. "I think you're asking

for more nightmares, but I'll tell the chief you'd like to take a look."

Minutes later, after Iliana had placed a quick call to Chief Valente, the card was brought to her in a plastic evidence bag. It was a black card with silver writing. The envelope it had arrived in was plain. Nothing about it was especially notable. The handwriting was a large scrawl, the words properly spelled. The card was made of black stock paper, thick and textured, the kind available at any craft store.

Serena wanted to appear in control. But this card made her want to retreat to her beach house. The outer envelope had been addressed to her with only her name, meaning someone had been close enough to the castle mail room to hand deliver it. Security was supposed to be tight around the castle. Had the assassins uncovered another vulnerability?

What if the police chief was correct and the threat came from someone inside the castle? She had to consider the possibility that the person who had arranged to have her father killed could be someone close to the family. It could be someone whom she passed in the hallways, someone who worked in her kitchen.

The castle had never felt more unsafe. There were a hundred different ways for someone to get at her and now that the overt threat had been made, it was hard to call her worries paranoia.

"Iliana, do I have any social engagements coming up out of the country?" Getting away, putting some distance between her and what was happening in Acacia, in Rizari and in Icarus would give her perspective and a sense of security, however false.

Iliana retrieved her tablet and tapped on it. "Your

father and sister were planning to attend the wedding
of the duke to his fiancée in Elion. I did not contact the
wedding coordinator about the event yet. Do you want
to go in their place?"

Serena liked the idea of honoring her father's obligations by attending as well as giving herself a breather
from the stress. Though being in a crowd was a source
of anxiety for her, she'd grow accustomed to it and,
unlike events held in her country, she wouldn't be the
center of attention in Elion. She would blend in with
the many other royals in attendance. She would force
herself to smile and appear happy to be there. A few
photo ops could sway public opinion of her for the better. Maybe some of the media who were questioning her
abilities as a leader would see her smiling and calm, and
write about her in a more flattering light.

Serena could just as easily talk herself out of attending. Public, well-attended events were rife with possibilities for failure. She despised small talk, she didn't want
to address issues surrounding her father's and sister's
deaths, and she didn't have a firm enough grasp on the
most pressing political issues to discuss them in detail.

Deciding she could handle this undertaking with a
little guidance, she dialed her minister of foreign affairs
to consult with him on the matter. If she needed to follow certain protocols, she wanted to know in advance.

Mitchell Wagner entered her office carrying a thick
folder of papers. He was thirty years older than she was,
a contemporary of her father's. He treated her with what
Serena interpreted as disdain, or maybe he was uptight
and surly by nature. Serena let most of his bad attitude
slide because he was good at his job and she didn't know
anyone with nearly as much experience to replace him.

"Thank you for meeting with me," she said.

"The pleasure is mine, Princess."

Now that they were meeting, more questions came to mind, those beyond the social and political implications of her attending a wedding in Elion. What did Wagner know about DeSante? Serena gestured for Wagner to sit. "I've had a run-in with President DeSante. There are rumors he wants to annex Acacia to have better access to attack Rizari. What can you tell me about him?"

Wagner appeared bored by the question and that annoyed her. "The president of Icarus won't back down until he accomplishes what he wants. He desires control of shipping lanes in this part of the Mediterranean."

"What is preventing him from attacking us?" The more powerful navy in Icarus could easily dominate the Acacian Navy. DeSante had flexed that muscle several times, perhaps to prove it.

"You're an unknown. No one knows what to expect from you. Perhaps he believes he can manipulate you or he's waiting to see how strong your bond with Rizari will become. DeSante is a vicious tyrant, but he isn't a stupid man."

Serena watched every dart of his eyes, twitch of his mouth and breath for a sign he was holding back. "What would you advise me to do?"

"I would suggest you keep DeSante at a distance, but close enough that we'll know if an attack is coming," Wagner said.

Serena considered that. She could make an effort to speak with DeSante more often, to keep her finger on the pulse of political movements. "I can do that."

Wagner wouldn't want his time wasted. She moved

the conversation along. "Tell me what I need to know about attending the Duke of Elion's wedding."

Wagner raised his eyebrows. "This is something you are considering?"

The doubt in his eyes made her question the choice. Did everyone believe her to be socially incompetent or was he concerned about her safety? Serena held her ground. "Yes."

Wagner settled in his chair. "I can provide the profiles of those in attendance and point out any political minefields that you'd need to avoid." He paused and rubbed his chin. "I think it would be good for you to attend. It may give you some ideas for your own wedding to King Warrington."

Again with the pressure to marry King Warrington. Why was everyone bent on it? Anyone who knew them had to see they weren't a good couple. A good political union perhaps, but nothing more.

"Your attendance would be noted and appreciated. The duke flew in for your father's funeral."

Serena didn't recall who had attended the service. Those days were a haze of decisions about psalms to read and songs to sing. "Is King Warrington attending the wedding?" She wasn't sure if his presence was a motivation to attend or a reason not to. She and Warrington had to appear a certain way in public, to look as if they were strong and reliable. Their countries wouldn't want to see a bickering, deeply divided couple running the countries.

"I believe he is planning to." Serena could do without the small smile that crept across Wagner's face. He, like so many of her countrymen, was eager to see her married, presumably because he had no confidence in her abilities to lead the country. She stifled the doubts that crept in at the slightest opening.

"I will attend." The words left her mouth feeling dry and her palms sweaty. She could have made an excuse, sent a lovely gift and a personal note, but she wanted Acacia—and herself—to be viewed as strong. She would prove that she was capable of running her country. She stood to lose too much otherwise.

Mitchell clasped his hands together. "I will communicate your intentions to the Duke of Elion and ask Iliana to make travel arrangements."

He left her office and Serena unfastened the top button of her blouse. It was too hot and the starched shirt was suffocating her. She reached for the phone and called Casimir.

The moment she heard his voice on the line, she felt better. "What are you up to?"

"What's the matter? You sound ill," Casimir said.

"I am ill. I agreed to attend a wedding. I can't go to a wedding. It's the Duke of Elion's. Lots of royalty will be in attendance looking elegant and refined, which will only highlight how ridiculously wrong it is for me to be there." She would make a fool of herself. She wouldn't say the right things. She would commit faux pas that would be printed in the tabloids, highlighting her ineptitude. Maybe she should call Wagner and tell him she had changed her mind.

"Cut yourself some slack. You can do this. I've seen you in social situations. I will be there, too, and you'll be fine," Casimir said.

Surely, he was exaggerating. She didn't feel fine in public. She felt unruly and loud and inappropriate.

A horn blared in the background and Casimir swore. "Sorry, someone just cut me off in traffic."

"Where are you?" she asked.

"Running errands."

"In Acacia?" she asked.

"In Icarus."

Why did that seem oceans away? She wished she could see him now. Her fascination with him had morphed into a crush, and it was becoming something deeper, stronger, the more time they spent together.

She had never felt this way about a man before. Their connection was intimate and she lived to see him again. She found him exciting and desirable. She had none of the same feelings for her future betrothed, the King of Rizari.

But even if the "right man" for her felt wrong, nothing could make what she had with Casimir right.

Casimir was enjoying the afternoon on *The Buccaneer*. Buying a boat had been on his mind for a long time. When he'd needed an excuse to be in Acacia, the purchase had filled in nicely. "You need to work on your charm," Casimir said to his old friend and handed him a beer.

"The princess was put off by my approach," DeSante said and twisted off the top.

Not a question. "Of course she was. You're treating her like a hostile and she isn't."

DeSante took a sip of his beer. "I am making it easier for you. The less she trusts me, the more she'll let you in. Are you making progress?"

He hoped he was. She was making time for him and confiding in him. "I'm getting to know her better every day. She trusts me." Knowing he had her trust and was misusing it bothered him. But this was for the greater good. It was all part of seeing his plan through.

"Learning anything I can use to persuade her to support our cause?" DeSante asked.

Serena was vulnerable. Her personal life was in shambles and her royal world was crumbling. He could give DeSante some information on how to get to Serena, which buttons to push, but he knew that DeSante would go for the throat and Casimir wanted to protect Serena. "Not yet. I'll keep working on it."

"I need you to work faster. She'll be in bed with the King of Rizari soon. Once that happens, I'm done. For that matter, so are you."

The image of her in bed with Samuel Warrington incensed him. Casimir was careful to keep his emotions concealed. President DeSante was not above using every weakness to his advantage and having feelings for Princess Serena was Casimir's flaw to be exploited. "I will not let her get into bed with that man. He's doing a grand job being a world-class ass to her. That helps."

"Make yourself a wedge. Do not allow their relationship to progress."

He wouldn't, though he couldn't take credit for how easy it had been. "What other methods would you suggest I employ to advance our cause?"

"Extortion. Play on her fears. Get inside her head."

DeSante's ambition knew no bounds. It was those extreme tactics that had garnered him the reputation for being cold, dictatorial and fierce. "I will get you what you want, but I will not hurt her or jerk her around."

DeSante sighed. "I should have sent Rolland."

The threat was clear and Casimir didn't appreciate it.

"Don't use him to pressure me. Rolland is a demon and I suggest you keep him in his cage." If Rolland showed up at the castle to convince the princess to bargain with the president of Icarus, he would take their goal to an extreme. Rolland didn't accept no for an answer.

"Consider him tamed. But if I don't see results soon, I'm sending in someone else to close the deal."

Casimir needed the afternoon to catch up on some tasks. From the time he'd left his place in Icarus, someone had been following him, so he made a good show of visiting a men's clothing store, a big box store, staying in character every moment and letting himself be photographed. Who was tailing him? It wasn't DeSante's style and DeSante had no reason to question Casimir's loyalty. Their conversation the day before told Casimir where he stood. He was still focused on his goals, but if he lost focus, DeSante would use someone else to get the job done.

Casimir didn't like the idea of someone digging into his life. DeSante had done a good job of establishing Casimir's fake identity, but nothing was bulletproof except the truth.

When Casimir was finished with his errands, he entered a busy part of the shopping district and disappeared. After he had doubled back twice to ensure he wasn't followed, he found an unoccupied bench in a crowded park and pulled out his smartphone.

He needed to check in with his spies in Rizari without anyone intercepting the messages and a public Wi-Fi network served the purpose.

Casimir was concerned about Serena and how she was affected by his schemes. He didn't want her destroyed when her plan to marry King Warrington fell apart, but he wouldn't allow her to make such a terrible mistake and marry a murderer.

He read his emails with a great deal of pleasure. Warrington had no idea what was coming. He thought he had stolen the throne and no one could challenge him. Casimir had every intention of making Samuel pay for killing his father.

Chapter 5

Elion was a beautiful green country. The fog hovered for most of the day and it seemed to rain often, as if precipitation was a constant. But Serena was glad to be here. Iliana was beside her, searching her schedule, ensuring none of her commitments were overbooked, while also setting aside time for Serena to be alone.

"The Countess of Provence is attending the wedding with a guest. Is Fiona's guest Casimir?" Iliana asked.

Casimir and Fiona seemed close, and though he'd said they were friends, Serena imagined Casimir being the perfect date. Good manners, textbook handsome and a total gentleman. Weddings could bring out a woman's romantic fantasies and having a man like Casimir close could fulfill them.

"Perhaps. It wouldn't surprise me. Casimir mentioned he was attending the wedding, but he didn't say if he was invited or if he was attending as someone's guest."

"Will it bother you if he's here with Fiona?" Iliana asked.

Serena didn't think that Casimir was interested in Fiona sexually. She was beautiful and charming, but Serena was more certain of her own connection to Casimir. "No more so than it might bother you if someone you liked was here with another woman." Serena had picked up on something between Iliana and DeSante. She was waiting for Iliana to admit to it.

"What are you getting at?"

"Just wondering if you have a crush on a certain president who will also be attending this wedding."

Iliana went ramrod straight. "A crush? On Demetrius?"

The use of his first name was telling. Serena reached across the car seat and took her friend's hands. "Iliana, you are my cousin and I love you. I've noticed things. Like how excited you become when you talk to him or about him. That you seem strangely giddy when his name comes up in conversation. The other day, I saw you lower your head to hide your smile when his name was spoken."

Iliana blew out her breath. "Is it that bad? Because I feel ridiculous when I'm around him. I can't help it. I know he is a jerk. Total jerk. But he's a cute jerk, you know?"

"I understand."

Iliana let her head fall back against the headrest. "I feel better that you know and it's out in the open. I've been worried but I can't talk myself out of it. This is the most absurd crush. Why would I like him?"

"I reserve the right to change my mind at any point, but I think he has some desirable qualities. He's strong and determined and resolute."

Iliana looked at Serena skeptically. "He forced you to speak to him. Again, that's a jerk move."

Serena shrugged. "He didn't harm me. I don't think his intention was even to scare me. I think he wanted his way. So, he's a little like a two-year-old having a temper tantrum, but definitely not evil-villain material. He hasn't moved on Acacia when we both know he could have and easily won."

"You were bent on hating him, but now you're cheering him on. What's changed?" Iliana asked.

Serena had never hated DeSante. Feared him, yes. But the more she learned about Icarus, Rizari and Acacia, the more she understood why the king and the president made the maneuvers they did. Her relationship with Casimir had also shed light on Iliana's relationship with DeSante. "We can't help who we're attracted to. Even when it's inconvenient and makes no sense, it's beyond us."

Iliana looked out the window. "I don't plan to act on my feelings."

"Nor do I," Serena said, thinking of Casimir.

As they drove up the driveway leading to their hotel, Serena was shocked by the crowd gathered outside the metal gate. "Why so many people?"

"The hotel has been fully booked for the wedding. The crowd is there to take pictures of the rich and famous guests that will be arriving," Iliana said.

Iliana was well informed on matters pertaining to this wedding and on social issues in general. When their car pulled through the gates close to the hotel, uniformed guards held back the crowd that tried to surge through.

Cameras flashed as photographers pressed them against the window of her vehicle.

"When we arrive at the front of the hotel, if you can, climb out of the car, turn around, smile and wave. Try to look relaxed," Iliana said.

Serena could do that. She wouldn't have to say anything, and appearing happy and in control for ten seconds shouldn't be hard. As long as she didn't trip or otherwise appear like a fool.

When the vehicle stopped to allow them out, she stepped out of the car, smiled, relaxed her shoulders and turned. She lifted her hand and waved to the crowd gathered.

Out of the corner of her eye, she caught a glimpse of King Warrington. Of all the terrible timing! Serena wanted to dive back in the car. Instead, remembering she was being watched, she smiled in his direction.

Samuel was a man with presence. As he strolled toward her, he wasn't smiling, but he seemed pleased to see her. The crowd grew louder and cameras flashed more incessantly. "Serena, what a happy coincidence."

The king bowed to her and she returned the greeting with a curtsy and the lowering of her head. "Your Highness."

"This will be our first weekend away together," he said.

He phrased it as if this was a romantic rendezvous between them and that made her terribly uncomfortable. They had not discussed this wedding or made plans to see each other while in Elion. "I am sure we will see more of each other."

King Warrington waved to the crowd and then set his hand on Serena's lower back, leading her into the hotel. As the doors shut behind them, he removed his hand as if he had been burned. "I'll have my secretary get in touch with Iliana to see when our schedules align."

With that, he strutted away from her. Serena gave him credit for knowing how to work a crowd. Serena would learn to do the same. So much was riding on her. It wasn't an option to appear a clumsy dope in public.

In her beautiful hotel suite, Serena pulled a bottle of water from the small refrigerator. She offered one to Iliana who refused with a shake of her hand. Serena twisted off the metal top and took a long swallow. Facing the crowd and running into King Warrington had been nerve-racking. She needed to keep her cool and not let a couple unplanned incidents derail her confidence.

The theme of the weekend was relaxed and happy. At least, *appear* to be relaxed and happy.

The bellhop arrived with her suitcases. Serena handed him a generous tip and he thanked her before leaving the room.

"I'll unpack your bags," Iliana said.

Serena shook her head. "We'll unpack together."

"Serena, you need to be more…"

"Mean? Rude?"

Iliana laughed. "No, not mean or rude. But you should let me do my job. You don't need to help me. Be a little more demanding to the staff."

Serena thought again of the possible mole in her midst. "Are you saying this for a reason?" Had Iliana heard something about the mole? Did she have suspicions about someone they worked with?

"I've been watching others and thinking about how they appear to their country," Iliana said.

"By others do you mean DeSante?"

Iliana rolled her eyes. "Not everything I think is about him. I believe the most successful leaders position themselves above the people around them and demand their respect. You want to rub elbows with everyone as peers. You are the queen. Try asking me to do something."

Serena liked doing things for herself. But she trusted Iliana's advice. "I'll start by asking you, firmly, to please show me what I'll be wearing tonight."

Iliana flipped through the dresses in the wardrobe case and frowned. She checked the other luggage. "Don't panic, but I don't see the dress I brought for you for the party tonight."

"I'm not panicking. Can I wear one of these other dresses? They're all so beautiful."

Iliana shook her head. "I have everything planned, the jewelry and the shoes. If you have to repeat clothes, it will reflect badly on Acacia. Don't worry. I'll check my suitcase and I'll be back. Maybe I have a few items mixed up with yours."

Iliana appeared rattled, but Serena was unconcerned. Iliana rushed to her room down the hall.

Serena returned to the living room and sat on the couch. She kicked off her heels and wiggled her toes. She couldn't let small bumps in the road turn this weekend into a nightmare. Staying focused on her goal, which was to make her father proud, represent her country and forge a few associations with others, was key. The rest of it, what she wore and what she ate, wasn't important.

A knock on the door brought Serena to her feet. Iliana had moved quickly.

Serena opened the door and came face-to-face with Casimir. He was wearing a black pair of pants and a crisply ironed, dark blue button-down shirt and tie. She had half a mind to grab the tie and pull him close.

He took her breath away. "Hey, you," she said.

"Hey, you." She stepped back and he came inside her room. If he lingered in the hallway, someone might see him and rumors would fly. Her guards were at their post and she hoped they would maintain their silence on the matter.

"Nice place. Much nicer than mine."

"Iliana booked it." Serena smiled.

"She's with you?" Casimir asked, glancing around.

"In her room." She was due back any second, but Serena didn't want to trample the moment by telling him.

He slid his hands into his pockets. "I'd heard you'd arrived and saw the bellhop bringing up your suitcases."

"How did you know they were mine?" Serena asked.

"Country emblem," he said.

Right. Not exactly traveling discreetly, but discreet hadn't been her goal.

"I saw you with King Warrington."

"Are you here with Fiona?"

The questions were asked at the same time. They were circling each other, not sure where they stood.

"I've missed you. It's been a few days, but I feel like weeks have past," he said.

Her heart surged in her chest. "I feel the same."

"You didn't call. But I know you are busy."

Was that hurt in his voice? Disappointment? "I have been busy." But also unsure if she should call, when she should call. When they were together, it felt right, but with distance came questions.

"I took a chance and came to your room, talked my way past your security guards, hoping to see you, wondering if everything we had was in my head."

So he felt it, too. "Not in your head."

"Can I see you tonight, after the party?"

Her heart thumped hard and loud, onboard with whatever he was offering. "Yes, of course."

Serena had so many questions, but she wanted answers to the one that roared the most: What did she mean to him?

Casimir's past kiss burned on her lips and she wanted to be in his arms so desperately. Would he reach for her? How could she tell him what she needed?

Casimir removed his hands from his pockets and extended them to her. She rushed into them and he folded them around her. "Did you get shorter?"

She rose up on her tiptoes. It was now or never. "No heels. Now kiss me."

He lowered his mouth to hers and she felt as if she was coming apart at the seams. Everything in her wanted this man in her bed. He made her feel so unspeakably precious. There was no comparison between Casimir and King Warrington.

Whenever she was with Warrington, she felt as though he was using her, as if he barely tolerated her. With Casimir, she felt part of something bigger and better.

Casimir's soft lips moved across her cheek to kiss her below her ear. She tilted her head, giving him more, wanting everything from him.

"Oh, my God."

He froze at the sound of Iliana's voice. He brought Serena upright and she straightened.

Iliana was looking between them and the door, a dress in one hand and her other hand plowing through her hair. She shoved the door closed. "Serena, are you okay? Do you want me to leave? What is happening? What is this?"

Serena held out her hands. "I'm fine. We're fine. Casimir stopped by to say hi."

"Serena, you can't do this. What if someone sees?" Iliana was hissing the words as if someone could overhear.

"No one will see. We're not doing anything wrong."

Iliana set the dress over the back of the settee. "I get it. I know where you're coming from. Things with Warrington have been—" she made a so-so gesture with her hand. "But this would be a huge scandal if it leaked."

"No one will find out. Especially not if you help us."

Iliana folded her arms across her chest. "I'll help you, but you know you are playing with fire. What about your guards? They know he's in here. What will stop them from telling someone?"

She made a good point. "They work for me. My guards can be trusted. You know I would help you if you needed it." Like if Iliana wanted to meet with a certain dictator and spend time alone with him.

Iliana heard her loud and clear. "Then let me return to my room so you two can finish…whatever this is." Iliana looked at the clock on the wall. "But you have four minutes, tops, because someone is coming to fix your hair." Iliana sighed. "Tell you what, I'll turn my back." She did and covered her ears, humming softly.

Casimir laughed. "Is she always like this?"

"Most of the time. She's the best."

Casimir wrapped his arms around her waist. "I want much more time with you than two hundred and forty seconds. I'll be thinking of you all night and counting down until our next rendezvous."

"Me, too."

He pressed another lingering kiss to her lips. Then he fled her room.

Iliana's eyes were wide. "I am not judging, but I had no idea that was happening."

"It's not something that's happening. It just happened."

Iliana removed the dress from the garment bag. "I need to steam this. But please be careful, Serena. This could be very bad. And we don't need anything else very bad to happen."

Serena's hands were shaking so hard, she couldn't button her dress. She had only glanced at the dress when Iliana had hung it in her closet, assuring her it was the appropriate dress for a royal cocktail party. Serena couldn't imagine how Iliana knew what was or wasn't appropriate for a specific event. Maybe there was a book on the matter that Serena was unaware of. But she wished she had chosen a dress more carefully, say, a dress with a zipper.

She hadn't slept well on the flight to Elion and now she had to attend the wedding festivities cranky, tired and nervous. Serena opened the door to the bedroom leading to the rest of the suite.

"Oh, Serena, you look a mess," Iliana said.

Since she had spent the past two hours being primped by makeup artists and hair stylists, Serena didn't want to hear it. "I'm fine. Just nervous." Thinking about being with so many people was enough to bring on a full panic attack. Serena fought against it. She would keep her calm.

"I wish I could go with you, but the invitation did not include me," Iliana said. "What's making you more nervous, seeing Casimir or seeing King Warrington or having to deal with the crowd?"

All of it. She wished she could fast-forward to 11:00 p.m., a good time to leave the party, especially with the wedding being held tomorrow morning. "I wish I was more like Danae." She turned around so Iliana could button her dress.

"Stop that. You are not Danae and she couldn't have been you. You each have your strengths. You're far more sensitive to others. That's a great skill. Use that."

"How will my sensitivity help me?" Most people were keen to tell her to toughen up and be more firm.

"If you sense someone needs a friend, be that friend. Listen. Don't worry about being entertaining. Half that room probably pays a therapist five hundred an hour to listen to their problems. You can do that for free."

At the mention of therapists, her thoughts flew to Dr. Shaw. Her shoulders tightened and she felt ill. "Do you think assassins will come after me tonight?"

Iliana hugged her. "No. You will be safe tonight. You have your guards in addition to the security for the wedding, and King Warrington and Casimir. And me. I'm a text away if you need anything."

Serena had come this far, she would go the distance. She would represent Acacia proudly.

As Serena entered the Great Hall where the party was being held, she was struck by its grandeur. She wished Casimir was beside her. She circulated through the crowd, clutching her handbag. It made her feel better to have something to do with her hands. In a room of famous faces and celebrities, she didn't stand out and it was the way she preferred it.

As if they had an invisible draw between them, Serena found Casimir. He was standing across the room, wearing a tuxedo as if it was made for him. She couldn't take her eyes off him. One of her guards was with her, walking close beside her. In a room of dashing, talented men, she only had eyes for Casimir.

Making it doubly a shame that King Warrington was in the room. He was speaking to a group and hadn't acknowledged or noticed her. Making a beeline for Casimir would be terribly obvious.

But she caught his eye and she felt as though he was looking into her soul. She would have given almost anything to be alone with him, to follow her heart and her instincts and run directly to him.

She considered her options. As the heiress to the throne, she should feel free to do what she wanted. Except the opposite was true. In matters related to her personal life and her political decisions, she was utterly caged.

Iliana had never been to Elion before. She might never have another opportunity to be in the country again. Instead of lying in bed, watching television and worrying about Serena, she pulled on her favorite jeans and a sweater, grabbed her handbag and planned to take a walking tour of the area, or at least the parts of it that she could reach on foot.

She opened her hotel room door and came face-to-face with Demetrius DeSante. "Oh." Her heart raced and her stomach dropped. Her handbag hit the floor and she bent to pick it up at the same time he did.

Their hands met as they were crouching on the floor. The air around them crackled and singed. They rose together, their eyes locked. Iliana struggled to compose herself.

Though he was flanked by two of his guards, she didn't feel threatened.

"Were you waiting outside my door?" Iliana asked.

"A happy coincidence that I caught you on your way out," he said. He had a lilting accent and her heart swelled a bit.

"Serena isn't with me."

"I am not here to see the princess. I am here to see you."

Iliana felt sure her heart would explode out of her chest. He cut an impressive figure, tall and darkly good looking. His face was that of a warrior, stern and strong. "How may I help you?" This did not feel like a professional visit. This felt personal. But Iliana wouldn't make the leap alone. He had to cross the line and then she would gladly cross it with him, if only for a night.

"Come with me to the party tonight."

Iliana looked down at her jeans. "I have nothing to wear."

"You look perfect in that."

Iliana laughed. "You are the only man to think that, I am sure."

"What can I say to change your mind? Of all the women I have ever known, you are the most difficult to persuade into doing what I want."

Everything the man said sounded sexual. "I can't go, tonight, Mr. President."

"Call me Demetrius. Please." He was looking at her with such intensity, she looked away for a moment and collected herself.

When her eyes returned to his, he was watching her. His tie was crooked and she reached for it.

His guards tensed, but he held up his hand. "I don't think she plans to strangle me."

Iliana shook her head. "Of course not. Your tie is uneven. But I like it. Very fashion forward. Where did you get it?"

"I have no idea."

"You don't do your own shopping, then?" she asked.

"No. For now, I have a personal shopper. One day, I will have a wife to perform that duty."

The word wife echoed in her brain. He wasn't speaking of her, but it did funny things to her heart. Iliana had never been a "take care of your man" woman. She was independent, lived alone and had never bought a man clothes. How could she imagine herself in that role, and for a dictator, no less? "Serena left for the party a while ago." Shouldn't he be there as well?

"Then I will be late."

"I was surprised to hear you were planning to attend," Iliana said.

"The duke is an old pal. He will understand if I am tardy."

It was strange to hear him speak of anyone as a friend. From what she had read and heard about De-Sante, he was cold and fierce. While she could see that side of him, he was showing her another side, too, one that was compassionate, warm and funny. "I should probably get going."

"Where are you going?" The question sounded casual, but she heard his concern.

"Touring the city."

"Would you allow me to accompany you?"

"I don't think it's a good idea." Except in some world where only they existed. But with the politics and the social issues between them, a relationship with Demetrius, especially a public one, would cause trouble for Serena. Serena didn't need more trouble.

"I will never force you to do anything you do not wish. But if you change your mind, here is my phone number." He took her phone from her sweater pocket and typed something into it.

She was startled by him offering the connection. She had called his office before and had thought that number was exclusive. This was beyond that. "Thanks. Thank you."

He bowed to her before leaving. When he'd disappeared down the hall, Iliana looked at her phone. He had typed *Yours*. And then his number.

Serena didn't like attending the party without a date. She should have considered this more carefully. It wouldn't have been appropriate to bring someone like Casimir, but she could have brought her uncle with her. King Warrington had technically attended alone as well, but he was not at a loss for company.

Serena circled the perimeter of the room and observed. Perhaps she would run into another wallflower and she could strike up a conversation. Her guard followed her, which made her feel a little less lonely, except like most of the other security present, he stayed silent.

Serena spotted Casimir speaking with Fiona. He was her date for the event. Her heart sank. Casimir could change his mind about Fiona, get swept away into an affair with the beautiful countess. Serena turned away, not needing to torture herself by watching them, and considered leaving. She had shown up. No one was tracking her. No one seemed to know she was there.

Her cell phone buzzed and she opened her purse. It was a call from the castle. Strange at this hour. She stepped out of the Great Hall into the hallway.

"Serena, I am so happy I caught you."

"Uncle Santino, what's wrong?"

"Are you safe, darling?"

She looked around. Her guard was hovering nearby. "I'm fine. You sound upset. What's wrong?"

"Terrible news. Someone tried to assault me!"

Serena's body tensed. "Are you okay? Were you hurt?"

Her uncle was breathing hard. "I'm fine now. I wanted to have a quiet, private dinner with an old college friend and asked my guards to wait in the car. I left the restaurant after my meal, walked to the car and someone jumped me from behind. I have a terrible headache and feel out of sorts."

Everything in her screamed in alarm. Another attack. "I'm coming home now," Serena said.

"No, no, there's nothing you can do. I only called to ensure that you were okay. I worried it may have been a conspiracy to strike out at the royal family again. After what happened to your father and your sister, I worry for you."

Serena shivered in the air-conditioned hallway. "I'll be okay. Are you sure you don't want me to return home?"

"No. Stay close to the king, though. He will keep you safe."

Serena frowned. Many, including her uncle, seemed to believe she had this amazing connection and relationship with King Warrington. Yet, a few hours ago, she had been kissing another man. "The king is quite busy."

"Never too busy for you. Remember, Serena, people will only treat you as badly as you let them."

"I'll do my best." That rarely seemed to be enough. "Please call if you change your mind and make sure your guards stay close," Serena said.

"It was a wise move to be out of the country. Give the dust some time to settle and give the police time to find who is behind these vicious attacks. You take time with the king and regroup. Your country is counting on you."

The city was so beautiful. Even with the heavy fog and light drizzle, the views were striking. Old buildings restored to maintain their character and charm lined the streets. No clutter littered the roads or sidewalks and every window had greenery to match the open fields and wide expanses of land surrounding the small town.

Iliana would like to live in a quiet place like this. She guessed everyone knew each other here and they were a close-knit and warm community.

"Give me your wallet," a man said into her ear. Something sharp pressed into her back.

Adrenaline kicked hard in Iliana's blood. She reached into her purse to hand him her wallet. The thief turned her around and grabbed a fistful of her hair. He held a knife to her stomach. She was afraid to breathe, for fear he would kill her.

"Let me go!" Iliana screamed.

"How lucky for me that a beautiful woman was stupid enough to walk alone."

"She isn't alone."

Demetrius DeSante came out of nowhere, fists flying. He had the thief on the ground and was pummeling him mercilessly.

The thief wasn't moving. Iliana grabbed his arm. "Stop, Demetrius. Stop. Please."

Demetrius landed another punch and then stood. His guards were ten paces away. They had not interfered and they seemed indifferent to the scene. Would they have allowed the dictator to kill the man?

Demetrius touched the side of her face with tenderness she wouldn't have thought he possessed after that display of violence. "Are you hurt?"

"I'm fine. Scared. Of him. Of you. What are you doing out here?"

"Following you."

Iliana blinked at him. Serena had messaged her to see if she was okay following an attack on Serena's uncle, so Iliana had been somewhat distracted. She had been walking the streets for close to two hours and hadn't noticed anyone following her. "But the party…"

"The party is just that. A party. But you are precious."

Her lips parted and she inhaled. He was looking at her intently and her heart fluttered for reasons that had nothing to do with fear. "Thank you. I didn't think…"

"This is not Acacia. You are a stranger in another land. You need to be careful."

He slipped his arm around her waist and led her to a black sedan parked at the end of the block. "Tell me what you'd like to see and I will take you."

Iliana felt she was in an alternate reality. "I was planning to walk the city and see the sites."

"Then may I suggest a place?"

"Sure."

"I know a small café on the edge of town that serves the most wonderful biscotti. Let's share some coffee, or tea if you'd prefer at this late hour, and enjoy the local specialties."

"You want to eat with me?"

"I want to do more than eat with you, but I am a gentleman."

She swallowed hard. Seeing this side of him was strange. What was his angle?

"You called me Demetrius."

Her mind was still reeling from the attack and fear was still trembling in her muscles. "Did I?"

"You did. When you were begging me to show your assailant mercy."

Iliana blinked at him. "You would have killed him."

"He should not have touched you. I wouldn't have beaten him for stealing from you, but touching you and threatening you is a grave offense."

"I was okay." Except she wasn't sure if she would have been.

"Iliana, I know you are afraid of me. But I want to undo those fears. I want to show you I am not a monster. I am a man, a driven man, and I will prove that you can trust me."

Iliana didn't know what to do with this information. Still rattled, she slid closer to Demetrius in the car.

Though he seemed surprised, he didn't move away. She laid her head on his firm shoulder and closed her eyes.

Inhaling deeply, she let herself relax. She had fantasized about Demetrius, dreamed of him, sparred with him verbally and now that she was in his arms, she didn't want any more drama. She just wanted him.

Despite being together for hours, Demetrius DeSante didn't touch her. He sat across from her in the café at the circular mosaic-topped metal table. He did not laugh easily and rarely smiled. But he made no attempt to end the evening. He asked interesting questions to further the conversation. He didn't look at his phone or the clock on the wall.

Demetrius was well read on a variety of subjects and strangely, they seemed to share several interests and were of like mind on many topics.

Best of all, his attention was completely on her.

Iliana wished she could text Serena about this, but she didn't know how to without appearing rude. And she already felt intimidated sitting across from the dictator. When the shop employees began wiping down tables, they reluctantly stood to leave.

Demetrius left a sizeable tip on the table. She wouldn't have thought he would tip so generously. Everything she had read about him seemed shaded and not representative of the real Demetrius DeSante.

When they returned to the hotel, Demetrius walked her to her room, oblivious to anyone who saw them together. Would he try to come inside her hotel room? Would he expect sex? She slipped her key card into the slot and the light turned green. She turned the door handle and cracked the door.

He did not advance forward.

"Iliana, I had a wonderful night. Thank you for the company."

She held the door open and debated inviting him inside. Reading him was difficult and it would be easy to make a misstep. "Thank you for rescuing me."

He seemed to blush and it was adorable. His hands were clasped behind him. He would leave without touching her or kissing her. Would it be wrong to kiss his cheek? To hug him?

She decided a kiss on the cheek was not out of bounds. She leaned up and pressed her lips to his cheek. He closed his eyes.

When she pulled away, she had left some lipstick on him. She wiped at it with her thumb. He caught her hand and kissed the inside of her wrist. "Leave it."

"It looks like I marked you."

"Perhaps I want to be a marked man. Good night, Iliana. You will call on me if you require anything."

He stepped back and she closed the door. After sliding the lock into place and taking several deep breaths to calm herself, Iliana peeked out into the hallway. Demetrius was gone.

She wouldn't know how to explain what had happened tonight. Was she being courted by the dictator of Icarus? Was he trying to use her for some ulterior motive?

If he was using her, what did she have that he needed?

As the party picked up the pace, wine and alcohol were flowing more freely and the volume of the room grew louder.

Casimir found Serena sitting at the bar. She looked bored. He seconded that emotion. He had spent time with Warrington, a task that taxed and angered him to no end.

"Having fun?" he asked.

Serena smiled halfheartedly. "I was planning to leave in a few minutes. I wanted to give you this." She pressed her room key into the palm of his hand.

The simple gesture meant volumes. Even after a night of socializing with the upper echelon of Elion, she still wanted Casimir in her room. The anticipation of being alone with her might kill him.

Casimir was pleased to know that if he was with Serena, she would not be with King Warrington. Demetrius DeSante would be pleased to know that information as well.

Serena slid off the bar stool and walked casually out of the room. Before he could follow her, DeSante approached.

"I almost killed a man tonight."

Casimir knew his old friend could mean that literally. "In what context?"

"I went out with Serena's assistant. A man touched her. I beat him senseless."

Casimir shook his head. DeSante rarely acted or reacted with pure emotion. There had to be more to the story. "You had a date with Iliana?"

"We were out together. It was not a date."

"What kind of man touched her? Like brushed by her on the street?"

DeSante gave him a droll look. "No, he tried to assault her."

The incident came more clearly into view. DeSante had no patience when it came to violence against women or children or anyone who could not defend themselves.

Zero threshold. It was a strange ethic. He would beat someone without guilt, but would defend to the death someone whom he believed deserved protection.

"Is Iliana hurt?"

DeSante shot him a look. "Do you think I would let someone hurt her?"

Casimir didn't know DeSante and Iliana had grown so close. DeSante's interest in Iliana was noteworthy because he rarely pursued a woman. "If you were out with her, I have no doubt she was safe."

DeSante stood taller. "I made it clear to her where we stand."

"And where is that?" Casimir asked.

DeSante touched his heart. Then he flicked his head upward to someone behind Casimir. "Excuse me."

Casimir didn't mind the abrupt end to their conversation. He and DeSante could be friendly. They made it their policy to be sociable with everyone. But they couldn't be linked together. It was too risky for their plan.

The last thread he needed to tie up was Fiona. She was having a good time, not drunk, but definitely feeling a buzz. He located her on the dance floor.

"I'm heading to bed," he said.

Fiona shook her head and winked at him. "Not unless it's my bed."

He wasn't sleeping in her room. They had booked separate rooms for a reason. "Not tonight, Fiona. I can't sully your reputation."

"Then make an honest woman out of me and put a ring on my finger." She threw her head back and laughed, but he heard the truth in the statement.

He had promised himself Fiona wouldn't get hurt

in his quest to destroy King Warrington. That might mean ending his relationship with her and giving her wide-open space to move on with her life. Not that he and Fiona had made any verbal commitments to each other, but Casimir knew that Fiona sometimes read into a situation and the more time they spent together, the more attached she became to him.

"Good night, Fiona." He kissed her cheek and she waved as he left the party.

He took the stairs to Serena's room. He needed to burn off some extra energy and give himself time to think about how to play this.

It had never been the plan to sleep with Serena. He didn't want to hurt her or put her in the middle of anything. He needed to be careful not to be seen entering her room at this hour by anyone other than her guards. They were, and should be, unavoidable.

Casimir stopped in his room, changed into sweatpants and a hooded sweatshirt. Then he went to Serena's room. He didn't see her guards. Were they posted inside?

Casmir entered the bedroom and he closed the door behind him.

Serena was in her closet, taking off her dress. His breath caught. She looked beautiful.

"Where are your guards?" he asked.

"In their rooms. Sleeping."

No one was watching her room? That seemed risky. All the better that he was with her.

She turned to show him the buttons. "I can't get my dress unfastened."

She was undressing in front of him? Score for his desire. He walked closer to her, trying not to appear too eager and trying to keep his lust in check. This might not mean what he thought it did.

"You picked a dress with the world's tiniest buttons. There's no way one person could get this off." His fingers brushed her bare skin as he worked with the tiny spheres, forcing them through the satin fabric loops.

"Maybe it's supposed to require two people. More exciting that way," Serena said.

Her tone was higher and she seemed anxious. "Everything okay?" he asked, still unfastening the buttons. They went down the back of the dress, well past the curve of her rear end. Should he unbutton every one, or leave some fastened? How far did she want this to go?

"I received some bad news from my uncle."

"About Dr. Shaw?"

Serena took a deep breath. "Thankfully, Dr. Shaw is stable and growing stronger every day. But my uncle was attacked leaving a restaurant."

Though he wondered if there was a connection, Casimir could not tell her about Iliana's near mugging without giving away his friendship with Demetrius. "He didn't have his guards with him?"

"He did, but they were waiting in the car," Serena said, emotion thickening her voice.

Casimir gently turned her by the shoulders. "I'm sorry." He drew her into a hug. She seemed as if she needed a friend and a support. He could be both. It wasn't exactly what he had in mind, coming to her room tonight, but he would be whomever she needed him to be.

"Do you want a glass of wine? Something to relax?" he asked.

"I've had enough to drink tonight," she said, turning again.

He had unfastened the last button. Her thong was exposed, giving him a peekaboo look at the rest of her.

"Have you looked in the mirror?" he asked.

She shook her head.

He led her to the mirror and she stared, mostly at him. They looked good together.

"You look like a princess," he said.

"I am a princess," she whispered.

Reading her signals and responding, he peeled the right shoulder of her dress away, letting it fall down her arm. She was wearing a black bra and now he could see the lace trim. Elegant and classy, exactly like her.

Then he slid the fabric down the other shoulder.

The dress fell to the floor in a heap. Still watching her face in the mirror, he kissed her neck, setting his hands on her hips.

She let out her breath on a sigh. He moved his hands to encircle her waist and she leaned into him. He had wanted her for so long, this could have gone lightning fast and been over in an instant. But he wanted to draw it out, to make his time with her last as long as possible.

Though he wasn't sure how this related to avenging his mother's honor or how it would impact his and De-Sante's plans, he knew exactly what he was doing with Serena. He knew how to please a woman, and tonight he would please Serena.

"Open your eyes and look at me," he said.

She did as he asked.

"Watch what I'm doing to you."

He reached into the front of her panties and found her hot and wet. His erection strained against his pants, but this was about her. He wanted her to come once, maybe twice. He massaged her and she swayed on her feet.

"Spread your legs."

She brought her legs apart and he plunged a finger inside her. She gasped.

Moving her panties aside, he knelt between her legs. Using only his fingers, he made love to her, his eyes never leaving her face. She reached for the full-length mirror stand to steady herself. She made the most astonished face when she came and pride tumbled over him.

He stood and kissed her and she melted against him.

"Let's go to bed," she said.

"My thoughts exactly."

Sweeping her off her feet, he carried her to the king-size bed. With a flick of his wrist, he pulled away the covers and blankets and laid her down.

She watched him from propped elbows, her back on the mattress.

He lifted her foot, removing her shoe and dropping it. Same for the other foot. He set her feet on the bed, her knees bent. He moved between them.

"What are you doing?" she asked.

"I want you to come again."

"I already..."

"That's why I said *again*."

She started to protest, but he ignored her and brought his head between her legs. After a few gentle laps of his tongue to gauge her reaction, he held nothing back, licking, sucking, tasting.

"I can't. I can't," she said, her hips thrashing.

But she could. He had seen it and now he wanted to taste it.

Adding his hand, he slid inside her. His free hand

reached to her breast and, pulling aside the delicate fabric, he stroked her. She climaxed in his arms.

He moved up the bed and lay next to her, feeling simultaneously tired and as if he could do this all night. The way she moved and the sounds in the back of her throat when she enjoyed him were awesome.

She rolled to the side and buried her head against his neck. "Casimir, please stay with me."

For tonight? Forever? His mind traveled to funny places and he considered what he had done. It complicated matters for sure. Was that bad?

Letting DeSante in on what he had done, not the details, just that his relationship with the princess had shifted, might give perspective, but Casimir wasn't ready to share this with anyone.

For tonight, Serena was his and his alone.

Chapter 6

Serena curled next to Casimir, basking in the heat of his body. The only light was from the closet. She was tempted to get up and turn it off, to pull on her pajamas and get more comfortable. But being next to Casimir was a comfort in itself.

She ran her fingers over his jawline, his beard tickling her fingers. Then she kissed him. Her skin prickled and the memory of the night they had shared simmered in her blood.

He looked so peaceful and handsome as he slept. "Casimir?"

"Yes, Your Highness?" He sounded groggy.

"Please don't call me that."

"What would you like me to call you?"

"My name. Call me Serena."

He brought his lips to her temple in a kiss that was as perfect as it was brief. "Serena, what's on your mind?"

"I was thinking about last night." Given the early-morning hour, it was an accurate description.

"About what happened with your uncle?" he asked.

"About what happened between us."

"It sounds like you're worried."

Of course she was worried. What did this mean? "I'm supposed to marry King Warrington."

He tensed. If she hadn't been touching him, she wouldn't have noticed the slight tightening of his muscles in response to the mention of the king. "I know that you do not and cannot belong to me. You belong to Acacia and the king." His voice was edged with ice.

The truth in his statement brought tears to her eyes. She blinked them back. "Can't I be yours for now? For a few days or weeks or however long we have?"

A dark expression passed over his face. She didn't know him well enough to say what it was, but he was holding something back. He had depths she hadn't fully explored and given the temporary status of their relationship, she couldn't demand he confide in her.

Secrets could bring trouble. "Will you tell me what you're not saying?" she asked.

He rolled to his side. "I'm worried about you. You don't seem cut out for this life. You aren't hardened and scheming. Everything you do is open."

"Is that wrong?"

"Not wrong, but not how most people play this game. You'll be hurt because someone will take advantage of your goodness and genuineness."

A warning traced up her spine. "Are you one of those people?"

He shook his head and closed his eyes briefly. "I have

no intention of harming you. But I see the path you are
on, and it's not good."

He wanted to put distance between them before her
path became tied to King Warrington's. Casimir seemed
to be one of the few people in her life who saw that she
and the king were wrong for each other. "Why are you
pulling away from me?"

"You ask this as you sleep in my arms?"

She was overwhelmed with emotion. Though he
didn't speak of love, he spoke of devotion and stead-
fastness when she needed it most. "You have been the
first person in a long time to become close to me. I can't
define why it's so easy to let you in."

He let his forehead fall against hers. "I feel it as
well."

"Stay close to me tonight," she said.

"I will. I promise. For tonight."

Inside the church and forced to make polite conversation with strangers, Serena was grateful when the string
quartet began to play music and she was escorted to her
seat by an usher. The church was filled with pink and
yellow flowers and a sweet floral scent hung heavy in
the air. The church had been built a few hundred years
earlier, its stained glass windows intricate and the fres-
cos on the ceiling beautiful and ornate.

Surprised at how close she was to the altar, she
looked around for Casimir, trying to appear noncha-
lant. He had left her room early that morning before
the sun rose.

No one could know they had spent the night together.
It wouldn't be proper. One of her reasons for attending
this wedding was to represent her country and to honor

her father's memory by stepping in to his place. Starting rumors or problems ran contrary to her intentions.

When she visually located Casimir inside the church, seated a couple rows behind her and next to Fiona, he met her gaze. The eye contact closed the distance between them and her skin tingled as if she were standing in his arms. Afraid someone else would notice the look, she broke it.

Serena faced the altar and tried not to think about her own wedding. Many of the same people would be in attendance, her father's and sister's absence too painful to consider.

The groom walked to the altar with the minister and Serena was struck by the expression on his face. He was happy, excited even.

How would King Warrington look as he waited for her? Stern? Serious? Resigned? She hadn't seen him yet today. Would he think about their wedding today with the same sense of disappointment and dread?

When the doors in the back of the church opened and the bride entered, the groom's face switched from excited to elated.

Serena's heart broke for her misfortune. King Warrington wouldn't stare at her with affection and love. Their wedding would simply be a means for them to fulfill their obligation to their countries. Would he even want to share the same bed on their wedding night? Would she?

A mild headache formed at the edges of her brain. She had ibuprofen in her clutch, but taking it now would cause a distraction.

The rest of the ceremony was a blur, but Serena stood, sat and kneeled along with the people around her.

As the church emptied, she remained in her seat. She wished the day were over. This was supposed to be a small vacation from Acacia and her troubles there, but she didn't feel refreshed. She felt stressed and burdened thinking about her wedding. Arranging for her private plane to take her home was a simple matter, but she had to attend the reception. It was a private dinner for close family and friends. Although, given that Serena was invited, she wondered how close those family members and friends could be.

Casimir approached and sat next to her. "Enjoy the service?"

"The bride was lovely. The groom seemed happy."

The guests were outside throwing bird seed and blowing bubbles. The church was quiet. Could she stay here? She had made an appearance. Maybe she could skip the reception after all.

She reached for his arm, but she drew back when she realized her mistake. He wasn't her date and behaving otherwise was inappropriate. "You were gone when I woke."

"I had to leave before your guards returned."

Fiona approached, smiling, but something in her eyes worried Serena.

"I see you're talking to your princess again," Fiona said, glowering at Serena. Fiona slid her arms around Casimir's shoulder in an obviously possessive manner.

"Ready to go to the reception?" she asked Casimir.

Casimir smiled at her. "Sure. See you there, Serena?"

"Yes. See you both there."

Serena waited for them to leave. She was alone in the church, save for her bodyguard standing nearby.

She could hear the sounds of excitement drifting farther away.

Being in a church made her think of her father and her sister. Her sister would have loved to be married in a church like this. She would never have the opportunity.

Serena wiped at the tears that came to her eyes. She fished in her handbag for a tissue. She missed her father and sister so much, she wondered if the pressure on her chest would ever fully go away. Serena thought of them a thousand times a day and today was no exception.

She composed herself and then walked outside to her waiting car. Serena didn't want to socialize. She had too much on her mind. Was she accomplishing what she had set out to accomplish? Did anyone see her differently now, having spent time with her?

Needing to hear a friend's voice, she called Iliana who answered sleepily.

"How was your night?" Serena asked.

"I went sightseeing and instead of the sights, I saw Demetrius DeSante almost kill someone."

Alarm rattled her nerves. "What? Are you okay?"

"Thanks to him, yes, I'm fine. He was worried about me and he followed me. Sure enough, trouble found me and Demetrius kicked its ass."

"The dictator of Icarus kicked someone's butt for you?"

"Sure did. One of the most insanely disturbing and yet shockingly romantic things that has ever happened to me."

"Do you think your attack is related to the one on my uncle?" She had messaged Iliana the night before so she would be extra careful.

"The guy was a street thug. He didn't know who I was."

"Are you okay now?"

"Physically, yes. Emotionally, I feel totally confused."

"Same here."

"Oh, did something happen with Casimir?" Iliana sounded more awake now.

Serena filled her in, glossing over some details. "I know we can't be together, but I can't stay away from him."

"Give in and stay there for as long as reality allows. That's what I'm thinking about with DeSante. See where it leads. What's the worst that can happen?" Iliana asked.

"DeSante could kidnap you, take you to his country and add you to his harem."

Iliana laughed. "He would never. I don't share men. And can you see me as a harem woman? Please. I look terrible in jewel tones."

Serena had known Iliana long enough to read between the lines. Though she joked about her relationship with DeSante, they had something real. "Maybe you should give him a chance."

"You're okay with that?"

Serena wasn't sure she could pass judgment on anyone else's relationship. She was making a mess of her own. "I'll think on it. But as long as you don't spill state secrets, what's the harm?"

"Since I don't know any state secrets, I think we're safe there."

"We just pulled up to the reception. I'll call you later, okay?"

"Have fun!" Iliana said.

Not a chance.

Fifteen minutes later, Serena was struggling to follow a conversation with the duke of someplace. He was talking about his plans to take his yacht around the world. Normally, the conversation would have interested her, but since he was simply listing cities and dates, she found it tedious.

If she didn't get away, she would fall asleep. Not the impression she wanted to make.

She cut into the monologue. "You'll have to excuse me. I see someone I need to speak with." The duke didn't follow her and she was grateful.

Serena threaded through the crowd toward the bar. She asked for a glass of soda, hoping the caffeine would rouse her out of her funk.

Casimir was the only person in the room she could focus on totally. When their eyes met, he moved toward her. Given the number of people in attendance, hopefully Fiona wouldn't notice him speaking to her. Serena didn't want to make an enemy of the countess.

Casimir stood by her casually. They hadn't touched and Serena longed to close the distance between them. Too many people to judge and too many cameras to capture the act to give in to that desire.

"Are you feeling okay?" he asked.

The crowds made her uncomfortable, but she was not the center of attention so it was tolerable. The bride and groom were drawing and holding most of the focus in the room, and deservedly so. "I almost didn't come. But I'm here."

A flurry of activity by the door caught Serena's attention. King Warrington had entered the Great Hall.

Serena's stomach knotted and she felt light-headed. The king of Rizari moved through the crowd, shaking hands. She wanted to disappear. She didn't want to talk to him, except decorum dictated she acknowledge him. She felt guilty for sleeping with Casimir and she resented Samuel Warrington for the hold he had over her life.

"Is it too late to leave?" she asked Casimir.

"He's blocking the main exit. I can take you out the side door."

Running away would look strange. Someone would notice and then Serena would have to provide a reason for her rude behavior. "I'm trapped." Today, tomorrow and in her future marriage.

King Warrington strode toward her and Serena took a slow, deep breath. Of all the times to feel dizzy and fuzzy, this was a bad one. She plastered a smile on her face and pretended she was happy to see him.

Extending her hands to him, she clasped his and leaned toward him, allowing him to kiss her cheek. He smelled of cologne, and she gagged a little.

"King Warrington, hello," she said.

"I've told you, call me Samuel. Even in public, we can be on familiar terms."

He had said no such thing, but it sounded good to anyone listening in on their conversation. "Did you enjoy the service?" Small talk. She hated it.

"It was well done. Hi, Casimir. I see you are keeping the princess company."

Casimir smiled in response.

People were moving closer to eavesdrop on their conversation. Serena hoped she was playing the role of his future betrothed convincingly.

Women, in particular, were jockeying for position to be near the king, openly staring at him and whispering to each other. His playboy reputation preceded him. She had to admit, he was handsome in a polished, preppy way.

But he was no Casimir.

"The bride is breathtaking," Serena said, trying not to become distracted by the thought of wearing a wedding dress herself.

With pleasantries exchanged, they were out of topics to discuss. They had little in common except her sister. It was inappropriate to talk about business or political issues at a wedding where others could overhear.

"My guards are signaling me, but I hope we'll share a dance tonight," Samuel said.

Serena nodded. "Looking forward to it." Not really. She would find some way to avoid it and him. Based on their interactions thus far, he would be thrilled to be relieved of the obligation. The women pouncing on him guaranteed he would have his share of women to keep him company.

One thing was clear: King Warrington wanted Acacia, but he did not want Serena as his wife.

Serena touched her hat to be sure it was in place. The room tilted and then Casimir's arm was around her waist and his hand on her forearm. "Your Highness, are you okay?"

In his voice, a worry. "I feel dizzy," she said.

Casimir was leading her somewhere, hopefully away from the crowd. She closed her eyes to dissipate the dizziness. When it grew darker, Serena opened her eyes. They were in the gardens outside the Great Hall.

Casimir led her to a marble bench and helped her

sit. He knelt in front of her. "Are you feeling okay?" Seeing him this way brought back poignant memories of the last time he had been in that position and desire stole the breath from her lungs.

Serena waved him off and tried to lasso her runaway libido. "I needed fresh air. It was hot in there."

Why had she come to this wedding? Why had she believed she could handle this? She had to prove something to everyone it seemed, including herself. "I don't want to marry King Warrington and when I think about it, I feel sick." She spoke the words in a whisper. She was sure this wouldn't come as a shock to Casimir. After all, he knew more about her relationship with the king than most. Serena set her hands in her lap. "Did you see how women frolic around him and throw themselves at him?"

"Frolic?"

"What word would you use?" Serena asked.

"Maybe another *F* word to describe what those women want, but why does that matter?"

Did he really not know or did he want her to explain it? "That's not a desirable trait in a husband."

"Some women would enjoy having a man who others desired."

"But that's the part we have wrong. Warrington doesn't desire me. I don't know that he ever will. What if he doesn't stop his dalliances after we're married?"

"That would be embarrassing for both of you."

Serena closed her eyes. She shouldn't have come to Elion. She should have sent a nice gift, a pleasant note and an excuse, like she had wanted to in the first place. "What should I do?"

"What do you want to do?"

She was almost never asked that by her uncle or her advisers. "I don't know." She considered her options. Could she demand more of King Warrington's time? Insist on fidelity being part of their arrangement?

Casimir shrugged. "You could offer him the country without the marriage."

She had considered that. "My people would revolt. They would fight a takeover and view it as hostile. They would feel they had no voice in the government."

"As his wife, will you have a voice?"

She had hoped they could come to terms and King Warrington would consult with her on matters involving Acacia. But who knew what would happen once the marriage papers were signed and their interests were merged? "I had hoped."

"You could live apart and lead your own life."

Her own life in her own house sounded good in some ways, but lonely. "You mean cheat on my husband?" Have a series of affairs that couldn't develop into anything real? She had that with Casimir now and it broke her heart.

She couldn't have a child with a lover. Did she want children? She hadn't stopped to make firm plans on the matter, although she had figured she would have children one day.

"Isn't that what he is likely to do to you?" Casimir asked.

Given the king's behavior during their first planned meeting, she guessed he wouldn't respect her feelings or honor their marriage vows. "I don't know him well enough to say."

Casimir slanted her a look.

"What do you want me to say? To admit I'm agreeing to a raw deal?"

His expression was unreadable. "I know you're getting a raw deal. But unless you force King Warrington to accept different terms, nothing will change."

"If someone sees us together and starts a rumor, something will change. I'll have let down my country. Warrington will marry someone else."

Casimir lifted his brow. "I doubt that. He still wants Acacia. He didn't agree to take it out of the kindness of his heart."

"He isn't taking it. It's a union." The words sounded flimsy, even to her own ears.

The music in the Great Hall stopped and Serena heard someone speaking on the microphone. Time to return to the party. Still feeling overwhelmed, Serena entered the hall, where the bride and groom were walking hand in hand through the crowd, speaking with their guests. Serena recognized the intimate body language between the bride and groom. They were in love. Actual love. Not trying to fool their countrymen and women or make a political alliance or please someone else. They had genuine warmth and affection for each other. Serena remembered reading that they had met at university and had been together since.

Watching them, loneliness descended on her. But that feeling was nothing new. Serena had been lonely since her last disastrous relationship.

To make matters worse, when Serena moved to her table, she saw she had been seated next to King Warrington. She should have expected it. Most members of their social circle knew about their pending arrangement. Few would stop and question how Samuel's history with Danae would impact their engagement, perhaps treating them as disparate relationships.

Serena sat and smiled at the king. Her worry increased when she noticed Fiona sitting across the ten-person table. If Fiona was at their table, then so was Casimir. Could she hide how she felt about him? She was accustomed to watching people and that had taught her that the smallest reaction, the lift of an eyebrow, a lingering look, a private smile, could give away so much. Too much.

"Where did you disappear to?" King Warrington asked.

Had he noticed her absence? Or was it that she hadn't followed him around the room as his other admirers seemed to do? "I'm jet-lagged and not feeling well. I went outside for some fresh air."

He leaned closer to her. Was she speaking loud enough?

"I'm sorry to hear that."

Nothing in his voice communicated real empathy. Serena worked to keep her voice low, but audible. "I know this is hard for you. I miss Danae, too."

Surprise registered on his face. Perhaps he had not expected her to mention her sister, but it was the big green-spotted pink elephant in the room and they might as well talk about it.

The king cleared his throat. "She was a good person." Now his voice held actual emotion. His eyes grew damp and she thought she detected some anger in his tone. At the situation? Toward her for bringing it up? "I know it puts us in an awkward position," she said. She felt better saying it.

"We'll make the best of it," Warrington said. He took

a sip of his scotch and looked straight ahead, avoiding eye contact with her.

Serena wondered why she had never considered the impact Danae's death would have on King Warrington. Perhaps some of his reluctance to spend time with her had to do with his lingering feelings for Danae.

The duke came to the microphone near the band. "Thank you for coming today. Many of you traveled a great distance to celebrate with my bride and me." He launched into a speech about how much he loved and cared about his new wife and how he looked forward to the days and years ahead. He was poised and collected. Serena wished she could behave that way in public, instead of floundering and stuttering her way through meetings and speaking engagements.

When he finished his speech, the duke pulled his wife onto the dance floor with him. He held her close as the music played. They seemed to move as one around the dance floor.

Casimir came to the table and sat. Fiona leaned into him, setting her head on his shoulder. He didn't push her away, nor did he slip his arm around her and hold her close.

Serena took a sip of her water and forced her attention on the bride and groom. Samuel Warrington didn't seem eager to talk about Danae, and Serena wasn't willing to give away anything about Casimir.

With her and the king harboring feelings for others, could they ever have an honest relationship built on trust?

Casimir could see the princess and King Warrington in his peripheral vision. Serena was leaning toward him, though she and the king weren't speaking.

The rage Casimir felt for Serena's future betrothed was potent, and knowing King Warrington was a liar and murderer didn't help matters. Yet rage had no place in revenge. It would skew his thinking, much as lust could.

Samuel Warrington tossed him several looks, but Casimir kept his expression neutral. He wouldn't tip his hand in Samuel's direction and give the king any reason to look deeper into Casimir's life.

King Warrington set his hand on the back of Serena's chair and Casimir forced himself not to look in that direction. He counted back slowly from ten. He had to stay calm. If he revealed himself now as the true heir to the throne, he would ruin the careful plans he had made.

When the bride and groom finished their dance, they motioned for their guests to join them. King Warrington extended his hand to Serena. She took it and he led her to the dance floor.

Casimir changed his position to keep Serena in his line of sight. He rationalized that he needed to keep her safe and therefore he had to keep her in view. But the room was filled with private security and few threats. He wanted to watch her for his benefit.

He needed to know that she wouldn't fall in love with King Warrington. A long line of lovers had fallen for Warrington's charms. Casimir couldn't stand the idea of Serena being in that line. Furthermore, he had promised Demetrius DeSante he wouldn't allow Serena's and the king's relationship to progress too far and once a promise was made to DeSante, it was a life-and-death matter to keep it.

When the song ended, a woman in a purple dress cut in between Warrington and Serena. Casimir saw the change in Warrington's posture. He pulled the woman to his body, he stared at her and rocked against her. She was one of his lovers. Did Serena realize it, too?

"Come on Casimir, dance with me," Fiona said.

Casimir escorted her to the dance floor and was lucky when the music changed and another man moved in to dance with Fiona.

Casimir let Fiona go, feigning disappointment. She winked at him. Fiona was a shameless flirt and loved men's attention.

Serena came to his side. "The king is awfully friendly with that woman. Do you know her?"

Casimir recognized her, but he couldn't place her. "She looks familiar, but no." The king and the woman in purple were practically grinding into each other. "Perhaps she is a friend."

"I don't touch my friends that way. They aren't strangers," Serena said.

"Perhaps she's an old girlfriend."

"Or a current one. I have been trying not to let the rumors bother me, but his reputation is making me wonder," Serena said.

He was glad she was more skeptical and questioning, but he hated the hurt in her voice. She was taking the king's behavior personally, when it had nothing to do with her and everything to do with the man's selfish motives. "She has nothing to do with you."

"Do you think he cheated on my sister?" Serena asked.

Casimir knew that Samuel had. One of DeSante's contacts in the government of Rizari had been following the king closely for years. It was easy enough to pinpoint when the king took a new lover. New lovers were sent flowers, gifts and given lots of the king's time for as long as the woman held his attention. "I don't know what arrangement your sister and King Warrington had."

Serena looked around the room. "There is so much I don't know. So much that is beneath the surface here. I can't really trust anyone. Except you. You've been there for me."

Casimir flinched. It was a knife to the gut. She trusted him? He would hurt her in the end. Casimir was lying to her, and while he was a grand liar, he hated that no part of her detected it. He wished she wasn't so trusting and naive. Anyone in power, especially someone new to politics, needed to question the people around them and keep some walls up. Serena's openness would get her killed. "You shouldn't trust anyone."

Her smile faltered but didn't fully fade. "What does that mean? Are you telling me I have misplaced my trust in you?"

Grossly misplaced. But Casimir needed to stay close to her. He searched for words that wouldn't hurt her, but that weren't an outright lie. Somehow, that seemed to cross a line. "I mean to keep you safe. I mean for you to understand that as the princess and soon the queen, people will want to hurt you and take advantage of you."

"I won't let that happen, but I was thinking it might be a good time for me to take advantage of you. Come to my room?" she asked.

A bold statement, coming from her. He went hard thinking of slipping into her room again. "Yes. You go first and I'll meet you at the hotel."

Casimir entered her room, his body keyed up and his arousal swollen to the point that it was painful against the fabric of his pants.

Serena rushed to him, throwing herself into his arms. He caught her and she wrapped her legs around his waist, her dress rising up around her hips. "I thought you wouldn't come."

"I'll come. We both will."

He carried her directly to the bed and laid her down, careful not to put his full weight on her. She rocked her body, simulating the act that his body wanted most.

"Casimir, please. Hurry."

He couldn't do anything except respond to her requests. Lust surged in his head, forcing out thoughts of caution. He was fully prepared for her to change her mind. Was this an emotional reaction to her sadness and hurt over King Warrington's behavior? There was no room for another man between them. "Are you sure?"

"I ache for you."

Simple, honest words. Casimir knew if he made love to her, he would never allow her to sleep with Warrington. They had spent the night together, they had fooled around, but they had never taken it this far. By sleeping with Serena, he was raising the stakes high. Everything was on the line.

She could not fall for King Warrington. She would belong to Casimir and Casimir alone.

If his revenge didn't unfold according to plan, he would lose the crown that was his birthright, his spirit would be crushed, his mother would sink further into darkness and he would fail Serena. She would marry King Warrington and if Casimir survived the inevitable backlash from the king, he would have to live with that knowledge.

Casimir would make her feel as good as he knew how, he would show her how a man should treat a

woman and every other man she came in contact with
would pale in comparison to him. He took great pleasure knowing that. If by some horrible twist of his
plan, Serena married King Warrington, at least Casimir would know that he had been with her first and he
had treated her like a princess, like a queen.

He ran his hand down her smooth hair. "I want you,
too, Serena."

In one even motion, he flipped her onto her stomach and worked on unfastening her dress, kissing her
skin as his fingers worked the dress open. "We need
to have a conversation about picking dresses without
so many buttons."

"Just rip it."

With a firm tug, he parted the fabric. Buttons
bounced to the ground. "Much better."

He unsnapped her black bra. The black did something to him. She rolled over and he peeled away her
dress and tossed aside her bra.

She was naked to the waist and he kissed her, brushing his lips over her cheeks, her chin and her throat.
The longer he kissed her, the more he wanted her. She
touched his hardness through his pants and let out a
gasp of surprise.

He moved her hand away. "This is about you." If
she touched him, he would embarrass himself. He was
that turned on.

"What about—"

He silenced her with another kiss. He skimmed his
hand between her legs. Serena lifted her hips into his
hands, demanding more. More he was willing to give.
Finding her ready, a charge of electricity burst through
him, mind-numbing pleasure taking over. His finger

easily slipped inside her and she cried out. They didn't need her guards coming to investigate, so he quickly returned his mouth to hers. Kissing was fast becoming his favorite way to spend his time.

He moved his hand, slowly at first, letting the tension between them build and grow. He watched her face, gauged her reaction to every movement. He slid her dress down her legs to give him more room to maneuver. Watching her was an utter turn-on. If he hadn't already been mad with lust, her gasps and sighs would have taken him there.

Nothing about this had been part of his plan. He had wanted to use her for information, but this act had nothing to do with his plan for revenge. He didn't want to consider his exact motives. She was beautiful and sweet and he was about to make love to her. That was enough.

The involuntary buck of her hips let him know she'd found completion. Gathering her close, he held her.

Her pulse was racing. When her hand moved to the tent in his pants, he shifted. "I'm fine." It would go away. Eventually. A cold shower. A bucket of ice. His hand when he was alone.

She didn't say anything else, just snuggled in tight. After a few minutes, her even, deep breathing indicated she had fallen asleep.

Serena rolled to her side and slung her leg over Casimir. "I'm cold." Based on the darkness that shrouded the room, sunrise was still hours away.

Casimir reached to the bottom of the bed and pulled the sheets and blankets over them. "When I was dancing with Samuel, I was thinking about you," she whispered.

Casimir watched her with soulful eyes.

"As the princess, you would think I would be allowed to make some of my own rules."

"When you are queen, perhaps you can."

She shook her head. "I'll be a queen in name only, a figurehead, but powerless."

"You have managed to have complete power over me."

He said the sweetest things that reached to her core. "Kiss me. Please."

He captured her mouth in a soul-stirring kiss. She felt the swell of his arousal against her belly. He deepened the kiss and she opened her mouth, letting his tongue stroke hers, lightly sucking on his lower lip.

"I have always planned to use great care with you, but you are making that impossible," he said.

His mouth found hers once again and their tongues collided and sparred. Her entire body was tuned to him. He had been attentive to her and she wanted to please him.

But Casimir seemed to have an agenda of his own. He palmed her breasts, sending molten heat surging through her. Instead of rising between her thighs and removing his pants, Casimir lowered his head between her legs. He took her into his mouth and she bit her lip to keep from screaming. His tongue moved up and down, swirling. He sucked her hard and she jerked against his mouth, desperate for release.

She had never felt this way about a man. The intensity, the intimacy, the incredible sensations were a whirl in her brain and in her heart. "Please, Casimir."

"Tell me what you need," he said, kissing the inside of her thighs.

"I need you." Every word was a pant. "You inside me."

He answered her plea by pressing two fingers inside her. He moved his tongue and fingers with expert precision. Serena knew she was close to finishing, but was unable to stop it. She looked at him and he lifted his head, making eye contact with her. She went off at that moment, tremors rocking her body, bringing every inch of her skin to attention and sending pulses of pleasure over her.

Casimir gathered her against him. He kissed her forehead. "Can I spend the night?" he asked.

"What about Fiona?"

"We have separate rooms. She won't know where I am," Casimir said.

"What if she comes looking for you?"

"Then I will tell her I was sleeping off an alcohol-induced buzz."

She rubbed her cheek against his shoulder. "I wish you would let me return the favor."

"I'm fine."

He didn't sound fine. Why didn't he want her to touch him? Casimir Cullen was a curious man. He had been a mystery from the very start, and Serena felt as if she was only beginning to scratch the surface of what lay beneath.

Chapter 7

The coronation of the queen was a grand affair in Acacia. It had been declared a national holiday. Banks, libraries and schools were closed. The formalities of the day were broadcast on television and streaming on news sites.

Serena tried to think about the day in pieces: the procession, the ceremony and the reception. She was hosting dozens of royals from around the world. The coordination of security, the staff and various events was a huge task.

Lucky for Serena, she had help. Iliana was handling her first major kingdom-wide event as Serena's personal assistant with poise. She'd provided Serena a detailed schedule, outlining where she had to be and with whom. Without her, Serena would be lost.

Her uncle Santino had overseen the details of her personal security and how to manage the crowds. Living through the day would be an accomplishment, as would her holding it together.

King Warrington was scheduled to meet with Serena before the procession. While he was not a part of the coronation, he had inserted himself into the day by making his travel plans known and arriving in Acacia by private airplane.

A physical reminder of her duties and future life, the Acacian crown, sat heavy on Serena's head. She had practiced wearing it, balancing it and walking with it. She would wear it today, but not many other occasions. It would return to the vault for safekeeping after the ceremony. Her biggest hurdle would be pressing through the coronation and the reception without stuttering and stumbling over her words. Her stomach was in knots. Someone might decide tonight was the day to take a shot at her. Or poison her food. Or slip into one of the private events and get close enough to hurt her.

A queen. The queen of Acacia. It was a position she hadn't thought she'd occupy. Immediately, her mind shot to Danae, sending grief to war with her worry. The crowning of the new leader of Acacia should have happened years from now, when her father was old and had decided to pass his crown to the next generation and live out his remaining days in the comfort of his seaside estate.

Her phone rang and seeing Samuel Warrington's private number, Serena almost didn't answer. But if she spoke to him now, perhaps she could avoid him later.

"Samuel, hello," Serena said, sitting on the chaise lounge in her bedroom.

"Good morning. I hate to drop in on you on such

short notice, but I'd like to congratulate you personally before the coronation. Stealing a moment alone with you later will be nearly impossible."

Why did he want to meet alone? She was immediately suspicious. Would he try to pressure her into agreeing to the engagement today? "My schedule is booked."

"It will only take a few minutes. I am sure you can squeeze me in. I'll see you shortly."

He ended the phone conversation. His tactics were strangely like Demetrius DeSante's. Why were the men in her life so quick to strong-arm her?

Iliana looked at Serena. "Everything okay?"

"King Warrington would like to see me before the procession."

Iliana squeezed her hands. "You need to bridge this gap with him at some point. I know it's hard and he hasn't exactly been Prince Charming, but you can make this work. I know you, Serena. You'll find a solution."

Like passing the crown to someone who wanted it and would happily marry King Warrington? "I've been trying."

Iliana pursed her lips. "Yes, but also no."

Serena knew what she meant. She was thinking about Casimir. Sleeping with Casimir wasn't helping her relationship with King Warrington.

Iliana consulted her tablet. "When he arrives, where would you like to meet?"

Serena considered her options. Not her bedroom—too personal. Her office seemed too formal. Many other parts of the castle were staged for various elements of the day's events. "The rose garden."

"Perfect. I'll message you when he arrives."

* * *

Serena was waiting in the rose garden's gazebo and stood as King Warrington approached.

He strolled as if he owned the castle and everything in it. She supposed it wasn't far from the truth. Soon, he would. She would struggle to keep control and fight hard to make her voice, and the voice of her countrymen, heard.

King Warrington sat on the bench across from her. "I won't keep you. But it dawns on me that we've been circling each other. We rarely talk. If we're to be married, this should be part of our routine, don't you think?"

What exactly did he mean? "I am not sure I follow."

"We'll share information. Figure out our best move."

Political strategizing was important if they would lead their countries jointly. "That seems reasonable. Did you wish to discuss something in particular?"

He sighed. "I received a call from the president of Icarus this morning. He wanted to discuss a meeting between the three of us."

DeSante wasn't showing his hand. What was his angle? "What did you tell him?"

"That I would think about it. Before we meet with him, I want us to present a united front."

Then King Warrington's reasons for being here weren't about their relationship or congratulating her. They were about ensuring she would side with him against DeSante. "On what matters?"

"All matters."

Unilaterally agreeing with King Warrington wasn't in her best interest. She didn't know what matters were most important to him and he didn't know those closest to her heart. "I think a meeting is a good idea. With my father unable to mitigate, we'll establish a new means of communicating."

Samuel ran a hand through his hair. "We need to move past this awkward formality between us. You look beautiful today and usually I am good with beautiful women."

There was a compliment in his statement somewhere, but she mostly felt uncomfortable.

"I can give you what you want if you'll just clue me in to what that is. Land. Money. Some heirloom jewelry. My advisers have been pressuring me to lock this down," he said.

How romantic. He was wrong, though. He wouldn't give her what she wanted because land and money didn't matter to her.

How could she be excited about this engagement? Samuel Warrington didn't love her. She wasn't attracted to him and he didn't seem interested in anything about her except her title. "We don't know each other."

"We can get to know each other if that's what it takes to make you comfortable," Samuel said.

He didn't want to spend time with her. He had made that clear. He treated her like an obligation he couldn't rid himself of fast enough. "How would you propose we do that?"

He leaned forward, snagged her around the waist.

"What are you doing?" she asked, pushing against his shoulders.

"Isn't this how husbands and wives get to know each other?" he asked.

Was he dense? Or maybe sex was how he became close to the women in his life. "This is not appropriate."

There was an awkward moment when he released her. "Figures you'd be frigid."

Her back went ramrod straight. "I am not frigid."

"Then let's sleep together, get it over with, and then work on the rest."

A man hadn't talked to her like this before and she was taken aback. "I am insulted you assume that sex is what I need to become close with you. What about finding common interests? Spending time on mutual hobbies?"

"Who has time for interests and hobbies?" He sounded angry.

According to what she knew of him, he spent much of his time throwing parties and vacationing. "I know this isn't easy because you cared for my sister. The pressure is making it worse for both of us. We can take things slow." How much slower, she didn't know. Perhaps they could start with a few conversations over email. Or text messaging. Become friends, which may lead to attraction.

Was it wrong to think attraction could be cultivated? She could find a trait in King Warrington that appealed to her and focus on that. She hadn't heard of anyone working that hard at a relationship, but she didn't know many women who had political marriages.

"We don't have months to waste. Demetrius DeSante is eager to attack you."

It wasn't far from her mind that the president was watching. But Serena hadn't been to war and her inexperience was a weakness. "I am aware of his intentions."

"Time is not your friend."

She didn't need threats and additional pressure from

King Warrington. "I know where my obligations to my country lie. I know what I need to do."

The king smiled as if he'd won. "I will call on you later this week. Perhaps you can articulate what other terms might make our arrangement acceptable to you."

He bowed to her. "Good day, Princess."

Serena watched him retreat down the landscaped paths of the garden.

Her skin crawled with revulsion and that was a terrible emotion to feel for her soon-to-be husband.

Casimir appeared and Serena gasped. "Casimir. How did you know I was here?"

"Iliana told me you were meeting with King Warrington in the rose garden."

Why did she feel she had been disloyal to Casimir? He knew about her impending arrangement with King Warrington. If he had seen them together a few minutes earlier, he would have seen that nothing happened except an almost kiss, which she had stopped. "He didn't leave me much of a choice about meeting."

Casimir said nothing with his words, but his look spoke volumes.

"Say what you want to say," Serena said.

"I have nothing to say that hasn't been said before. You said you didn't want to marry him, yet you're pursuing a relationship with him."

Was he hurt? She was unsure where they stood, but his presence renewed her feelings for him. Serena grasped the lapels of Casimir's suit jacket and pulled his lips to hers. He resisted for a moment, but then he returned the kiss, the heat of his mouth infusing her with a burning desire. She wished she had an extra hour to pull him away and do unspeakable things to him.

When she broke the kiss, she searched for the right words. "Some sad twist of fate has forced me into being queen. If I had my choice, you would be my future. I would be with you. But we know that's out of my control. I can't run this country alone. I can't protect us from Demetrius DeSante and his army without a better military. All I can do is make the best possible decisions for my country, given the circumstances."

Casimir ran his knuckles lightly down her cheek. "You underestimate yourself. But I am honored to know you would choose me. I know it's wrong to touch you and kiss you. I know I shouldn't but I can't stop myself."

Serena's phone chimed. A text from Iliana that she was needed in the solarium. "We will talk about this later. We will meet tonight?"

He didn't nod or indicate he would meet her, leaving her filled with uncertainty. "Good luck today. Be strong. Be the queen you were born to be."

His words infused her with confidence. "Thinking of you will get me through today."

Coronation Day was a blur of activities. Serena held it together through the procession and the ceremony, the pictures, the questions and endless small talk.

There had been a few incidences where her social awkwardness and lack of grace had been a problem. Serena had forgotten names, confused people and had been too nervous to eat, but she'd forged on, remembering Casimir's encouraging words.

She'd smiled until her cheeks hurt and waved to thousands of people. This day was about keeping Acacia on the path to a bright future. But Serena could not think of her own future. She could not think about Casimir leaving her, or about her marriage to King Warrington or her fears of what would happen when Acacia united with Rizari.

Prior to today, Iliana had warned the media not to ask questions about King Warrington, Rizari or her father's and sister's deaths. The press had complied.

During the ceremony those in attendance, dignitaries and commoners alike, held a moment of silence for their former leader. Serena had kept it together, but barely. At several different moments during the day, she'd felt the urge to burst into tears. The weight of her new title and the importance of this day was heavy on her shoulders.

One of the brightest moments of the coronation had been seeing Dr. Shaw in the front row when she was crowned queen. He had been seated beside his wife in his wheelchair. Though he needed rest and hadn't stayed long enough for her to greet him, she was pleased he had been in attendance. He was healing and that lifted Serena's spirits.

The final event of the day was an elegant party in the throne room with the doors opened to the lower level patio, which had been decorated with beautiful potted plants.

Serena needed to change her clothes before the evening's festivities. It was her seventh clothing change of the day. Iliana was waiting for her in her bedroom and she seemed distraught.

"What's wrong?" Serena asked. Iliana had planned the ceremony and related events to every last detail. Now that the coronation was almost finished, Iliana should be congratulating herself, having a glass of wine, and taking the next week away from work.

"Nothing."

Iliana had answered too abruptly. "Iliana..."

"It's nothing with the coronation. It's about Demetrius. A personal matter."

"You can tell me about it if you wish."

Iliana shook her head, fresh tears forming in her eyes. "I'm not ready to talk about it. Let's get you into your gown. It is my favorite. The most elegant by far. But it comes with a warning. I know that Casimir is here. Everyone is watching you tonight. Don't say or do anything that will start rumors."

Serena hugged her cousin. "Thank you for the reminder. I will be careful."

The morning after the coronation, Iliana had planned to sleep in late, maybe spend the day shopping in town or catching up on the errands she had neglected over the past weeks. When she'd received a message that Demetrius DeSante was planning to visit Serena, she rearranged her schedule, showered and beat feet to the castle.

She was upset with him because he had been so distant lately, but she wanted to see him. To confirm that their fling was over? To see if he still cared about her? She was a masochist, seeking out a situation that would inevitably hurt her. But like a moth to a flame...

Demetrius DeSante was waiting for Serena in the solarium on the first floor of the castle. He had finagled another meeting, perhaps by strong-arming any number of people. His official reason for the meeting was to congratulate Serena and formally acknowledge her as queen.

Iliana couldn't get over it. Serena as queen. Iliana was biased, but she thought Serena would rock the position. She was compassionate and warm and she cared about her country. Once she found her footing and some confidence, she would shine.

But her warm feelings for her cousin didn't negate her annoyance with DeSante. Demetrius hadn't informed her he was coming to the castle. She had seen the appointment on Serena's calendar that morning.

He had been so romantic and sweet in Elion and then Iliana hadn't heard from him. Being involved in a hot affair one minute, a freezing one in the next wasn't her jam.

Iliana entered the solarium. Demetrius's guards were in the room. Iliana nodded to them and they made no movement toward her.

"Good morning, Demetrius."

If the use of his first name when he was visiting in an official capacity offended him, he didn't indicate so. "Iliana."

"You didn't tell me you were coming by the castle this morning."

"I utilized the official channels to make this appointment."

What a load of crap. He hadn't wanted to see her and that stung. "I am the queen's personal secretary."

"Protocol and precedence dictate I book appointments with the queen through the minister of foreign affairs."

Iliana lifted her head proudly. "I must have misunderstood our relationship." He had alerted her to his official visits most times in the past.

"What did you understand our relationship to be?"

Iliana wasn't sure she could say it aloud without sounding like a perfect idiot. "In Elion you said... I

mean, I thought we were…friends." What a weak word
to describe what her imagination had led her to believe.

"We are friends. But you didn't call me," DeSante
said.

"Was I supposed to call?"

"You are supposed to do whatever it is you want to
do. You are strong enough to take what you want. I gave
you my number to use at your leisure. You did not do the
same for me. I would not use your professional contact
information to pursue a personal matter."

He was putting the silence on her. "I coordinated the
coronation. You didn't RSVP."

DeSante threw his head back and laughed. "You'll
find a way to keep me in line. No infractions are acceptable. Even trivial social ones."

"That's right," Iliana said, unsure if he was making
fun of her. "And the coronation was not trivial." She
had spent long, hard and confusing hours planning that
event, reading the details of past coronations and official protocols.

"My apologies. I know for you, it was a significant
occasion. For me, it was an inevitable event that drew
other matters to a head. I was dealing with those matters."

What did that mean? What was he getting at? "I see."

"Do you, Iliana? How would you feel if I told you I
plan to speak to the queen about you?"

Her heart raced. "And tell her what?"

"That I wish for you to be our intermediary. I find
Mitchell Wagner to be dull. I find you to be stimulating
and infinitely more suited to negotiate affairs between
the queen and me."

"What makes me more suited to that position?"

"It's my preference. I think you are glorious. Speaking to you excites me." He moved toward her like a panther stalking its prey. When he was close, he set his fingertips lightly on her hips. "I mean to have you, Iliana. I will court you and win you over."

Her legs felt boneless, but she remained standing. She wasn't a swoon-and-faint type. She was, however, a suspicious type. "Why?"

His eyes studied her face. "You never think of me?"

She'd be lying to deny it. "I think of you."

"In bed? When you are sleeping alone?"

"What makes you think I sleep alone?"

She expected her words to shock him, but he appeared unfazed. "You are a matter that concerns me and when matters concern me, I make sure I know everything about them."

She stepped back from him and shoved his hand away. "Are you spying on me?"

"Yes."

"That is so...rude!"

"For your protection."

"You know what, Demetrius? In Icarus, maybe women like that high-handed, man-is-king crap, but here, in Acacia, men and women are equals. I don't need a dictator peeping in my windows at night."

"I don't peep in your windows. I have hired parties watching out for you."

As if siccing strangers on her was any better. "Why? Why are you are so interested in me?"

DeSante inhaled and let out his breath slowly as if mustering patience. "You are of more importance than you know. One day, you will understand. Until then, I will keep you safe."

She should be creeped out, but he believed she required protection. "If pictures of me in the shower show up on the internet, I will blame you." Except somehow she knew he would demand lines and boundaries be kept to protect her privacy.

"If pictures of you in any compromising positions show up anywhere, you will see no end to how I will defend your honor and protect you."

Before Iliana could fully process or respond to that, Serena entered the solarium.

Seeing her cousin and the president of Icarus in intense conversation, Serena felt she had walked into a private exchange. Iliana seemed upset, but she could hold her own, regardless of her emotional state. Serena half expected, and would have found it highly amusing, to see her cousin let loose on DeSante.

DeSante and Iliana looked at her, and both went silent and still.

"Iliana, is everything okay?" Serena asked.

Iliana stepped away from DeSante. "Just confirming the president's plans."

Serena knew his unofficial reason for the visit was to pressure her again about merging Acacia and Icarus. Using the guise of offering his congratulations was flimsy.

Serena was firm in her resolve not to allow her country to become a dictatorship, least of all with Demetrius DeSante at the helm.

"I will take my leave," Iliana said. She glowered at DeSante and Serena hid her chuckle. Later, she would ask her cousin what their conversation had been about. She sensed a certain tension between the two. Perhaps it was the early stages of their relationship and they were smoothing out the kinks.

Serena and DeSante sat. Serena's steward rolled in a cart of tea and cookies.

"Thank you for meeting with me. I would like to extend my congratulations to you. Our previous meetings have not been productive. I am hoping that will change now that you have power of your own," DeSante said.

Their previous meetings had been forced by him and she had been unprepared for them. "I do not like to be manipulated."

"I have an offer for you that you might find more pleasing than others under consideration."

She doubted he had anything new to bring to the table. She gestured for him to continue.

"We will arrange an alliance without a marriage between us to muddy the water."

"I would like an alliance. Acacia is not spoiling for war."

"Neither is Icarus," DeSante said.

She didn't believe him. He wasn't looking for a war, but he would not turn away from any provocation. In her experience, provocation could be anything: a ship drifting too close to Icarus, an unintended flyover by a commercial plane slightly off its route or unfair trade arrangements. "Would our alliance leave me as queen of Acacia and the Assembly in place?"

"You would be queen in name and the Assembly would retain some limited powers."

Meaning she would be a figurehead with no power and no voice to speak for the people of Acacia. "I do not think that is an arrangement that will work for my country."

DeSante moved closer to her. Her guards were in the room, otherwise she might have felt threatened. "You will regret an alliance with the king of Rizari."

She would personally, but she believed it would be best for her country. "They have favorable trade arrangements with most of Europe and Asia. The king is offering us a part in those arrangements."

DeSante shook his head. "A part? Meaning you will sell what you have to him and he will take the lion's share of the profits."

Serena wouldn't listen to DeSante tear down every reason she was leaning toward a union with Rizari. "If you wish for me to consider your position, tell me why you are threatened by this arrangement."

DeSante leaned back in his chair. He regarded her carefully. Would he lay his cards on the table? Serena could guess why he didn't want her to marry King Warrington. The two countries being united would put Icarus in the weaker position. A man like DeSante did not like being in the weaker position. "The king of Rizari wants control of the Mediterranean. He will take Acacia and it will put him geographically closer to Icarus. When Acacia and your father provided a buffer, I had some degree of confidence that Warrington would keep his distance. My country does not want to waste resources defending ourselves from Rizari. We have more pressing goals and objectives."

His explanation was what she had expected. "I do not believe that the king of Rizari has plans to attack Icarus."

DeSante stared at her as if she were daft. "You have a lot to learn, Your Highness. Your naïveté is refreshing, but I won't like to see you taken advantage of, especially when it affects me."

"I am not alone in making decisions. I have my advisers and the Assembly."

"I will ask you to consider another offer that involves your secretary."

Serena was surprised he would bring up Iliana. Did this have to do with their blossoming relationship? She had no opposition to it as long as Iliana was happy. "What about Iliana?" She worked to keep her temper calm. She would protect her cousin at all costs.

"I believe her loyalty to you is preventing her from being loyal to me."

"Why would she be loyal to you?" Serena asked.

"I have power and am in a position to protect her."

"As am I. I would never allow someone to hurt Iliana. She is family."

"But you must realize that you do not know everything that happens in this region. I receive more intel. She is important and when critical information comes to light, she will need protection."

Serena didn't follow. Was he referring to the assassins who had killed her father and sister? "Tell me what danger Iliana is in and I will see to it that she is safe."

DeSante shook his head. "Only I can ensure her safety."

"You seem certain of that."

"I am."

Was he making a threat against her? It didn't sound as if he was implying he would harm Iliana, yet he was withholding important information. What game was he playing? "If information comes to my attention that makes me fear for Iliana's safety, I will see to it that I counter any attempts to harm her. But if you are simply maneuvering to have a personal relationship with her, I will tell you that I have no objection to her being friendly with you, as friendly as she would like. You have helped her on at least one occasion. For that, I thank you. But her life and her choices are in her hands. I will not stand between her and happiness, wherever she thinks she may find it."

"Would you consider brokering a marriage arrangement between myself and Iliana in exchange for an alliance between our countries?" he asked.

Serena blinked, feeling more than a little thrown. He could have knocked her over with a feather. "You want to marry Iliana?"

"Yes."

A dozen emotions played through her. She would not pressure Iliana into accepting any proposal or offer her to DeSante in exchange for the union. It let her off the hook, but Serena would not sacrifice Iliana's happiness for her own. Given her personal struggles, she wouldn't put another woman in that position. "My answer is the same. It is my cousin's choice to do what she wants with her life."

DeSante stood. "I will not take more of your time. Thank you for clarifying your position on Iliana. With regard to King Warrington, your future betrothed, I hope that you are correct and that he doesn't have war on his mind. When you realize I am your best option, I only hope it will not be too late to come to terms."

Chapter 8

Serena sat next to Iliana at the head of the table in the formal dining room. They were waiting for her lunch meeting to begin. Her uncle and her advisers wanted to speak with her. Given that she was newly crowned, it made sense to touch base on the most important issues the Acacian Assembly was working on.

Iliana handed Serena her tablet. "Bad news."

Serena took the device from her. Splashed across the local news website was a split photo depicting her with Casimir and King Warrington. The headline said, in bold capital letters, QUEEN'S NEW LOVERS.

Serena groaned and scanned the article. The picture of her and the king had been taken in the rose garden before her coronation. His arms were around her. The second image was a compromising shot of her and Casimir. Her face was visible, while his was shaded. It was hard to tell what exactly she and Casimir had been doing, but it didn't look innocent.

"Can I ignore it and hope it goes away?" Serena asked.

"Is it Casimir?" Iliana asked.

"Yes."

"Serena, you have to be more careful." Her rebuke was obviously out of concern.

"I made a mistake. I shouldn't have kissed him in the rose garden. But it may have been for the last time. He didn't come by last night after the coronation." And he hadn't returned her messages. Was it over? She couldn't imagine him abruptly ending the relationship, but she was unsure and saddened.

"Is there a way to spin the story, perhaps explain that he's a friend and the angle of the picture makes it look worse than it is?" Iliana asked.

Serena didn't like lying, but stating outright that she had been kissing another man on castle grounds would create massive problems for her administration and for her arrangement with King Warrington. "I should at least discuss it with the king."

Serena sent him a message, asking him to call when he had a free moment.

The door to the dining room opened and her uncle entered. "Serena, you are looking lovely this morning," her uncle said. He greeted her with a hug.

Two more of her advisers entered and sat to her left.

"Your Highness, I don't know if you've seen the paper this morning," one of her advisers started.

Now was the time to stop this story from spinning out of control. "I have. I think it is a flagrant attempt to discredit me."

Her uncle took Iliana's tablet from her and narrowed his eyes at the picture. "Have you spoken to King Warrington about this yet?"

"No, but I will," Serena said. She was tired of being questioned and prodded. She was capable of handling some matters on her terms.

Did anyone recognize Casimir? It would be ideal if she could keep his name out of this. Serena didn't know where they stood, but dragging him into a royal scandal would be the death of their relationship.

"I want to stay on topic today. I will not address rumors about my personal life," Serena said, channeling Iliana's advice to remember her position and stand her ground. Not that she had any idea where she stood. Her uncle cleared his throat as her remaining two advisers entered the room. "The purpose of this meeting is to discuss your personal life and how it will impact Acacia."

She was the queen of Acacia and that held power. Letting herself be steamrolled by her advisers or lowering her head and nodding in agreement to the king of Rizari's demands was unacceptable.

Her uncle slid a thick document in front of her. "Legal has reviewed the terms and conditions and marked the clauses that need our attention."

"Is this the king's marriage proposal?" she asked, glancing at the document. Not that she'd had high hopes from Samuel Warrington's proposal, as he had failed on the romance side of their courtship spectacularly, but this was dreadful, not even conducted in person.

"Not a marriage proposal exactly. The forms to become part of Rizari. Our laws must be followed and with your approval, the merger will be voted on by the

Assembly. We've polled the members of the Assembly and we believe we'll have majority agreement."

"I haven't seen this document before," Serena said, feeling caught unaware.

"We didn't want to worry you with anything before it was reviewed," her uncle said. His voice was gentle and in direct contrast to how she was feeling.

Worry her? She had been worried about this marriage since learning of its possibility. "I will need to read this." And have more time.

Her uncle frowned. "We don't want the king to think we are not interested. The picture in the news this morning will start rumors and he might decide to believe them."

The king couldn't think she would readily agree to anything he proposed. Unless he had deluded himself, he couldn't believe she was eager to become his wife— or hand over the reins of her country. "I will address this matter with the king."

"A few days won't make a difference," her uncle said.

A few days? She'd need a month. Or an entire quarter of a year. Her heartbeat quickened and she felt left out of an important conversation. Did everyone else in the room know about this contract? Was she the last to receive it? Why hadn't she been told the moment it had arrived so that she could read it and bring her concerns to the king?

She knew the answer and it saddened her. It was not brought to her because no one felt she was capable. They believed her only asset to her country was her gender because she could parlay it into a marriage to King Warrington.

"We'll start the marketing campaign immediately.

We'll need you to pose for pictures with King Warrington in our country and in his," her uncle said.

A marketing campaign? "Does the king know about this?"

The men and women around the table exchanged looks. Her uncle answered. "Yes. He thought it was a good idea for Acacians to see him and Rizari as an ally. Same for the people in Rizari. We want them to trust you."

Trust her? She wasn't the one drafting documents and negotiating with someone else's life! She took a sip of the water on the table in front of her. The room felt small and crowded. "I need time."

When half the room started speaking at once, her uncle held up his hand to silence them. "Please give me and my niece a few moments alone."

After waiting for Serena's nod, Iliana left reluctantly.

Her uncle might be upset about the picture in the news, but Serena was still the queen. She could hold her ground. If she couldn't with her uncle, how could she with King Warrington? Or Demetrius DeSante?

When they were alone, Serena looked between her uncle and the document. "You should have told me about this sooner. I feel blindsided."

"And I feel blindsided by the knowledge that you're rendezvousing with Casimir Cullen in the rose garden," her uncle said.

Her uncle had recognized Casimir in the picture. King Warrington may have as well. "Casimir and I are friends. He saved my life."

"That doesn't mean you should sleep with him."

Outrage surged hot and heavy in her blood. "That is not an appropriate way for you to speak to me."

"Yet I don't hear you denying it."

How had he known she had spent the night with Casimir? "What I do with my free time is none of your concern."

Her uncle appeared frustrated. "You are wrong, Serena. You are the queen now. Every moment of your time is the concern of the kingdom. Everyone wants to know what you're doing and who you're doing it with. If you're smart, you'll stay away from Casimir Cullen and any other man who decides to take advantage of your trusting nature."

"Does that mean I should stay away from Demetrius DeSante, too? Because he visited this morning. Do I have to worry that someone will accuse me of sleeping with him? Is that what I am? A woman who sleeps with every man she comes into contact with?"

"Calm down, Serena. The president of Icarus went through official channels to meet with you. From the looks of your meeting with Casimir Cullen, he did not."

Serena held up her hands. "I won't discuss Casimir with you. I need more time to think about the proposed arrangement with King Warrington."

"You don't have more time. Demetrius DeSante is not backing down. He's made his position clear."

"He thinks that Rizari will use Acacia to attack Icarus after my marriage to King Warrington," Serena said.

Her uncle quirked a brow. "That's ridiculous."

"How do you know?" she asked. Had her uncle spoken to Warrington about that issue directly?

"King Warrington isn't spoiling for war. He wants to merge our countries for the mutual benefit of both nations. Putting Acacia in the middle of a war wouldn't benefit us."

Serena didn't know what to think about Samuel Warrington's intentions. "I'll need to speak with the king directly."

And Casimir. She needed to call him and warn him that their relationship was no longer just a matter of speculation. If the media believed the picture held any truth or if a story was buried inside it, they would dig, looking for information about Casimir and their affair. What other damning evidence was out there waiting to be revealed?

Casimir swore aloud when he saw his picture on the front page of the newspaper. From the angle and graininess of the shot, it wasn't obvious who he was, nor was it obvious what he and Serena were doing, but it would raise questions.

His phone rang. It was Serena. He had missed several of her calls, having been working on some issues involving Icarus and Rizari. And since he didn't know where he stood with Serena, he had wanted to think about his next move.

He answered with a greeting, trying to sound casual.

"Have you seen the news this morning? There's a picture of us in the rose garden."

"I saw it," he said.

"Are you upset?" she asked.

It would drive a wedge between her and King Warrington, which helped his cause. But he didn't want to be exposed to scrutiny by reporters and King Warrington either. "I wanted to wait and talk to you about it."

"The picture is hard to see clearly. I hope it will blow

over without the media making it into an ordeal. Where are you now?" she asked.

"In Thorntree." He hadn't left Acacia yet. He hadn't been back to see his mother in a couple of weeks. He dreaded seeing what condition she was in and having to explain why it seemed no progress had been made. "Come by the castle?" she asked.

He wasn't sure how to answer.

"You didn't come over last night," she said.

"You're the queen. That changes things."

She sighed loudly. "It doesn't have to. Not yet."

The worry in her voice struck him. "It's not a good idea for us to be seen together. Why don't you meet me at the beach house?"

"Thirty minutes? Key is in the lockbox attached to the railing." She gave him the key code to open it and the code to disable the house alarm.

"I got it. See you then."

Casimir drove to the beach house, plotting his next move. He and DeSante were still working diligently to destroy King Warrington, looking for solid evidence of his involvement in the death of Casimir's father and uncle and proof of his launching a smear campaign against his mother. A scandal could bring their plans to a crashing halt. Problem was, he wasn't sure he could stay away from Serena if he tried.

Casimir entered the beach house and circled the front room, not touching anything, but taking in Serena's decor. She liked pale, soft colors and delicate things. He took the stairs to her bedroom. Her bed was covered by a white comforter with ruffles. Her curtains were a lightweight, shiny material. On the porch were fresh potted plants, some in bloom, and an empty easel.

She had another easel in her room, this one holding a painting of the sea. He could see the talent in her work.

"Casimir?"

He heard her voice from the main floor. Heard her drop her keys in the turquoise bowl on the entryway table.

"Upstairs," he called.

Serena ascended the stairs and appeared in the doorway. "I have terrible news I wanted to tell you in person."

"Worse than the picture?"

She nodded and looked on the verge of tears. "King Warrington sent over the agreement to unify our countries."

He didn't like that, and not just because he wanted to see King Warrington fail. "Unify your countries, meaning you marrying him."

Serena nodded. She seemed out of sorts, as if she had not fully considered the implications.

"What are you planning to do?" he asked. He had a response in mind. She would not sign the papers and she would stand strong and run her country alone.

She tossed a folder on the top of her dresser. "Read it if you want. I'll work something out that leaves me with power and ensures Acacia isn't swallowed into Rizari."

She was considering signing the agreement. She would marry him. Casimir hated that on so many levels.

The truth rose in his throat. Could he tell Serena the truth about who he was and what he'd planned? If he did, she might never trust him again. He didn't have the proof of Samuel Warrington's guilt and confessing his motives now could ruin what he and DeSante had planned and worked for. "Have you considered doing nothing?"

"Doing nothing? Like ignoring it?"

"You'd buy time." Time he would use to topple King Warrington. Though Serena would be angry that he had hidden his identity, she may be pleased to have control of her country without threats of war. She would rule Acacia without a marriage or interference from Warrington or DeSante and she would forgive him. Eventually.

"If I do nothing, Rizari and Icarus may make a play to take over Acacia. We'll be in the middle of a war. There will be casualties. I couldn't live with myself."

"You think the king of Rizari would attack Acacia unprovoked?" He hadn't considered that a possibility. Should he?

She ran her fingers through her hair. "I don't know what to think."

Casimir sat on the edge of the bed. "I think you should tell the president and the king you need time. You're still grieving for your father and your sister. I think that's enough of a reason."

"My uncle thinks postponing anything will show me and, by extension, Acacia as weak. Besides, I've spoken to King Warrington. After the picture went public I had no choice. He is coming for dinner tonight so we might discuss the matter privately and in detail."

No! Time alone with King Warrington was the last thing Casimir wanted for Serena. "Will he show up?" Perhaps if he reminded her of his past behavior he could keep them apart. Though he would have time before the actual marriage, he couldn't tolerate the idea of Serena promised to another man or in another man's arms. Especially a monster like Warrington.

"I don't know."

She moved toward him and he pulled her into his arms where she belonged. She laid her head against his chest. "You'll be okay. It will work out."

"I have to accept my duty." She looked up at him. "But I'm not married yet. I'm not engaged. For a few more days, I'll be a single woman."

She shifted, looped her hands around his neck and drew him down to her mouth. She pressed her lips to his and moaned. He was well aware of what she wanted.

DeSante wanted him to consider every angle before making a move that could be a game changer, but he couldn't do that with Serena now. Sleeping with her would have nothing to do with the plan and everything to do with desire and lust.

"The bed is right behind you," she said.

White candles in glass surrounded the space, helping to set the seductive mood. He hadn't planned for this to happen and while sometimes being caught in the moment could be great, she was worthy of so much, more than he could give her. "Let me light the candles." A small gesture.

She nodded and handed him a lighter from a drawer in the bedside table. She deserved romance and affection. When the last candle was burning, he laid the lighter on her dresser.

He looked at her in the dresser mirror, kneeling on the bed, watching him. He turned and they collided. In a frantic grabbing of clothes and unfastening of buttons, they tumbled onto the mattress.

"Do you need anything?" he asked. The desire to make this moment perfect and right for her was preeminent in his mind.

"Everything I need is here in this bed."

Casimir produced a condom from his wallet and slid it on. He kissed her, claiming her lips how he would claim her body.

"Why can't I have this? You and me, in this house. No crown, no title, no responsibilities?"

Because they both had crowns, titles and responsibilities. His were unclaimed. Could he confess to her his true identity? She was trusting him enough to sleep with him in her beach house. The impact wasn't lost on him. "Because that is not our fate."

She kissed him. "Then we'll pretend for now that we can have this together."

He bought into the idea because he knew that his confession would ruin her. Though it had not started this way, he had come to care for her. Deeply. He wanted her to be his. Some distant thought made him wonder if making love with her would prevent her from agreeing to marry Warrington. "Open your legs for me."

She slid her knees apart and he positioned his body over hers. His tip nudged at her entrance and he let out a low moan. "You're so wet," he said.

"I've wanted you for so long."

As he came into her, she spread her thighs wider. Her body beneath his was delicious and lithe. As he moved, it seemed to be in time with the waves as they lapped against the beach.

He rocked slowly and he loved the sensations of filling her. Their eyes met in an intensely intimate moment.

She lifted her hips, encouraging him to move faster. He responded to her silent plea, delving deep. Her fingernails dug into his shoulders and she closed her eyes, crying out her release.

Casimir groaned and finished moments later.

He collapsed on top of her and kissed her neck and collarbone. When he rolled away, he excused himself to dispose of the condom. When he returned, she was sitting on the bed, looking out her window at the water.

He came behind her and gathered her close, letting her settle against his naked body.

"I have to meet with Warrington in an hour."

He didn't want her to go. He didn't want this night to end. "Call and tell him you can't make it," Casimir said, hating the idea of Serena meeting Warrington tonight. He wanted this night to belong to them.

Serena groaned. "Don't tempt me. You know I can't. It would raise too many questions. I've been given enough passes."

He didn't think she'd been given anything. She had been expected to behave like a veteran leader of her country when she'd had less than a month in the position. She'd had to bury her emotions with her father and sister, and ignore the fear that multiple attempts had been made on her life and the fact that she was about to marry a stranger.

The marriage proposal had been delivered. It was up to her to sign and seal it.

Casimir hadn't intended to use sex to stop her. No room for regrets or second thoughts or the residual guilt he felt over his initial interest in her and his plans to use her. He had genuine feelings for her now and sleeping with her had been a natural progression of their relationship.

"I could stay here forever, but I have to return to the castle. I need to change before my dinner with King Warrington."

"Wear clothes you have here," he said.

"Like shorts and a tank top? I think that would be inappropriate."

"I think you should let him see the real you."

Serena pushed her hair away from her face and looked at him, bewildered. "You believe that."

He wouldn't have said it if he didn't. "Yes."

"Even though it would turn him off even more?"

"Even if that were true." If King Warrington shut Serena out of his life, then Casimir couldn't use her to gather more information about the king. The idea upset him less than the thought of losing her to Warrington.

Serena deserved a chance at real happiness with a man who could love and care about her.

Like him.

He threw the brakes on his thoughts. Like him? He didn't want to marry Serena. That hadn't been part of the plan. He cared about her, but he didn't see how he could have avoided that. She was so shockingly authentic and kind, he'd liked her immediately.

But he wouldn't fall for her. He didn't want a complicated love match. Love sharpened emotions like jealousy, anger and resentment.

Serena climbed out of bed and started dressing. He watched her with lazy fascination.

She circled the bed and kissed him. "You can stay as long as you'd like."

But not forever. Their romance was ending and he needed to turn his full attention to his revenge.

Serena smelled Casimir on her skin. Could King Warrington? She'd had enough time to change her clothes, but not to shower. King Warrington was waiting for her in the dining room and she needed to be prepared to discuss matters of grave importance: their marriage, their future, and the photo of her and Casimir.

Serena entered the dining room. A tense energy charged the air. She and Warrington's rocky relationship was about to be dragged through a storm.

Serena sat across from him. She had arranged for dinner to be served, but she guessed that neither of them had much of an appetite. "I assume you saw the picture in the media."

King Warrington's face was drawn into a hard line. "I saw it."

"He is a friend."

"Tell me his name."

Serena hedged. "I want to respect his privacy."

King Warrington seemed indifferent, as if he hadn't expected an answer to his question. "Maybe this isn't an ideal situation, but perhaps we understand each other better than I thought."

Serena didn't catch his meaning. "I don't follow."

"If you want to date other men, I don't have a problem with that."

Her heart sank. He wanted to use her indiscretion to justify his own philandering. "Even after we're married?" she confirmed.

"Right. I would ask that you be more discreet. I don't want my wife's picture splashed all over the media. It makes me look foolish. But carry on your affairs in private and I will turn a blind eye to them."

"You will expect that I turn a blind eye to your affairs as well?"

"Naturally."

Serena felt sick. She had slept with Casimir and

while she knew that was out of line, she had drawn a distinction between her relationship with Casimir and her arrangement with King Warrington. After she and Warrington were engaged, she would end her affair with Casimir. "Then you and I won't have a relationship?" Just a marriage on paper?

"We can play that however you wish. I will need an heir, of course, so perhaps you'd have to tolerate me for a few nights." He sounded repulsed by the idea.

Serena shook her head, trying to dash away her confusion. She had not expected this conversation. "I had a strange visit from President DeSante after my coronation."

"He did not attend the coronation in person."

"He sent a representative. But he was interested in speaking with me about our…merger." She wouldn't call it a marriage. Not after Warrington's declaration that they would openly cheat on each other.

"What did you tell him?"

"That we were working on it."

"Then he knows that if he wants to strike, it should be soon."

"If he were to strike before our merger, would you not protect Acacia? You have much to lose if Icarus occupies my country."

"You have more to lose," King Warrington said.

Then Samuel wouldn't help her country without the bonds of an official union. That didn't sit right with her. Wouldn't a man of honor protect Acacia no matter what, given what he stood to gain? "Demetrius DeSante seemed to believe that you would initiate a war against him once our countries were allied."

Warrington was quiet. Serena watched his mouth,

his eyes and his posture for any signs of truth to the statement. Several moments passed and Serena didn't fill them with idle prattle. She stared at Warrington, waiting for him to speak.

"It's a different world once we are merged."

Not answering the question. He was withholding something. "You believe Icarus will be a threat once we are united?" Serena asked.

"Don't you believe him to be a threat now?" Warrington asked.

Serena tilted her head. "He wants an alliance with us badly enough to make threats, but I don't think he would let those threats escalate into war. He has to know if he starts a war, neighbors will take sides and since he's made enemies with his hardline tactics, many will side with us. Perhaps not by sending troops or aid, but they may cut ties with Icarus completely, leaving them isolated."

"That's quite an analysis from someone new to the political arena."

Why did everything from his mouth sound like an insult? Warrington had an agenda and though Serena didn't know what it was, she was sure that whatever Warrington had planned, his needs would come first.

The king plowed his hands through his hair. "This is not how I envisioned our first date alone. I was hoping we could talk about more pleasant things. I suppose with you, that's impossible."

Serena wanted to throttle Warrington. It wasn't a good omen for their arrangement. Every time they were together, their relationship grew a little more hostile. She didn't know how to respond to Samuel's comment.

She stood. Listening to his insults was a waste of

time. "I suppose that gives you more time to spend with your girlfriends." Serena fled the room, regretting leaving Casimir at the beach house and regretting meeting with Warrington at all.

"A peace summit?" Serena asked.

Iliana set a leather folio in front of her. "The proposal arrived today. The summit is being organized by, get this, Demetrius DeSante." Iliana's excitement gave away how much she liked the president of Icarus.

His offer to marry Iliana replayed through her mind, but Serena wasn't sure what to think of it. Until she understood DeSante's angle, his actions were subject to suspicion.

"He sent this to you directly?" Serena asked.

Iliana nodded. "He's invited you and King Warrington to meet with him in Langun at a friend's ski resort."

Serena didn't understand DeSante's latest ploy. "Does DeSante want you on the premises as well?"

Iliana's eyes were bright. "Yes."

"I don't have a problem with you and DeSante seeing each other. My problem is that I won't go to this meeting in Langun and be blindsided. What does DeSante have planned? Has he said anything to you?"

"He seems like he genuinely wants to meet with you and King Warrington on neutral ground and no country is more neutral than Langun."

"Can you see what else you can find out?"

"Absolutely. Give me a list of questions and I'll call him."

Serena didn't like forcing Iliana to be the intermediary, but Iliana and DeSante had a good rapport and Serena would take advantage of it. That was as far as she would allow herself to request anything of Iliana in regard to DeSante.

After a busy day, Casimir met Serena in her beach house. Wrapped in Casimir's arms, Serena told him about the summit meeting in Langun.

"I hope you'll go," he said.

Serena groaned. "You sound like Iliana."

"It's a good opportunity. The three of you can speak on neutral ground."

"Warrington hasn't agreed to attend."

"If he finds out that you and DeSante are meeting, he won't miss it."

That was true. The three of them were circling each other, looking for allies and bonds. "I suppose it can't hurt. If DeSante tries to strong-arm me, I'll leave."

"That sounds reasonable," Casimir said, kissing the top of her head.

"Here's the follow-up question. Will you go with me?"

Casimir shifted her so he could look at her. "Of course. I'd love to."

Serena wished she had the same relaxed response to the summit that Iliana and Casimir seemed to. She couldn't shake the feeling that DeSante or Warrington would drop bombs on her.

"Are political and work conversations over for the day?" Casimir asked, shifting on top of her.

She slipped her hand around the back of his neck. "Conversations over. Time for some relaxation."

As their lips met, Serena turned her worries off and turned her body over to Casimir.

As Casimir had predicted, King Warrington had been quick to agree to the summit once Serena had informed him she was attending. Serena and the king's relationship remained tense.

Given the conversations and negotiations over the next twenty-four hours, she expected tense to shift into troubled.

Iliana was staying in the resort's main hotel and Serena was booked in a private château. Casimir had made his own travel arrangements, flying into Langun. He had texted Serena when his plane had landed. He was driving directly to the château. It was risky inviting him along and they would keep his presence a secret, but Serena needed his strength and his support. She needed him with her.

Her bedroom in the château overlooked the mountains. While the view wasn't as comforting as the sea, Langun was a beautiful country. DeSante had picked a calm, relaxing place for them to speak. Smart man. Then again, she had never questioned DeSante's intelligence. Only his morality.

Serena turned from the window and jolted when she came face-to-face with Casimir. She hadn't heard him come in or come up the stairs. He pressed a hand over her mouth to keep her from making a sound that would alert her guards.

"How did you get in here?" she asked.

"I used the front door." He was already pulling at her scarf and vest, tossing them to the floor.

"Did anyone see you?"

Casimir shook his head. "Did he try anything?" he asked, looking her over as if the evidence would be written on her clothes.

"I assume you mean Warrington, but no, I haven't seen him since I arrived."

She enjoyed the streak of possessiveness that whipped across Casimir's face. She removed her sweater and let it drop to the floor.

"Let's turn on the fire. I'm cold." The gas fireplace, located on the other end of the room, was operated by a remote.

"I'll keep you warm."

He folded her into his arms and she inhaled the scent of him. They stumbled to the bed, a tangle of arms and legs and kisses.

"I want you, Serena. I…"

She unfastened the buttons on his shirt. "You what?"

He stilled her hands, taking them in his. "I'm falling for you."

His words sucked the air from her lungs. She felt the same for him, but she didn't feel capable of returning the words. Too much was at risk. She couldn't back up the words with a commitment and it felt wrong to say them.

"I think of you when I wake up. I think of you when I'm sleeping alone. I miss you when we're not together."

The words sang to her, a bittersweet melody. She had found someone she trusted and cared for, who made her happy, and they couldn't be together.

She lifted her mouth kissed him. The kiss spoke the words she couldn't say and her body moved with his. "We're together now, let's make the most of it."

That night, while Serena lay in bed with her laptop open, Casimir sat on the edge of the mattress. "Could you see our arrangement as more than temporary?"

He hadn't planned to tell Serena he was falling for her, but the words, the truth, had sprung from his lips.

He had been disappointed that she hadn't returned the notion. She'd made love to him as if she cared for him, as if he was important to her, but that could be reading between the lines. Casimir didn't know what to think of her or of their relationship.

"So much of my life is not my own."

It could be hers. Why couldn't she see how far she had come in the past several weeks? How much further she would go in the next months? She had grown into a leader, and every day she was stronger, more dignified and confident. Casimir didn't believe she could be easily manipulated. She had held her own against a powerful dictator and a lying, murdering king.

Why couldn't she see that she could rule her country with grace and strength? That she didn't need someone at her side, telling her what to do, guiding Acacia forward? Casimir dispensed what advice he could. "When you meet with DeSante and Warrington, you need to remember that you are their equal in every way. You owe them nothing."

Serena closed her laptop. "Those are fighting words."

"I don't want you to fight with DeSante or Warrington. But I want you to stand your ground. Take what you want and give nothing, unless it is something you want to give."

"Is that so?" She set her laptop on the nightstand and stood from the bed. She positioned herself in front of him and pulled his shirt over his head. She ran her hands over his shoulders and down his arms. The past several times they'd had sex, he had done most of the work, seeing that she was taken care of, picking the positions she liked best. He'd wanted her relaxed and he wanted to win her over. The nagging thought that she would sleep with Warrington would not let go.

She gripped his biceps in her hands. "Let me take what I want now. I want you."

She wasn't quite smiling, but the corners of her mouth were turned up. Her eyes seemed to see deep into his soul. She had his head turned around. When he was alone, he could think clearly, but when they were together, his resolve and his intentions flew out the window and he only wanted her. In his bed and in his life.

Giving into the attraction, knowing he couldn't fight it, he let her push him back on the bed. She threw her leg astride him. With her knees on either side of his hips she lowered her mouth to his neck.

A sound of contentment escaped her lips and he went from intrigued and amused to rock hard.

He didn't reach for her. He didn't make advances to hasten it. He watched her, propped on his elbows, enjoying the show. "I had hoped this would happen. That you would see."

"See what?" she asked, and kissed his chest.

"That we are good together. That you have power over me. Power of your own."

She lifted her head and met his gaze. Taking the hem of her shirt in her hands, she pulled it over her head and tossed it on the ground. She removed her clothes, item by item, taking her time. When she was finished undressing, she unbuckled his belt.

She climbed into bed and threw some of the pillows to the ground. The bed had at least a dozen and they would be in the way. He and Serena needed room to maneuver. She slipped beneath the sheets. Casimir joined her, but he didn't remove his pants.

His eyes were fastened to hers. "There are some lines that once they are crossed, there is no returning."

"I don't want to return. I like where this is going," she said.

Serena grinned. She unzipped his pants and withdrew him. Her mouth came over him, hot and wet and slow. As she took him deep, he counted backward in his head, trying to control his release.

But Serena was persistent. Her hand and the suction of her mouth felt incredible. She moved faster, lifting and lowering her head. He touched the ends of her hair, threaded his fingers through the long strands, tangling them.

She moaned and the vibrations shot around his erection. Another few noises from her throat and she brought him to completion.

She moved onto the bed beside him. Casimir could have fallen asleep like that, with her tucked under his arm, her soft hair brushing the bare skin of his neck and her sweet scent surrounding him. But their time was limited and he had brought her a gift. "I have something for you."

He left the warmth of the bed and grabbed his duffel bag. He removed the navy velvet box. The necklace inside had been his mother's. It was a gift from his father to her on their wedding night. The king of Rizari's seal was engraved on the back of it.

If Serena recognized the seal as authentic, she would be curious where Casimir had acquired such a rare treasure. Perhaps he wanted to tip her off, to expose his lies, so they could muddle through those dark waters and face the future with truth between them.

Serena opened the box and gasped. She removed the

necklace from the satin liner inside, and held it up, letting it dangle between her fingers as she looked at it.

The necklace was platinum and diamonds. The setting was antique, but the style was becoming more popular. "What is this? It looks like there is a story here," Serena said. As the necklace spun on her fingers, she stopped and looked at the seal on the back.

"It's my family crest. The necklace belonged to my mother."

Serena's lips parted. "I don't know what to say. I am so touched by this beautiful gift."

It was the one item of value his mother had taken with her when she'd fled Rizari. She could have sold it, but she had been concerned someone would think it was stolen and she'd be arrested or her identity would be revealed because of it. "Take it. Wear it. It's yours."

Casimir was playing with fire. If Serena wore it and Warrington saw it, especially the back of it, he would question Serena about it. The necklace had to have been reported stolen due to the value of the diamond.

If Serena admitted the necklace was a gift from Casimir, this game would come to a head. Serena would know the truth and Casimir needed her to believe him and forgive him for keeping it from her.

"I can't accept this. It's so precious."

"Please wear it. For me."

He looped the delicate chain around her neck. She held her hair up while he fastened it.

Casimir reclined on the bed and Serena moved into his arms.

"What would you say if I told you I want to ride you?" Serena asked.

He tensed as jolts of anticipation shocked him. "I'd

be surprised to hear such frank words from your lips, but I would happily oblige."

She shifted on top of him. Casimir fumbled to find a condom quickly. He rolled it on and let Serena take charge. She rose above him, wiggling into position and sinking her body onto his. When he was deep inside her, she rocked her hips.

He held onto her, but let her set the pace. Like it was every time with her, emotions and feelings assailed him. Casimir placed his hand where their bodies were joined and moved them the way she liked, evoking as much pleasure from her as possible.

Release was just out of reach.

A tap on the door had her freezing. "Just a minute." Her eyes wide with panic, she rolled away from Casimir.

"Serena? It's Iliana."

Casimir had half a mind to let Iliana see them. She knew they were carrying on an affair. She would keep Serena's secret, wouldn't she? Though DeSante hadn't elaborated on the subject, he seemed to trust Iliana and DeSante trusted almost no one.

Serena gestured toward the bathroom. Though Casimir felt otherwise, he did as she asked. Still sporting a raging hard-on, Casimir darted into it and closed the door lightly.

Serena pulled on her robe and checked her appearance in the mirror. Her cheeks were flushed and her hair was a mess. She opened the door to her cousin.

Iliana was clutching a tablet in her hands. "I'm sorry to bother you, but I was surfing the web and I found something you should see."

Serena braced herself. Iliana turned the computer toward her and she gasped.

Posted on the main webpage of a local media site in Acacia was a picture of her and Casimir at the wedding in Elion. This time, the photo clearly showed him and he had been named in the accompanying article.

"How should we respond?" Iliana asked.

"To what?" What could she say that would explain away a picture?

"The press will want an explanation. This picture makes it look like you and Casimir Cullen are involved. King Warrington will ask. What should we say? The press knows he was the man in the rose garden." Iliana sounded distressed.

Serena didn't want a lurid story about her and Casimir spread over the internet. "This picture was taken out of context. We were photographed at the wedding of the Duke and Duchess of Elion. I spoke to many people that weekend."

That statement was loaded with lies, but she had no choice. To protect herself and Casimir, they had to deny their involvement with each other.

Iliana looked at the picture. "I will communicate that. But I have a hard time believing it and since the press connected the picture of the mystery man in the rose garden to Casimir, it will be a hard sell."

"We'll tell the press we're friends. Nothing more," Serena countered.

"You're protesting too much."

Serena wasn't great with lies on her feet, but when she caught the thread of one she hung on for dear life. "I know this could turn into a media circus and an outright scandal."

Iliana straightened. "I'll speak to your press secretary and see if we can't minimize the fallout. Would you like me to hire a local photographer to take pictures of you and King Warrington to counter what the news might print about you and Casimir?"

A good idea, even if the thought of acting as if she were in love with King Warrington made her sick. Could she fake that emotion? "That would be great. Please see if King Warrington is amenable."

When Iliana left and Serena closed the door, Casimir stepped out of the bathroom. He looked flushed.

"Hot in there?" she asked.

"Cold, actually."

He was still naked. It turned her on. "You know what game we're playing."

"I do," he said. "But sometimes, the lines between lies and the truth become blurred and it's hard to remember what's real."

"That's why we need to stay focused on the endgame," Serena said.

"The only endgame I can think about is the one tonight," he said, gesturing toward the bed. He scooped her into his arms and plopped her onto the soft sheets. Parting her robe, he buried himself in her and Serena lost herself in his intensity and passion.

Iliana muted the television when she heard the knock on her door. "Come in."

Her suite at the resort was top-notch. She was having a great time. Their host had mentioned that he'd have his butler check on her before bed to see if she needed anything.

Instead of the resort's butler, Demetrius DeSante

entered her room. He motioned to his guards to stay outside.

Iliana rose to her feet, grateful she was wearing fleece pajamas that, while not overly attractive, were decent. "Hi, Demetrius. Is everything okay?"

His dark eyes held her. "Everything is fine now that I can see that you are safe."

"Why wouldn't I be safe?" she asked.

Demetrius's eyes narrowed. "Many reasons. But I did not come here to upset you. I wanted to make sure you were pleased with your accommodations."

She shrugged. "Sure. I made the arrangements. This is a nice place." Television, internet, spa-like bathroom and room service. Everything she needed for a relaxing weekend.

Demetrius clasped his hands behind his back. "Would you be more comfortable in one of the châteaus?"

Iliana hesitated. She had been to Serena's château that night and it was gorgeous. The details and the luxury amenities were top of the line. "I am fine here."

"I don't want you to be fine. I want you to be happy. Pleased."

"What are you suggesting?" She could have stayed in Serena's château, but Serena liked her privacy and was insistent on having time alone. It was when Serena did her best thinking, so Iliana didn't press the issue.

"Come stay in my château, in your own bedroom, but close enough that my guards can watch over you and I can know you are safe."

Iliana wanted to say yes. She wanted to agree, toss her few items into her suitcase and follow him out the door. But how would that look to Serena and King Warrington? There could be no divided loyalties. "Your offer is very generous, but I need to remain here."

DeSante sighed. "Then you leave me no choice but to also stay here. I will be across the hall should you need anything."

DeSante turned and left the room leaving Iliana in stunned silence.

Chapter 9

Serena was filled with frustration when she returned to the château late in the afternoon. Warrington had abandoned the discussion with her and DeSante and was returning to Rizari, leaving many issues unresolved.

Casimir was sitting by the fireplace, a book open on his lap. "Rough day?"

Rough and unproductive. "No progress. I spent the morning dealing with two hotheads. Neither of them wanted to compromise or discuss anything. They shouted accusations. Waste of time."

"Why do you think that is?" Casimir asked.

Serena slumped into the plush couch next to Casimir. He set his book on the coffee table and reclined, putting his arm around her. "That's a matter of speculation. They don't want to say out loud what they want for fear the other will resist on principle."

"What do you speculate they want?"

"DeSante? I don't know. He's a blank slate. I try to read him and get nothing. Strangely, the only time I've seen him display any real emotion was in relation to Iliana. I've asked her if he's revealed his thoughts on the leaders' ability to reach an agreement, but she says their conversations aren't related to politics."

"What about King Warrington?"

Serena groaned. "My personal issues with him are coloring my judgment. DeSante suggested Warrington is planning to start a war between our three countries."

"Do you think that's true?"

"I can't be sure. Whenever I've tried to talk to Warrington, we argue. I don't see how our relationship will ever progress past that point."

"Samuel's mother's sixtieth birthday party is tomorrow night."

"I know." Serena's interactions with Katarina had been less than stellar. But Serena was planning to attend the party, especially since she wouldn't have the excuse of the summit to give her a valid reason to cancel. "I was planning on going. Do you think I should snoop around his office? See if I can't find something to hint at why he is resistant to talking and what exactly he wants out of our merger?"

"I don't like the idea of you undertaking that task alone. Can you ask someone you trust for help?"

"Like you?"

"Like me," he said.

She considered it. With her access to the party, she would be given more opportunities to move around the palace. Employees of the king, the king and his mother would be distracted by the party.

Her father's birthday party crossed her mind and she

shivered. She leaned into Casimir. "Do you think it will be safe to be in the palace?"

"I am sure Warrington is taking the necessary precautions. What happened at your father's birthday is fresh in everyone's memory."

It was never far from her mind, and Serena wondered if Katarina's birthday would be the stage for another assassination.

Serena was accustomed to being unseen in social situations, but as queen, her status—and visibility—had shifted. By the nature of her position, people were interested in her. Katarina's birthday party was no exception, making it difficult for her to operate in stealth mode.

If Samuel's guards spotted her where she was not supposed to be in the palace, she would give the excuse that she'd needed time alone. If she was caught in the king's bedroom, she would pretend she'd been planning a seduction. But Serena didn't want to wave the black-and-white-checkered flag for him. Despite their mutual dislike, she had no doubt Warrington would sleep with her for kicks.

Then there was the matter of slipping past her guards. If she was out of sight, they would be worried and actively search for her. An idea popped into her head, so crazy that it actually might work. She would need to use Iliana to help distract them. From a certain angle, she and Iliana looked alike. If her cousin could fool her guards long enough, she could accomplish her goal.

A quick call confirmed that—albeit hesitantly—Iliana would help.

When Serena arrived at Samuel's palace, she was immediately escorted to Samuel's side. She would have preferred a few minutes alone to collect her thoughts, but she'd been running late.

"After what happened at the summit, I was worried you weren't coming," he said, patting the hand she had slipped over his arm. When he kissed her cheek, he smelled of cologne and scotch. The scent made her dizzy and slightly nauseated.

"We ran into some traffic from the airport."

"My mother is anxious to see you."

Anxious to dole out more criticism? Based on how Katarina had spoken to her every other time they had met, she would have no problem commenting on the recent scandal involving Casimir in the rose garden and in Elion.

Serena kept her shoulders pinned back and her head high. She was queen of Acacia. She wouldn't be intimidated or cowed by anyone tonight.

She wished Casimir was beside her, but at least he was at the party, somewhere with Iliana, waiting for her to finish with her obligation. Samuel led her to where his mother stood, sipping from a glass of champagne and talking to the people around her.

As they approached, the guests speaking to Katarina moved away, bowing slightly. Katarina was not titled royalty, but at times, Serena wondered if she knew the difference.

"Katarina, it's a pleasure to see you again," Serena said, extending her hand. She took care to inject some warmth into her voice. "Happy birthday."

"Your Highness." Katarina Warrington accepted Serena's hand and clasped it.

"Everything looks wonderful. Your son did a nice job arranging the evening." Serena pulled her hand away.

Katarina laughed sharply. "My son didn't arrange this. The king doesn't have time to plan parties. We have event coordinators on staff to handle these affairs. When you're ready to start your wedding preparations—" Katarina said.

Samuel cut in. "Mother, not now."

Serena didn't want to think about wedding preparations. "It's customary to be engaged before planning a wedding." She tried to keep her tone light, but the look Katarina gave her indicated she'd failed.

His mother pursed her lips. "Engagements are merely a formality. Tell me, Serena, what is preventing you from agreeing to the engagement?"

Serena was taken aback by Katarina's willingness to put her on the spot in front of other guests. She hadn't anticipated this meeting would take a hostile turn so quickly. "Samuel and I are taking our time." And arguing and fighting and seeing absolutely everything differently.

"I see. I have some additional topics I'd like to speak with you about. Perhaps we can talk in private later?" Katarina's eyes were cold and hard.

Serena would rather chew glass. She gave a nod of acknowledgment, but she wasn't planning to follow through on a private whining session with Katarina. "If you'll excuse me, I need a drink." Releasing Samuel's arm, she strode in the direction of the bar. Being verbally accosted wasn't how she would spend the evening.

Samuel caught up to her. "You'll have to excuse my mother. She's protective. You know how mothers can be."

"No actually, I don't." Serena's mother had died when she was three and it stung that Samuel didn't

know that. She strode away from him and didn't turn
to see his expression. Maybe it was time for Samuel
to put some genuine effort into their relationship. Or
maybe it was time for Serena to think of other ways to
secure Acacia's future.

Serena fled the drawing room, feigning that she was
upset after the incident. Guests were flowing in and Serena pretended to be on her phone and distressed. When
she was away from the crowd, she texted Iliana to meet
her in the bathroom on the first floor. They would trade
clothes and places. Iliana would have to take care not
to show her face, but a walk in the darkened garden
should accomplish that.

Serena waited a few minutes and following a quick
tap on the door, Iliana slipped inside the bathroom. She
locked up behind her. They traded dresses, Iliana wearing the formal purple gown and Serena slipping on Iliana's simple black frock.

"It's not too late to change your mind," Iliana said,
adjusting her wig. "It's dangerous what you're doing."

"This is my opportunity. I can't let it pass," Serena
said. She had to know for sure what Samuel wanted
before she signed those papers, agreeing to marry him
and turning over control of Acacia.

Checking her red wig and dress in the mirror, Serena slipped out of the bathroom. Samuel's office was
on the second floor of the palace. She used the servant's
stairwell, moving purposefully and quietly. Most everyone was working in or around the drawing room, so the
hallways were clear. Serena took slow, deep breaths and
tried to stay calm. Every footstep sounded loud, every
creak of the stair echoing in the space. She rehearsed

what she would say if caught. She wasn't a great liar, but she was prepared to sell it.

Once on the second floor, she strode toward Samuel's office. She set her hand on the door knob and turned it, hoping it was unlocked. It was! She entered the room and someone grabbed her hand, pulling her deeper into the office. She was composing her excuse, when she recognized his scent. "What are you doing here?"

Casimir pointed to the desk. "Searching."

"I told you I would look for evidence. You're supposed to be downstairs with Iliana."

"Iliana and I agreed. We couldn't let you do this alone."

"Great, now we'll both be arrested," she said drily.

"You're assuming we will get caught. We won't. Are you wearing a wig?" he asked.

"My guards won't be looking for a redhead. They are following Iliana in a blond wig." She patted the red hair.

"I thought you were pretending to be yourself on a mission of seduction. How will you explain the getup if you're caught?" Casimir asked.

"I'll tell Samuel I was shooting for a kinky role-playing evening."

"What role are you playing?"

"Red-haired, fiery seductress."

Casimir grinned. He kissed her then, pressing her up against the back of the closed door. Serena relaxed beneath his touch, letting his mouth plunder hers. His lips massaged hers, his tongue stroked against her tongue and his body rubbed with the right friction, the right movement to excite every nerve ending. A mewling sound filled the air. Did Samuel have a cat?

"Shhh," he whispered against her lips.

"I wasn't talking."

"You're moaning."

She straightened. "If you want me to be silent, you shouldn't kiss me."

"Shhh," he said again and went back to kissing her.

Her head was filled with Casimir. Kissing Casimir. Grinding against Casimir. Touching Casimir. When he broke away, she leaned against the door to keep from melting to the floor in a puddle of heat.

"I needed to get that out of my system," he said.

He strode to the desk and looked through papers using a flashlight.

It was out of his system, but now it was strongly in hers. She wanted to finish what he had started. They didn't have time now, but maybe tonight they could meet at the beach house. Being there with Casimir was one of her favorite ways to relax. But before they could relax, they had to finish this task and find something to clue her in to Warrington's agenda.

"I'll check his bedroom," Serena said.

Casimir glanced at her. "I need a few more minutes. I'll meet you there."

Serena wished they were rendezvousing in her bedroom. Instead, she was searching the bedroom of a man she hoped to never be in the position to share a bed with.

Samuel wouldn't leave incriminating information in the open for anyone to discover. Casimir had heard from one of DeSante's spies in the palace of Rizari that Samuel used this smaller office for the majority of his work, including personal matters. He had a larger office in the palace for official meetings.

Casimir had felt an instant connection to this space.

For good reason. It had once belonged to his father. His mother had some pictures of the palace, old, grainy photos, faded with age. The room was unfamiliar, yet being here was bringing to the surface emotions he'd thought long buried. He had never known his father, except in descriptions from his mother and stories in the news. He was torn between anger at his father and the crippling loss of never having met him.

Casimir heard a noise in the hallway and darted behind a plush couch, crouching to the floor. He should have been aware of approaching footsteps. His lapse in concentration might cost him dearly.

The door to the office opened, and Samuel and a black-haired woman entered. Casimir didn't recognize her, but she was tall and slender and wore a long black dress that was tied around her neck. Her breasts were spilling from the fabric and Samuel grabbed at her as they stumbled in the near darkness into the room.

She giggled and Samuel hushed her. After he closed the door behind him, he again advanced on her. She clawed at his clothes. Within seconds, she was bent over the desk, her dress around her waist, with Warrington behind her, moaning and groaning.

Casimir closed his eyes and tried to block out the noise. Even with his hands over his ears, the rhythmic thumps and high-pitched moans penetrated his hearing.

The episode was over in less than two minutes. Casimir gave his cousin no points for stamina or creativity. After a disgusting exchange of lurid compliments, Samuel and his fling left the office ten seconds apart. Casimir waited in case Samuel decided to return. When it remained quiet, Casimir resumed his search.

How was Serena doing? She hadn't messaged that

she'd found anything, but Casimir worried about her. He glanced at the time on his phone. It had been twenty-three minutes since Serena had left the office. Having found nothing himself, he sent her a message and then slipped out of the room to meet her in the king's bedroom.

Serena had a difficult time picturing Samuel sleeping and residing in his bedroom. It was almost hard to believe it was his. She had expected modern decor, possibly primarily neutral colors with a splash of bold tones, like red.

Instead, the room was decorated in soft fabrics, heavy drapes, and shades of green and blue. The decorations were simple and understated, though Serena had no doubt they were of high quality. The painting across from his bed was of a ship on the water, struggling against a fierce storm. What had compelled Samuel to choose that piece?

Serena opened his drawers, peeking inside. She found impeccably folded clothes that smelled of laundry detergent. Moving them aside, she looked underneath. She didn't know what she was searching for. He was unlikely to have saved documentation detailing his private thoughts on the future of Rizari. Samuel wasn't the type to keep a handwritten diary.

Pulling aside the curtain to the window, Serena took in the view. It was too dark to see anything except the dots of lights from the palace outbuildings. No view of the water. Serena released the curtain and returned to her search.

She opened the bedside table and found condoms, candles and lubricant. Feeling as if she had crossed a line, she closed it quickly. Serena knelt and looked under the bed. It was empty, save a condom wrapper.

"What are you doing here?"

A female voice. Serena rose to her feet. Samuel's mother was standing in the doorway, her silhouette outlined by the light from the hallway. Her hands were folded in front of her and she waited, watching Serena with narrowed eyes.

Serena had practiced her cover story so many times, it snapped to her tongue. "I was waiting for Samuel."

Katarina flicked on the light and stepped farther into the room. "Why are you dressed like that? What did you do to your hair?"

"Part of the surprise."

His mother lifted her brow.

Serena would let his mother think whatever she wanted. Let her believe it was a kinky fantasy, a lover secretly visiting in the night.

"I don't think you should be in my son's bedroom."

Serena lifted her head and tilted it to the side. She had seen her sister intimidate many foes with that same look. Would it work for her?

Samuel's mother set her hands on her hips. "We could call my son and speak to him about this."

Serena debated her next move. "That's a good idea." She could feed Samuel her story, that she was trying to smooth over the problems they'd been having by injecting a little fun into their relationship. Then she could pretend to be embarrassed or annoyed that she had been caught and return home.

His mother placed the call. Serena, astonished that she hadn't collapsed in a pile of nerves and sweat, sat on the chaise longue positioned under the window on the far side of the room.

Katarina spoke quietly into her phone, too low for Serena to hear. Serena tried not to let that add to her terror. She inspected her nails as if bored.

Katarina gripped her phone at her side. "You're not the good girl you pretend to be."

Serena glared at Samuel's mother. The woman knew nothing about her. "I am the queen of Acacia. I would appreciate if you'd show me respect. If you don't like me as your son's choice for a wife, that's your problem."

"His choice? My son doesn't have a choice. He has to marry you."

Serena saw another angle to explore. Katarina might know more about Samuel's motives than he had revealed to her directly. "We don't have an arrangement yet. He is free to marry whoever he chooses."

Katarina looked positively apoplectic. "That isn't true. My son sees the writing on the wall. War with Icarus is inevitable. He needs Acacia on his side."

Was Samuel expecting to defend himself against a war with Icarus or was he planning to be the aggressor? The information ricocheted around Serena's brain and made her feel dizzy. It wasn't the evidence she was looking for to implicate Samuel in wrongdoing, but it was more evidence that DeSante's suspicions were correct. Samuel had war on his mind. "I don't see it that way."

"Then you are a fool. Your sister would have made a better wife and a better queen. At least she had charisma and charm."

Serena tried not to visibly recoil. At the mention of her sister, Serena was assaulted by grief and curiosity. How much had Danae known about Samuel Warrington's plans for their countries? "I didn't realize you and Danae were close."

Katarina sniffed. "We weren't. But my son tells me everything. Everything."

The fact was unsettling, but Serena waited to see what else his mother would reveal. Perhaps in her attempt to assert herself as the most important woman in her son's life, she would step too far and divulge one of the king's secrets.

"You aren't my son's type."

Serena knew that. Samuel wasn't hers. "I see."

"Do you? Because I am not buying this act you're putting on tonight."

Samuel entered the room and appeared confused as he looked between his mother and her. His hair was mussed. "What are you doing in here?" He addressed Serena.

Serena folded her hands and tried to appear exasperated. "Being thwarted by your mother. I took our last conversation to heart and I had hoped to arrange a surprise for you. Your mother didn't seem to think it was a good idea."

He narrowed his eyes. "What surprise?"

Serena gestured to herself. "Me."

Samuel's lips quirked and his eyes lit up. It was the first time she had seen genuine interest from him. Figured he'd be attentive when sex was implied. Serena had opened a door she didn't want to walk through. She rose to her feet. "But this is a mess. I'll be returning home. It's your mother's birthday party. I didn't mean to upset anyone. I wanted to have time alone with you, but I can see that this is bad timing."

"Right. That sounds logical," Katarina said sarcastically.

Samuel looked at his mother. "Mother, you need to give Serena some latitude."

His mother straightened. "Aren't you planning to address the issue of her other lover?"

Samuel glanced at Serena. "I am aware of it and we've addressed it. That's all you need to know."

Surprised at the way the king had spoken to his mother, Serena stood and crossed the room to the door. "I'd rather not make another scene tonight and ruin your mother's evening. It is her birthday, after all." For once, Katarina had the grace to stay silent.

Serena fled the room and Samuel didn't stop her.

Serena ran into Casimir in the hallway. She shook her head and indicated he should turn and run.

She messaged Iliana to meet her in the same bathroom. This time, Iliana was waiting for her. They switched dresses again, and Iliana shoved both wigs into her oversized handbag. Serena exited the bathroom. Her guards were looking around for her and seemed relieved when they spotted her with her cousin.

Three hours later, at her beach house, Serena shared with Casimir and Iliana what she had learned. "King Warrington anticipates war with Icarus. I don't know if he plans to start it, but he expects it's inevitable."

Speaking freely in front of Iliana brought her cousin deeper into the circle of trust. She wanted both her and Casimir's opinions on the matter.

"He said that?" Iliana asked.

"His mother told me," Serena said.

Iliana made a noise of disgust. Casimir watched her with his deep intelligent eyes.

"I don't like his mother. She's strange," Iliana said.

"She's protective," Serena said, despite her feelings toward the woman.

"That's one way to describe it," Iliana said.

After discussing possibilities for an hour, Iliana rose to her feet. "I need to get going. I have an early morning tomorrow and the boss won't like it if I'm late."

Serena hugged her. "See you tomorrow. Drive safe, okay?"

After Iliana left, Serena was alone with Casimir, save for Serena's guards posted at the front and back of her house.

"I need to change out of this dress," Serena said, extending her hand to Casimir.

He took it, and followed her up the stairs to her bedroom. Her passion and her feelings for him were stronger than the confusing thoughts swirling inside her.

She unfastened her dress and let the satin pool on the floor. She was naked beneath the dress except for a thong and Casimir's eyes widened with lust.

She stroked his cheek and he closed his eyes, leaning into her touch.

He kissed the inside of her wrist. His lips trailed up her arm, moving their bodies closer together. "I want you, Serena."

She wanted him, too. He unbuttoned his shirt and let it fall over his broad shoulders. She kicked off her shoes, wiggled out of her underwear and pushed back on the bed, waiting for him. Watching him move, the sleekness of his muscles and the intensity in his eyes was throwing fuel on the fire burning hot and wild inside her. Casimir removed his pants and slid onto the bed with her, covering her with his body. He kissed her deeply, intensely, stroking his hand up and down her body.

Then he shifted, sitting with his back against the headboard and pulled her astride him. Her core touched his arousal, yet he made no motion to push inside her.

His kiss was ravenous, in direct contrast to the gentle caress of his hands on her bare back. She wanted his hands elsewhere on her body. Casimir palmed her cheeks. "I was worried you would have to protect your cover and stay the night with him."

She would have rather been arrested. "I wouldn't spend the night with Samuel. We haven't even shared a kiss. I think we'd have a few steps in between."

"Those steps can blur and blend," Casimir said.

"I'm with *you*. I don't want another man," Serena said, capturing his lips and kissing him.

Casimir rubbed his hips against hers and the friction hit her in the right places. She moved harder against him and she rapidly became frustrated. She wanted Casimir inside her. She'd come to associate him with mind-blowing orgasms and she was craving another.

Serena reached for a condom from her bedside table and fumbled to remove it from the packaging. After a few missed tries, Casimir took the foil from her hand and deftly handled the task. She lifted herself over him. He licked each of her nipples and reached between her legs, slipping a finger inside her and circling the tight bundle of nerves at her core with his thumb.

If he was checking if she was wet, the answer was obvious.

"Ride me," he said. The request came like a growl in his throat.

Serena lowered herself onto him in one clean motion.

Buried deep inside her, he held her close and kissed her. She swiveled her hips and broke the kiss, letting out a moan of pleasure. Passion and arousal were a hot blaze, urging her movements harder and faster.

Desire shuttered his eyes and she felt bolder with every response of his body. He was thick and hard inside her and she had the power to move how she wanted.

Timid at first, and then forgetting everything except how incredible it felt to be joined with him, she moved. His hands were at her hips, guiding her, sliding his body inside hers.

She felt the pressure between her hips and an orgasm built and exploded, ripping through her. Casimir swept her into his powerful arms. He flipped her onto her stomach and slid a pillow beneath her hips. He entered her from behind.

He thrust slowly. "Is this okay?"

Her overexcited body was tingling. She thought she would burst from his thickness. "It's good." She gripped the sheets to keep from sliding at the strength of his thrusts.

He increased his pace. He was taking her to new heights in his relentless pursuit of pleasure, bringing her with him. His thickness and length were almost too much, pushing her to the edge of another release. Casimir let out a growl and shoved hard into her, pausing for a beat before withdrawing and pressing inside her again.

Knowing he had finished, she let herself go, turning her body over to him.

How could she ever marry another man when her heart belonged to him?

Chapter 10

Santino burst into Serena's office at seven the next morning.

Serena stood to greet her uncle. "Good morning, what brings you by?" Serena had already skimmed the news that morning and saw no further mention of scandal related to her and Casimir, not even after he had attended Katarina's birthday celebration. Not that it was far from the minds of the press, but it didn't get top billing anymore.

Santino handed her a thick envelope.

"What's this?" Serena asked.

"The paperwork for the merger with Rizari, ready for your signature."

The merger, in other words, her marriage to King Warrington. "I haven't had time to review it." She had read it. But she wasn't on board with everything stated in it.

"You can't drag your feet on this. Enough time has passed. If we let too much time go…"

"Then what?" Would King Warrington change his mind? Would he attack Acacia and take it by force instead of by marriage?

"We are exposed. Icarus could attack while we dawdle and debate trivial details."

The summit meeting had not gone well. But Serena had hope that Icarus, Rizari and Acacia could still come to an agreement. Her marriage to King Warrington wasn't a done deal and she hadn't lost her bargaining power. She wasn't convinced that Demetrius DeSante and Icarus were the prime threats. She sensed more scheming and treachery from King Warrington.

Her uncle appeared worried. "If we renege on the arrangement with Rizari, that is an insult that King Warrington will not forgive."

"Do you think he will respond by attacking us?" Serena asked.

Her uncle seemed unsure how to answer. "I don't know what to think."

Serena tilted her chin proudly. "Maybe I'll run Acacia myself." She said it to test his response, to see if anyone would believe it was possible, aside from her and Casimir.

Her uncle shook his head. "How in the world do you intend to do that? You have no experience. You get nervous giving speeches. The press makes fun of you, constantly comparing you to Danae."

His lack of faith in her cut to the core. She had much to learn and she was open about that, but she was smart and capable. Her father had run the country for decades, just as her grandfather had before him. It was in her blood. She had watched her father all her life. She had learned from him and that counted for something. "I'll do everything I can. Our Assembly is strong and I have great hopes for the future."

"How can you possibly think you are capable of running a country?" Her uncle slammed his fist against her desk. "You've behaving like a spoiled child. You're wasting time pining for some commoner and imagining some fantasy where you're with him. You have a duty and an obligation to your country. This isn't an experiment for you to attempt. This isn't about making you feel good about yourself or boosting your self-esteem. The few times you've been in public, you've looked like a bumbling dolt."

His harsh words struck at her deepest insecurities. "I realize how important this country is and how important my position."

"If you realize it, then sign the papers. Stop exposing us to attack!"

Serena heard the shaking anger—or was it fear—in her uncle's voice and couldn't believe it was directed at her. "I will when I am ready." Then she thought about what finalizing the merger would mean for her and Casimir.

"You'll sign them now. The enemy is at the gate. The enemy has been in this space. In our home."

Serena felt tears come to her eyes. It wasn't solely her uncle upsetting her. The painful emotions that tightened her chest were rooted in her unresolved feelings for Casimir, her raw grief for her father and her sister, and the tremendous responsibilities that had been set upon her shoulders. "Give me time." Perhaps her uncle felt responsible for her and that stress was affecting him.

"Serena, I have always tried to protect you. This is a time where I need to protect you from yourself."

Serena stood and strode toward her office door. If her uncle wouldn't leave, she would. Santino grabbed her arm and his grip tightened. "Sign the papers, Serena. You won't be a good queen on your own."

She tried to shake him off, but his grip held. "You have no faith in me."

"Neither does anyone else in the country."

Serena felt as if she'd been slapped.

"You were practically estranged from your father and you've been dragged back to a position you don't want. Why are you resisting?"

"Because what I want has changed," Serena said.

"So help me, if you make this about some puppy love with that man, then I will have to take drastic action."

"Drastic action?"

Her uncle's expression was menacing. "I will do whatever is necessary to protect the people of Acacia, even if it's from their queen."

Casimir's judgment was clouded. He had set out on this path of vengeance years earlier and thought he knew what he wanted: to avenge his father's death and his mother's honor.

Serena had unexpectedly become part of that plan, a game changer. She was supposed to bring him closer to Warrington and the evidence he needed to take his rightful place as heir to the throne in Rizari. His father's killer would be brought to justice and his mother would have peace.

Serena wasn't supposed to be hurt in the process. She wasn't supposed to know anything about him. His goal had been to get in and out, with zero emotional ties and nothing to trace him to Rizari.

Casimir couldn't see Serena as a piece in a chess game. She was a woman, a strong and beautiful woman, who was coming into her own. She could handle so much more than the people around her gave her credit for. He had underestimated her and he had been wrong about her.

Casimir needed to tell Serena how he felt about her. Tell her the truth about who he was. Serena's beautiful face filled his thoughts. Could he find a way to come clean with her without hurting her? The truth was brutal.

He walked toward Serena's office, needing to speak with her. He didn't know what he would say, but he needed to clear his conscience.

"What are you doing here?" Iliana asked, standing from her desk.

"I need to speak to Serena," Casimir said.

Iliana glanced nervously at the door. "She's talking with her uncle."

That didn't matter. Casimir needed to see her. He burst inside the door. Santino was gripping Serena's arm.

"We're in the middle of something. Come back later," Santino said.

Not a chance. "Let her go. Now."

Her uncle released her. Lucky for him. Casmir had killed a man for less.

"What exactly is going on here?" Casimir asked, feeling his protective instincts rising.

"I'm handing this," Serena said.

"This is none of your concern, commoner. I'm trying to prevent my niece from ruining her life and running this country into the ground."

"By forcing me to sign the marriage agreement," Serena said.

"Instead, she is caught up in a fantasy about you and refusing to sign," her uncle said.

"I am not a girl caught in a fantasy. I am queen of this country and I am trying to do what is best for Acacia," Serena said.

Her voice was strong and clear. Casimir was proud of her for standing up for herself.

"Name your price," Santino said to him.

"Price for what? Walking out of here and leaving you alone with Serena? I have no price for that."

"Your price to walk out of her life completely," Santino said.

Even if Santino offered to kill Samuel Warrington in exchange for abandoning Serena, Casimir wouldn't do it. That truth felt like a bowling ball in his stomach. She meant too much to him. "You can't buy me off."

Serena smiled at him. Santino glared.

Iliana stepped inside the office. She was deathly pale. "Serena, it's happened. There's been an act of aggression between Rizari and Icarus. This will mean war."

The words *act of aggression* rang loud in Serena's head. What had happened? She couldn't reach either King Warrington or President DeSante.

Serena called for the heads of the Assembly and her advisers to gather at the castle. She wanted to be prepared to make decisions quickly. Though her uncle had not left, he was quiet.

After several more tries, she finally reached King Warrington.

"I need to know what is going on," Serena said. She was shocked by the hardness of her own voice.

"One of DeSante's submarines came too close to our shores and we fired at it."

"You opened fire on an Icarus sub?" Serena asked. She had anticipated Icarus being the aggressor. If they had traveled close to Rizari's shores, it was provocation, but a full-on attack was a declaration of war.

"We didn't open fire. Our navy is trained to respond to attacks and follow protocols, and they did." He didn't sound happy. He sounded angry and bewildered.

"Have you spoken to DeSante?" Serena asked.

"No."

Serena wanted to scream in frustration. It was absolutely critical that communication stay open between the two leaders. "Stay on the line. I'm calling him."

She put Warrington on hold and called for Iliana. "Get DeSante on the phone." Using her cousin's connection to him had never been more important.

Iliana nodded. When DeSante came on the line, he didn't sound upset.

"I warned you that Warrington wanted war."

She hadn't gotten the impression from Warrington that war was the goal. "I just spoke to him. I think we need to discuss this incident. It may have been an unfortunate training issue."

DeSante scoffed. "Training issue? No, Your Highness. If you believe that, you aren't the intelligent woman I believed you to be."

She was momentarily struck by the compliment, but she pressed on. This wasn't about her. "DeSante, no one wants war." Especially not her. Acacia would be the loser in this scenario.

"Aren't you supposed to back your boyfriend?"

Serena thought of Casimir first, then realized De-Sante was referring to King Warrington. "I am behind peace."

"At any price?"

"I am willing to do whatever you need to keep this discussion going and not have the situation turn violent."

"It has already turned violent. My sub was manned. Four deaths."

"May I conference in Warrington so we might speak about this together?" Rationally and calmly as three leaders who didn't want additional casualties.

"The time for speaking was at the summit. Now it is time for action."

Serena tried again. "Please, President DeSante, if you would reconsider your position."

"Demetrius, please listen to Serena. You know that this is a difficult time for our administration. If you attack Rizari, you will force Serena into marrying Warrington." Iliana was on her extension and had jumped into the conversation. She sounded desperate and scared.

Though Serena thought it was inappropriate, given Iliana's relationship with the president and his soft side when it came to her, it might help. Peace at any price.

"Iliana, I did not realize you were on the call," De-Sante said.

"I wasn't supposed to be. But I couldn't help it." She didn't sound sorry.

"You understand that Rizari destroyed one of Ica-

rus's submarines today?" DeSante said. His tone when
speaking to Iliana was a hundred times softer and
warmer than it had been when speaking to her.

"We don't know the circumstances."

"I know the circumstances."

"Demetrius, please, don't do this."

"Iliana, you cannot play on my affection for you to
manipulate me. I have a country to protect."

Iliana hung up the phone with a growl of outrage.

Serena didn't know how to play this. She was hope-
lessly lost. "President DeSante, before any further action is taken, we need to discuss this with Warrington."

"No, Your Highness. You do what you must, and I
will do the same." DeSante disconnected the call.

Serena returned to her call with Warrington. He was
no easier to talk with. She received the same hard-line
response from him.

The best she could do was meet him to speak in person. Though she had previously declined the invitation,
she agreed to meet Warrington in Rizari at the symphony hall, where he had scheduled a performance of
the country's most popular orchestra, an annual event
held the day after Katarina's birthday celebration. Warrington was unwilling to cancel the event, though there
were clearly more pressing matters to attend to.

It was a strange place to meet, but if it brought King
Warrington to the negotiation table, then she would go,
talk, listen and try to defuse the situation. Serena didn't
want war for Acacia and she had to stop this potential
disaster before it spiraled out of control.

Casimir felt the shift in the atmosphere at the castle.
Serena was doing her best to hold it together. As the

Mediterranean inched toward war, Casimir felt even more urgently that he needed to tell Serena who he was.

If he made his move and overthrew Warrington, he could prevent war. DeSante would back off if Samuel Warrington was no longer in power.

But overthrowing Warrington was not a simple task. Perhaps with Serena on his side, it would be easier. Would she support his play for power? Or would she be caught up in her anger at him for having lied to her and turn a blind eye to the benefits of helping him?

When King Warrington had requested that Serena meet him at the Grand Symphony Hall in Rizari, Casimir had followed her. He was not leaving Serena unprotected and he felt something was amiss. Though he had barely spoken three words to her, he'd stayed close. She'd been conferencing with one person after another—leaders of other countries in the region, the highest ranking members of the Assembly and her advisers. Her meeting with Warrington was next.

Of all the places King Warrington could meet Serena, why a musical performance? Samuel couldn't be trusted. Certainly, this event wasn't more important than the rapidly declining political situation between Rizari and Icarus. He was planning something and Casimir needed to get ahead of whatever it was.

Upon entering the theater, Casimir promptly spotted Serena. Seated in the king's balcony, she didn't know Casimir was watching her and he found her even more beguiling. She was quiet and unassuming, but her eyes were sharp. She had a guard on either side of her, the king's guards. Warrington had not yet arrived at the hall. Behind her was a heavy blue curtain, the same blue painted on the walls of the circular room. The gold trim was subtle, lining the balconies and stage without detracting from the aura of simplicity. Casimir's father had commissioned the symphony hall in honor of his brother, Samuel's father, and his love of music.

Out of the corner of his eye, Casimir caught a glimpse of Rolland, Demetrius DeSante's favorite and most trusted assassin. Rolland's most notable trait was that he was not notable at all. Average height and build, his dark hair was cut short, his eagle eyes sharp. Casimir tensed instinctively. His methods were unpredictable and he was loyal only to money. Raising the body count with innocents and bystanders wasn't a problem for him if it got the job done.

Rolland wasn't the type to patronize music and he did not exclusively work for DeSante. Which meant he was here on a job. Who was his target?

Casimir followed him in the crowd, while calling DeSante on the phone. But the president of Icarus wasn't answering. Casimir lost track of Rolland as people socialized and milled around.

He tried texting DeSante instead. Why is Rolland in Rizari?

The response came moments later. He's providing backup.

For? Who's his target?

Backup for you. You've lost focus and I need to get this done. No war. Target is Sam.

Casimir didn't need backup. Rolland would shoot first, ask questions later. He wouldn't care if he killed Serena and while assassinating Samuel held some appeal, a bloody coup made Casimir no better than Samuel. He wanted the throne in an honorable way. I have this.

Serena is meeting with our enemy to discuss an alliance. You had time. You failed. DeSante didn't mince words.

DeSante wouldn't stop Rolland. He had decided that Casimir wasn't moving fast enough. Rolland was exceptional at what he did. Accurate to a fault, he could slip away from any place unnoticed. He was untraceable and had so many contacts around the world, he could hide for months to let the fallout die down before reappearing somewhere else.

I am in control, Casimir texted, hating that he was being argumentative. His actions should speak for themselves.

Rolland stays on post.

DeSante was holding the line. Casimir knew his old friend too well. When DeSante set his mind to something, he rarely wavered. He had decided to kill Samuel and had sent in his best to do the job. If Casimir wanted Samuel alive so he could get the answers he needed, he would have to find Rolland and stop him.

When the members of the symphony began to tune their instruments, the lights in the hall blinked a few times. The crowd moved toward their seats. When the aisles were clear, the lights lowered and then the hall went dark. Casimir scanned for a red dot anywhere near Serena that would point to Rolland planning to take his shot at Samuel. He could have night vision goggles to assist him, but even a good marksman needed tools to hit his target in the dark.

The sounds of the orchestra rose up through the hall. Casimir moved from his position. He didn't want to be pinned down by trampling people if shooting started.

When the lights came on, Samuel Warrington was standing on the conductor's podium. Serena was in her seat. She appeared confused.

Noticing the king, the crowd erupted in applause. Samuel held out his hands to quiet them. "Welcome to you all, my dear friends, and please allow me to borrow the stage for one minute before the performance begins. This day holds a lot of meaning for me. As you know, this concert is a long-standing tradition held in the hall built for my father. He honored my mother with private performances here and I have continued that tradition in his absence. I have selected the score and heard some of the rehearsal. But before we enjoy the music, I have an important question for someone special."

Casimir felt panic for another reason, a reason besides an assassin roaming the crowd. The king was planning to propose to Serena. Though Casimir knew this was inevitable, he hated what was coming, hated that he would have to watch it. Most of all, Casimir hated the idea that Serena would belong to the king and the king to her.

Adding to his anxiety, given that the king had made himself an easy target, Rolland would take his shots.

"Serena Alagona, queen of Acacia, you have become the light in my world. If I have learned anything from the past several months, it's that life is too short. But it can also be sweet with the right woman at my side.

Together we can do great things. We can vanquish a common enemy. Will you be my bride?"

He had shoehorned in the problem with Icarus by reminding Serena and the crowd of their enemy, and forced the issue of the engagement.

Serena stood and appeared shell-shocked. She turned, presumably to exit the balcony to meet the king onstage. She would hate being proposed to in this public manner. Casimir hated it for a different reason. She would be close to Samuel, the target, while Rolland was somewhere in the building, probably gleeful about the spectacle he was about to make. Rolland liked his work to be appreciated and his efforts couldn't be fully valued when his directives included killing someone inconspicuously and hiding the body. The assassination of the King of Rizari would be in the open, in front of a live audience. It would be front page news for weeks.

Casimir rushed to intercept Serena. She was descending the stairs with the king's guards flanking her. "Serena!"

She whirled in Casimir's direction. "What's wrong?"

"No time to explain. There's an assassin here. You need to stay away from the king."

"Are you threatening the queen?" one of the guards asked. Casimir didn't recognize or know him. The man might think he was some nut stalking the queen.

"She is in danger. Not from me. Someone wants to kill the king."

"Every person here passed through security. The king and the queen are safe," the guard said haughtily.

Serena held out her hand to the guards. She addressed Casimir. "I need to talk to Samuel. He's waiting for my answer. Did you hear what he asked?"

He'd heard and though it wasn't the most pressing issue, he wanted to know her thoughts. "What will you say?"

Everything inside him needed her to say no. Despite what that could mean for their plans, no was the only acceptable answer. Her eyes were wells of sadness. "I will say yes. Our countries are on the verge of war. I can't rock the boat. I have to go, Casimir."

She wasn't thinking clearly because she was nervous and tense.

Three other guards swarmed closer and took him by the arms, dragging him away. Casimir had to find Rolland. The hall presented too many angles and too many places to hide. Struggling against their hold, he broke free of the king's guards and chased after Serena. The guards pursued, but they wouldn't shoot into the crowd, especially when the king was in range of flying bullets.

Serena wasn't wearing a vest. Casimir should have refused to allow her to pass him. He should have fought harder, but her answer had disarmed him for a moment too long. The king's guards, who were likely wearing vests, could take a bullet for her, but Casimir questioned their loyalty. The king's safety would be their chief concern.

Serena met the king on the stage. She was shaking and pale, but the nodding of her head was unmistakable. She was saying yes to his proposal. She would marry Warrington.

Casimir raced to the stage to warn them. The king's guards tried to stop him, but he was bigger, stronger and more determined. He stood in front of Serena and when the unmistakable sound of gunfire filled the hall, Casimir felt the impact when a slug landed in his chest.

Screaming. More gunfire. Casimir felt dizzy and had trouble pulling air into his lungs. He fought to take a deep breath. Serena was kneeling over him, cradling his head in her lap. He was in Rolland's eyeshot. She needed to go somewhere safe.

The king's guards were dragging the king to safety. The corners of his vision blurred and darkened. He tried to explain, tried to warn Serena to move to another location, to run to a safer place.

He couldn't make his mouth form the words. They came out as a gurgle.

Hers was the last face he saw before he lost consciousness.

Casimir felt as if he had been hit with a sledgehammer in the chest. Twice.

Serena was slapping his cheeks. "Casimir!"

Her hands moved down his body, poking and prodding. He moaned when she pressed his chest. He had taken a bullet in the vest. Rolland didn't fire tiny guns. He would have shot with serious power.

Serena was stroking his face. He preferred that to her prodding his body. "An ambulance is on the way. Just hold on."

Casimir opened one eye. They were behind the performance stage, as evidenced by a panel of lighting equipment on the wall and heavy blue curtains to his left. Serena was leaning over him, and he focused on her, her beautiful features filling his view.

"I'm fine. Vest." His bulletproof vest had taken most of the damage, but the impact would leave a deep bruise and maybe a few broken or cracked ribs.

Serena let out a cry of relief and threw herself on top

of him. He winced and she pulled back. "What were you trying to do?"

"Catch a bullet for you," he said, feeling out of breath.

Casimir closed his eyes, trying to think only of her face and not the throbbing in his chest.

When he woke, he knew immediately he was in her bed in her beach house in Acacia. The softness of her sheets and the scent of her surrounded him.

Serena was next to him on the bed, watching him. "How are you?"

Medical equipment was at the bedside, a blood pressure cuff was wrapped around his arm and a pad was taped to his chest.

"I feel like I've been shot," he said.

She touched his forehead. "You were shot. Twice. I have a nurse checking on you, but I thought you would be more comfortable recuperating here."

"I like it here. The smell and the sound of the waves. Where's Samuel?"

"I don't know. Not here. When the doctors confirmed you were stable, we took my plane back to here. I had X-rays taken of your chest. You've been in and out of consciousness. You hit your head when you fell."

He didn't remember much of anything. "Did I say anything stupid?"

She kissed his cheek. "No more than usual."

He smirked at her joke. "Can I see your hand?"

She held out her left hand. It was bare.

"No ring?" he asked. Had he misunderstood? Perhaps she and Samuel were not engaged. Had she refused him? Or had Rolland interrupted her answer?

She gestured to the white dresser across from the bed, against the wall. "It's there. On the dresser."

His chest ached all over again. "Why aren't you wearing it?"

"Are you trying to put yourself in more pain?" Serena asked.

He was fine. He'd had the wind knocked out of him by a couple powerful bullets. He wasn't down for the count. "You said yes." To King Warrington. To the man who had killed his father and destroyed his mother's life and who was seated on the throne that belonged to him.

"I had no choice. If I had said no to the king, it would have made the tensions between Acacia, Rizari and Icarus worse. I have to think of more than myself in these matters. If I get closer to Samuel, I can convince him that war is not the right response to the incident with Icarus."

Casimir would have preferred not knowing she belonged, at least in words, to King Warrington. "Run away with me."

"What?" she asked. "I had them look at your chest and your head. They said everything would be okay, but you sound crazy."

He felt crazy—and desperate. He had lost focus on his plan and his goals had changed. But the moment when he'd known Rolland was taking a shot at King Warrington, possibly gunning for Serena, too, nothing had been more important than her. "Run away with me. Let's leave this all behind."

"We can't do that," she said, but she sounded like she was considering it.

"You could have been killed today," he said.

"But I wasn't."

"Did they find the trigger man?"

She shook her head and laid her hand gently on his arm. "Everyone is looking for him. He won't get far. Someone snapped a picture of him."

"He's an assassin named Rolland. I know him."

Serena's brow creased. "What do you know about him?"

"That he's a sick, sadistic killer. He won't stop coming after King Warrington and I suspect he may come after me now," Casimir said.

"Why you?"

The ache in his chest was second to his worry. "You don't know Rolland. He's resourceful and slippery. I screwed up his assassination. He'll take that hard." Casimir didn't want to tell her that DeSante had sent Rolland. Keeping the peace between Acacia and Icarus was critical.

"You saved my life. Again. You have a funny habit of doing that. But my guards are here. They will keep us safe. It's my turn to protect you."

"I told you I would look out for you," Casimir said. She looked suspicious, as if she had more questions. If pressed, Casimir would answer them and then all the cards would be on the table. With the truth laid bare, Casimir would be taking a risk. He wanted to tell her. Wanted to give her a chance to be the woman he knew she could be, to see that he was a good man. "This isn't the life you deserve. Run away with me," he repeated, hating the begging in his voice.

Serena stood. "You don't mean any of this. You were hurt and you need to recover. Rest now. I'll wake you to eat in a little while."

Serena lifted his hand and kissed his knuckles. Casimir felt an ache in his chest, her rejection and the bruise of the bullets twisting in an unfamiliar combination of pain.

Casimir was talking crazy. It must be the medications he had been given for his injuries. Serena couldn't run away. It was her duty to serve as queen. She had taken an oath to serve Acacia. Walking away now was unacceptable.

She tried to reach Warrington again on his phone. He wasn't answering. Rizari and Icarus continued to circle each other and it was a matter of time before one took a swipe at the other and catapulted their countries into a full-on war. She had heard Warrington accusing Icarus of sending the assassin. If he confirmed it, war was inevitable.

Since she was engaged to Samuel, she would be dragging Acacia into Rizari's war with Icarus. Would he consider that before declaring war on Icarus? Would he consult her?

She had too much work to do and she needed to stay on top of the military and political situation between Rizari and Icarus, but she couldn't leave Casimir alone in the beach house. He was resting and injured. Could she bring him to the castle?

Serena looked around the kitchen. She needed to fix Casimir a meal. Her cooking skills were rough, but she had the ingredients to make soup. As she chopped vegetables, she thought again about what he had said to her.

Run away with me.

As if it was that easy. As if she could pack a bag and take off with him. Where would they go? What would they do for money? What about Acacia?

Yet he had seemed so earnest and so serious. He struck her as a man who thought through plans. Maybe his injury had affected him. Or maybe he had been telling her the truth. She couldn't wrap her head around it.

An hour later, she had a serviceable vegetable stew. She carried two bowls, two spoons and two cups of juice upstairs on a tray.

She watched Casimir sleep for a few moments and briefly considered letting him sleep as long as he needed to. He sensed her in the room—his protective instinct wasn't completely quiet—and he rolled over. He'd removed the blood-pressure cuff and pulse oximeter. He wasn't wearing a shirt and the location where the bullet had struck his vest was red and turning blue in places.

"I brought some soup," she said.

"Smells great."

He shifted and she caught his wince. She set the tray on her dresser and stacked the pillows behind him to make him more comfortable. She heard a creak on the stairs. Casimir said nothing, but tensed.

She brought the tray to Casimir. "Relax. My guards are watching the house. It's just the house settling."

A man with brown hair and weasel eyes appeared in the room brandishing a gun. "Your guards aren't watching anything. Your guards are dead, darling."

Serena turned and knocked the tray of soup off the bed. It splashed to the ground, burning her legs. "Get out of here!"

Casimir rolled to his feet. Gone was any sign he was in pain. "Rolland, you don't need to do this."

Rolland, the man who had tried to kill Samuel Warrington earlier that night had found her home. Were her guards dead or was he bluffing? If they were alive, where were they?

Rolland inclined his head. "DeSante didn't tell me you were sleeping with the queen. I thought she was engaged to the king of Rizari."

DeSante had hired Rolland. Serena touched her bare ring finger and put as much distance between herself and Rolland as possible. He had a wild look in his eyes. She didn't have any weapons in her bedroom. Throwing a lamp at him might distract him for a moment, but it wouldn't be effective against a gun.

Casimir didn't have a weapon to defend them either. Could he talk his way out of this without anyone else getting hurt?

"A marriage to the king of Rizari is a bad idea. I plan to put a stop to it," Rolland said. "Killing Casimir will be a bonus. He royally screwed up my plans. Excuse the pun."

"I'm not marrying the king of Rizari," Serena said calmly.

Rolland nodded toward the dresser where her engagement ring was sitting. "That ginormous rock says otherwise. And you forget. I saw you say yes to him." Rolland lifted his gun at her.

Casimir launched himself at Rolland. The assassin fought back, pinning Casimir to the floor and whipping him across the face with the gun.

Serena was about to throw herself at Rolland when Casimir roared up from the floor, slamming Rolland into the footboard of the bed. Relief washed over her. Casimir seemed to be in control.

Casimir grabbed Rolland's hand, pounding it against the floor. The gun popped free and Serena scrambled to grab it. It felt heavy and awkward in her hands, but she held it straight out, in Rolland's direction.

"Don't move," she said.

Casimir climbed to his feet and came to her side, taking the gun from her. He was breathing hard and covered in sweat.

"Serena, call for an ambulance. Rolland needs one."

Santino rushed to Serena and hugged her close. The police were on the scene and Casimir was speaking to them. Serena was worried about Casimir being up and around with his injuries, but he was handling the questions about Rolland. The bodies of her four guards were being loaded into ambulances. Rolland hadn't been lying about that. Tonight four men had died protecting her.

Their sacrifice wouldn't be forgotten. She would contact their families soon and offer her condolences and what she could to help them.

"I was so worried when I heard," Santino said.

"Worried because you feared I was with Casimir?" It was an unfair statement, but she wasn't ready to forgive her uncle for the mammoth pressure he had put on her to marry King Warrington and what he had said about her and Casimir.

In the end, Santino had what he wanted. She and King Warrington were engaged and she would sign the union agreement soon enough.

"I was worried about you being with Casimir, but not in the manner you mean."

Her uncle cleared his throat and extended to her a large envelope. "I've had Casimir followed. He may not be who he claims. I thought you should have eyes wide-open about that man."

Serena took the envelope, not sure of her uncle's intent with his accusations. "Who do you think he is?"

Her uncle didn't answer. He pointed to the envelope.

She sighed her displeasure and pulled a stack of photographs from the envelope. A few were impossible to place, close-ups of Casimir shopping, a couple from the wedding in Elion, a few with Fiona close to him. "What are you angling at?"

"Do you think it's strange that Casimir is always around when you need someone to rescue you? First, your father's birthday party. At the symphony hall during your engagement and then tonight."

Serena shook her head. If her uncle was implying Casimir was an assassin targeting her, he was wrong. "Someone is targeting me and Casimir is staying close. He cares about me and wants me to be safe."

Her uncle reached into the stack and drew out one of the pictures from the bottom. It was a picture of Casimir speaking to Demetrius DeSante.

"Casimir has been social with DeSante. I've been to those same functions and seen them speaking."

Her uncle rocked back on his feet. "Serena, you are painfully dense. They are more than casual acquaintances and you need to speak with him about that."

Serena would ask him about the extent of his relationship with DeSante, but Casimir had proven himself loyal. She felt bad about questioning him. Rolland had implied that DeSante had sent him. Casimir would not be part of a plot like that; his life had been in danger, too.

Her uncle held up a recording device. "If the pictures don't convince you, then you need to listen to this."

Serena's stomach tensed. "What's on the recording?"

"It would be better for you to listen to the recording. I don't want to give you the wrong impression or confuse you with my interpretation of what I heard."

Serena tried to process yet another bomb of information.

"Do you want me to alert King Warrington that we have a situation? How much have you told Casimir Cullen about your plans for Acacia?"

Too many questions. Serena looked at the recording device. Should she ask Casimir about it first and give him a chance to explain? Or listen to the conversation and draw her own conclusions? Serena couldn't remember every word she had spoken to Casimir about Acacia. He had never told her he was friends with Demetrius DeSante and they behaved like near strangers when they were in each other's company.

At best, Casimir had been hiding something from her. At worst, he was conspiring against her with DeSante as his partner. Was it the reason DeSante had positioned himself close to Iliana?

Serena held up her hand, silencing her uncle. "Enough. Give me time. I need to think about this."

Santino nodded once, bowed slightly and left her alone on the porch. Shoulders heavy, she entered her house and closed the doors behind her. She could see Casimir through her front windows, speaking with the police.

He looked handsome and strong but what she might hear next could devastate her. Her heart ached. Could

Casimir have been fooling her this entire time? Was he involved with her because of a hidden agenda?

She had given her heart to Casimir. She was thinking of ways to be with him, to escape her marriage arrangement with King Warrington. Was her uncle right that she was naive and overtrusting?

Feeling as if she was betraying Casimir, she pressed Play.

Some static and then Casimir's voice clear and strong. "I understand."

A long pause, then Casimir's voice again.

"She knows it's a mistake, but she's in a difficult position."

A pause.

"I haven't wavered from our plans."

What plans? If Casimir was indeed talking to De-Sante, it sounded as if they were working together. Working together against her? Why? What did they want?

More static on the line and then the recording ended.

The recording didn't prove much to her. How could she be sure that Casimir had even been speaking to DeSante? The recording was from her uncle, so considering the source, she gave it some validity. Was Casimir talking about her marriage to Warrington? He had expressed to her that he didn't want her to marry the king. That was nothing new. But what were the plans he'd mentioned?

She called to question the past several days. She and Casimir had made love. Was that only to keep her and King Warrington from growing closer? Was Casimir giving her advice based on his loyalties to President De-Sante and whatever they were conspiring to do?

Anger swamped her, mixing with sadness. She needed answers and only Casimir had them. She strode out of the house, directly to Casimir.

Maybe it was the look on her face or the fact that she was shaking with anger, but the entire yard fell silent.

"Leave us," she said. She was looking at Casimir.

The police and others fell back.

His scent, heartbreakingly delicious, lingered on her skin, tantalizing her. She grappled for her resolve. Casimir needed to explain to her what was going on between him and DeSante.

"What's wrong?" he asked and extended his hand to touch her.

She moved out of his grasp. "I need to know something from you. Whatever you tell me had better be the truth."

If he was a liar who was worried about being caught doing something wrong, he hid it well. His face was impassive.

She handed him the pictures. He glanced at them. "You had me followed?"

No accusation or hurt in his voice. Had he expected it because he was a liar who knew the truth would one day come to light?

"Do you want to explain what it is you're doing?"

He looked at the pictures again. "What do you want to know?"

He was pretending nothing was wrong and it infuriated her. She held up the recorder. "I have a recording of you talking to the president of Icarus. Care to explain that?" She felt shaken and broken, but her anger urged her forward.

"May I listen to the recording?"

She had hoped he would deny talking to DeSante. "Why do you need to listen to it?" So he could figure out what she knew and what lies he could tell to keep her in the dark?

"I think you may be misinterpreting things or taking words out of context."

Her anger was hot and she struggled not to escalate the conversation into shouting at him. "Explain how you know President DeSante."

"He and I are friends."

That would have been important information on day one. "Friends? You're friends with him? Are you also friends with King Warrington? Doesn't that make you a traitor? This recording makes it sound like you work for DeSante." And that he was working for him in a task that involved her. "Did you know the assassin's name because you were part of the plan to kill Warrington? Were you part of the plot to kill my father?"

Casimir lifted his chin and squared his shoulders. "I had nothing to do with your father's or your sister's deaths. I work for myself. I am friends with Demetrius DeSante."

When faced with the truth, why was he holding back? "What are you two planning?"

Casimir clasped his hands in front of him.

Silence? Didn't she deserve more? "If you do not answer me, I will have you arrested." Though the idea of Casimir in a jail cell almost gutted her, she couldn't allow someone—even the man she was falling in love with—to conspire against her and Acacia.

Casimir's eyes narrowed slightly. "Serena, there are matters you don't fully understand and can't possibly know. I need your trust. I need you to trust me."

He was withholding information and keeping secrets and he wanted her trust? "I cannot trust you if you will not tell me everything." The words burned in her throat.

Hurt flickered in his eyes. "I cannot tell you everything. I have too much on the line."

She had wanted him to bring her into his confidence. "Deceiving me sits well with you?"

"My plans have nothing to do with you."

He could not have spoken more hurtful words. She had believed that they had some future together, however difficult it might seem. But he was making his own plans; he was carrying out his own agenda. "What arrangement have you made with the president of Icarus?"

He hedged. "I cannot tell you that except to reiterate I had no hand in killing your father or your sister."

She fought against the negative thoughts that clouded her: Casimir was using her. He had been using her from day one. She had made a terrible mistake in judgment by trusting him. Her uncle and her detractors had been right about her.

Those soul-sinking ideas were too easy to hold on to. She went for broke. "Do you have feelings for me?"

"Yes," Casimir said. Except his face was once again impassive. If he cared for her, wouldn't he scramble to make this right?

"Why did you come to Acacia?" she asked.

"The answer is complicated."

"Lies usually are."

He met her eyes, but didn't respond.

She threw her hands in the air. Her emotions were a tangled mess. "Say something to convince me that you aren't a liar and a coward and a thief." A thief who had stolen her heart.

"I have not stolen from you."

She wouldn't admit she had lost her heart to him. "You have taken a great deal from me."

"The less you know the better."

Now he was insulting her. "Why do people say that to me? Because you think I'm an idiot who can't handle the truth?"

Casimir extended his hand to touch her and she jerked away before he could.

He didn't try again. That she wanted him to spoke of the depth of her feelings for him.

"There is a history you don't understand. There are situations that have unfolded and I don't want you caught in the cross fire. Look what happened tonight because you were in the middle of DeSante and Warrington!" Casimir said.

"How noble of you to want to protect me," she said, letting the sarcasm drip from her voice.

"I have honorable intentions for you. I don't want to hurt you."

Yet he had. Deeply. "You can tell me the truth or you can be escorted from here by the police."

Casimir stared at the sky. "You are asking me to either drag you into a war or keep you from it."

"But haven't you heard, Casimir? There will be a war. Countries are choosing sides and I will be dragged into the middle of this no matter what I do next. The only thing I know, here and now, is that you are guilty of crimes against Acacia."

She summoned her police and pointed to Casimir. "Arrest him for espionage and treason against Acacia."

Her heart broke at the words, but she made sure her

face betrayed no emotion. She had finally mastered the
art of wearing her queen facade, but it wasn't a triumph.
She felt as if she had lost everything that was important.

Chapter 11

Serena paced in her office. Iliana was sitting on the window seat watching her.

"You have something to say. Say it," Serena said. She was in a foul mood and hated to take it out on Iliana.

"You need to talk to him to find the truth," Iliana said.

"I asked him for the truth and he refused to give it to me."

"Give him another chance."

Give another chance to the man who had conspired against her with President DeSante?

"Are you hearing this from DeSante?" Serena asked.

Iliana shook her head. "No, Serena. My loyalty is to you. First to you. You know that. I haven't spoken to DeSante about this."

The hurt in Iliana's voice struck her. "I'm sorry, Iliana."

Her cousin waved her hand dismissively. "Don't be.

I feel like a moron. I blew things with DeSante out of proportion. He was using me and I think that's never been clearer before now. Please, don't mention DeSante. I'll just feel more stupid."

Serena understood. It was how she felt when sorting through what had happened with Casimir. "What was Casimir trying to accomplish?" Was his agenda to influence her to ally herself with Icarus? Was there more to his motives? Had she given away anything, said anything in front of him that gave Icarus leverage over her?

She had been foolish to fall for Casimir's charms. The setup and everything he had said and done had been too perfect. He could have studied her for months.

"The only person who can answer that question is Casimir," Iliana said.

"He's been lying to me. Why tell the truth now?"

Iliana stood. "You're right. He doesn't have to. But he cares for you. He saved your life." She pressed her lips tightly together and sighed. "The way he looks at you and speaks to you. He can't be pretending all of it. So give him a chance to come clean. Then decide."

Serena's heart ached to talk to Casimir. War was on her doorstep. DeSante and Warrington were ready to pounce on each other. Now was her chance to find the truth and ally herself with the right side.

Perhaps Casimir knew something about Icarus and DeSante or Rizari and Warrington that was critical. As a queen, Serena needed to know what that was. As a woman, she needed to know how he felt about her.

Casimir was inside a jail cell in the castle, with bars on the windows and the door locked. He wanted to speak to Serena, explain who he was and what he wanted. Outside at the beach house, he had been caught off guard. He had been scared for her after what had happened with Rolland and he had shut down his emotions and tried to think like a king and not like a man who wanted to protect the woman he loved.

He needed to speak with her now.

Yet asking one of the guards to see or talk to her would rush her. Serena had a methodical approach to everything. She would think and then would come see him. He would wait.

Casimir didn't have to wait long. The lock on the door creaked open and Serena entered the room. He noticed a change in her. Her timidity was gone. He read anger and hurt in her eyes. She moved like a predator and he liked seeing her strength.

He stood from the bare metal cot where he'd been sitting.

Serena remained near the door. "You will not be given another chance to talk. Tell me everything."

Casimir kept his hands at his sides. He wanted to reach for her and draw her into his arms, assure her that he had no intention of hurting her. He didn't want to manipulate her.

He started with the truth, the simplest fact. "My name is Constantine Casimir Warrington the fourth."

He gave her a moment to digest his last name. Her eyes flickered with recognition.

"My first cousin on my father's side is Samuel Warrington. He inherited the throne from my father, but I am the rightful heir. My mother was forced to leave Rizari while she was pregnant with me. My father never knew I existed. Samuel killed my father and his father in a hunting accident he arranged. His mother is partly responsible for my mother's exile from Rizari. I want revenge on both of them. I want what is rightfully mine," Casimir said.

"You believe the throne should be yours?" she asked.

"Yes." He was encouraged that she didn't immediately call him a liar and storm out of the room.

"How did you become involved with Demetrius De-Sante?"

"My mother and I lived in Icarus after she was exiled from Rizari. When DeSante was a general in the Icarus military, I served under him for five years. I made a name for myself. I worked to become close to Demetrius, then I helped him topple the previous government and take over as president."

"He's a dictator," Serena said.

"Call him what you want. I told him the truth about who I am. He knows what I intended to do. He has been my ally in this matter because he knows that I will be a better king than Samuel. Better for Icarus and Acacia and Rizari."

She inclined her head. "What about me? What did you intend to do with me?"

"I didn't intend to hurt you. I came to your father's birthday party planning to kill Samuel Warrington. When my plans were interrupted by the assassination of your father, I realized I had an opportunity to find out what happened to my mother and my father and expose the truth."

"You planned to use me to do that?"

"Yes. But what's happened between us has been genuine. I didn't sleep with you to acquire information. I did it because I wanted you. Want you still."

He could read nothing on her face, but her knuckles were white from clasping her hands so hard.

He was getting to her and while he didn't want to use their chemistry to manipulate her, he ached for her. He ached to take her to bed. To make love to her and talk until they had cleared the air and she again looked at him with affection and respect. Would she ever look at him that way again?

He knelt at her feet. "I know you're hurt. I should have confided in you sooner."

She shook her head. "I can't trust you."

Her nipples were puckered under her blouse. It was strange to notice it now, but he was tuned in to her. "You can."

She shook her head. He would remember the look on her face for the rest of his life. Sadness, hurt and longing, all mixed into one.

"I need you to forgive me," he said.

"No." Her mouth said one thing, her body another. She reached for his shoulders and drew him closer.

"I want you, Serena. I'll always want you."

"What you want isn't relevant."

"Then tell me what you want and I will make it happen."

Serena narrowed her gaze on him. "You plan to take the throne from Warrington?"

"Yes. I will take the throne and expose him as a liar and a murderer."

"And then what? DeSante is spoiling for war."

"He is not spoiling for war. You have it mixed up. It's Warrington who wants war."

"If you become king of Rizari, you will make amends

to DeSante. Then you will release me from any obligation to Rizari. I will rule Acacia."

He nodded. "I can promise you peace and I have no quarrel with you ruling Acacia. I have told you before that you are the right woman for the job. I am glad that you've accepted it."

"Are you behind the assassination of my father and the attempts on my life?"

He had denied it before, but maybe she needed the words again. "No." The denial was immediate and adamant because it was the truth. The idea of hurting her was revolting to him. "I will never hurt you. If you trust me to do as I say I will, I will make it my goal to never, ever cause you pain again."

Serena closed her eyes for a long moment. "That is a promise you will keep, but only as the leader of Rizari. I will never again be yours in any way other than as the queen of Acacia."

The words burned through him, but Casimir wouldn't push now. He couldn't lose her, but it would take time. She was angry and lashing out. "I will need your help."

She tensed. "Now you want my forgiveness *and* my help?"

"To grow closer to King Warrington and expose his lies. To take my place as the rightful king."

He waited for her answer, knowing his plans hinged on her saying yes.

Serena understood anger. She understood wanting revenge for pain and loss. Her need to settle the score with whoever had killed her father and sister was dimmed by the overwhelming sense of grief that seemed to take up every spare inch of her emotional capacity.

She had to do what was right for herself and right for Acacia. Regardless of what Casimir had wanted, her country came first.

Serena entered her solarium, her head held high. Samuel and his mother were waiting for her. "Thank you for meeting me this morning."

Katarina took a sip of her tea and smiled thinly. "We are very busy and surprised by your invitation. After the assassination attempt on Samuel, we've been trying to stay out of the spotlight. Please explain what was so important that you must speak to us today."

Serena took her seat kitty-corner from Samuel and his mother and tried not to let Katarina's words annoy her. "I've read the merger agreement."

"I think you've found it's more than fair, given your position?" Samuel asked.

Serena laughed and shook her head. Samuel and Katarina exchanged looks. It was Serena's intention to set them off-kilter. "Not equitable at all. You have too many demands for me. You think I'm in the weaker position, but I have something that you need. I think this will make you feel more open to negotiations. Guards!"

Her guards escorted a handcuffed Casimir into the room. They stood on either side of him.

"What is this supposed to be? You're arresting your lover?" Samuel asked.

Serena clucked her tongue. "You misunderstand our relationship. I wanted to expose this man for the fraud he is. You know this man as Casimir Cullen. I've learned his identity is Constantine Casimir Warrington the fourth, rightful heir to the throne of Rizari." She took a moment to let Samuel and his mother chew on that before continuing. "If you want this information to remain between us, you will offer me better terms." She picked up her merger paperwork from the coffee table and handed it to Samuel. "You can read this over, but it's not negotiable. If you want Casimir in your custody, you will agree to do what I have spelled out in that document."

Katarina rose to her feet. "This man has no claim to the throne."

"The law of Rizari says otherwise."

"I'd heard rumors…but I thought they were just that," Katarina mumbled. She straightened. "That is ludicrous. You can't make demands. I will not let you destroy what we have worked for."

Serena inclined her head. "What is it that you've worked for exactly?"

Katarina narrowed her eyes on Serena. "You think you're so smart and you have it all figured out. I could kill you right now and no one would stop me."

Since both Casimir and her guards were in the room, she doubted that. "You would threaten me in my castle?"

"You seem fit to threaten the king of Rizari," Samuel said.

Katarina grabbed the gun from the guard to her left. She leveled it at Serena. "You've overplayed your hand. I have had more time to build allies. One very important ally who will swear that whatever I speak is truth. I won't cow to your threats. We will take this man, this fraud, as our prisoner and I will kill you to keep the truth silenced."

Confused by Katarina's declaration, Serena rose to her feet.

Santino entered the solarium. "Looks like I've arrived in time. Ladies, please. Let's not let this fly out of hand. Katarina, don't let your temper spoil our plans. We've worked far too long and hard to clear the way to allow a misstep to ruin us."

The familiarity between Uncle Santino and Katarina disturbed her. How did they know each other?

Katarina lowered the gun. "You have two minutes to convince me why I shouldn't kill your niece."

Santino glanced at Serena, his eyes flat and cold. "Because we can use her. Because if you kill her, the next heir is that twit Iliana. She is far less pliable and already close with Demetrius DeSante."

"Mother, what is this about? Someone had better tell me what's going on!" Samuel said.

Katarina held up her hand to her son. "Samuel, just shut up and let me handle this."

"Let you handle it like you handled killing King Alagona and Uncle Constantine? Like you killed my father? Like you killed Danae?" His rage was white-hot and Serena sensed he had known the truth, and it had been killing him.

"You monster!" Serena leapt onto Katarina, landing a punch across her face. The gun popped free and skidded across the floor. Casimir dove for it, his handcuffs swinging from his arm.

Casimir was now armed, as were her guards.

Before relief could settle on her, her guards turned their guns on Casimir. "Do not shoot him. He is not our enemy. Katarina is."

Santino came at Serena, grabbing her by the arm. "You little idiot! What game are you playing?"

"Let her go, Santino, or I will shoot you."

Santino threw her to the floor and whirled on Casimir. "You've made a grave miscalculation. The guards in this castle work for me. They always have. At my command, they will kill you before you have a chance to get a shot off. They've been following you at my direction. I knew you were more than a wealthy playboy. I was right. I should have had you killed weeks ago."

Katarina rose to her feet and appeared smug. "Everything I've done has been for my son and the good of Rizari. If that means I have to kill the queen of Acacia and her lover to clear the way, I have no problem with that."

"Enough! All of you!" Samuel said. "Danae was murdered because of you." He choked back a sob. "I won't allow this to go any further. I should have stopped you after she died. When she died, a piece of me did, too." Grief underscored every word.

Samuel had loved Danae. Seeing his behavior in that light shed nuances on his behavior and explained much of his distance and his treatment of her. Somehow, knowing he had loved Danae was a salve on that hurt.

"Don't be weak," Katarina said. "I've done this for you, Samuel, so you could be king."

"So you could have control of Rizari and use me to do it!" Samuel screamed. He picked up a crystal vase from the table next to him and swung it at Katarina. She screamed in pain as it shattered across her face.

Casimir aimed his gun at Santino. "As the rightful heir to the throne in Rizari, in union with the queen of Acacia, I command you to drop your weapons. You will be rewarded for your loyalty. Disobedience will be punished."

"Shoot him! Shoot him!" Santino screamed.

The guards exchanged confused looks. They didn't know whose direction to follow.

Casimir shot Santino in the knee and he dropped to the ground, screaming.

"Last warning!" Casimir said.

The guards laid their guns on the ground, raised their hands, and backed away.

Serena picked up the guns, never letting her eyes leave her uncle. Samuel sat on the couch and wept.

Santino was being loaded into an ambulance. He was handcuffed to his gurney. Katarina was being treated by another paramedic on the scene.

In exchange for a lesser sentence, Samuel was spilling everything he knew about his mother and Santino's plot to make him king.

Years earlier, his mother had driven a wedge between Casimir's parents, forcing Anna out of the country by accusing her of having an affair with the king's brother, Katarina's husband. Katarina had arranged for the murder of King Constantine and her husband while they were on a hunting trip.

Katarina had then planned the murder of King Alagona, hoping to put Samuel in a position of leadership and power when he married Danae, the heir apparent to the throne in Acacia. Danae's death had been an accident. The threats against Serena had been tools to scare her into agreeing to marry King Warrington and merge with Rizari.

Casimir had a legitimate claim to the throne and an investigation was under way to prove it. Demetrius DeSante and Casimir had already been working on building the case. The matter should be simple to verify.

When Casimir assumed power, Acacia, Rizari and Icarus would have true and stable peace in their region for the first time in a century. His mother would have peace in her heart.

Casimir strode toward Serena, his shoulders back, his head high. He looked regal and unburdened. "I want you to know that I will do everything I promised. I will support Acacia as an ally and you as the queen. I will make peace with Icarus."

Serena folded her hands in front of her to keep from reaching for him. "Thank you, Casimir. You have everything you want now." He would be king of his nation. Why didn't he seem happier? Was he masking his emotions to appear in control?

"Not everything I want." He knelt in front of her, taking her hands gently in his. "I was bent on seeking revenge. But I've discovered that, more than revenge, I want you. I want you in my life. I will do anything you ask if you will give me another chance. I will walk away from all of this. I'll live with you in Acacia and be your faithful servant."

He was offering to abandon everything he had worked for. "What about Rizari? What about the throne?"

"I will pass the crown to someone else." The ease with which he could give up his kingdom told her that she was far more important to him than she had believed.

She ran her fingertips down the side of his face. "Casimir, you can't do that. You can't walk away from Rizari. Your country needs you."

His eyes shone with longing. "What about you? Do you need me?"

She felt tears welling in her eyes. What was being offered to her was rare and precious. All she had to do was reach out and accept it. "I do need you. I want you at my side whether that's on the throne, on the beach or in bed."

"Come here," Casimir said, dragging her into his arms.

"Don't you have work to do?" she asked.

He pressed a kiss to her lips. "Never too much work for this. Never too much to take time to tell you that I love you."

"I love you, too, Casimir."

"Then will you do me the honor of marrying me and being my wife?"

Joy erupted in her heart. She didn't think she could have been happier until that moment. "Yes, I will marry you, Constantine."

He groaned. "No one calls me that."

"But you're the fourth in a line of kings. What would you think about starting a family and giving you a fifth?"

Casimir kissed her long and hard. "I've always loved how your mind works."

* * * * *

Don't miss these other suspenseful stories by C.J. Miller:

TAKEN BY THE CON
UNDER THE SHEIK'S PROTECTION
TRAITOROUS ATTRACTION
PROTECTING HIS PRINCESS

Available now from Harlequin Romantic Suspense!

*Read on for a sneak preview of FATAL AFFAIR,
the first book in the* FATAL *series by*
New York Times *bestselling author*
Marie Force

One

THE SMELL HIT him first.

"Ugh, what the hell is that?" Nick Cappuano dropped his keys into his coat pocket and stepped into the spacious, well-appointed Watergate apartment that his boss, Senator John O'Connor, had inherited from his father.

"Senator!" Nick tried to identify the foul metallic odor.

Making his way through the living room, he noticed parts and pieces of the suit John wore yesterday strewn over sofas and chairs, laying a path to the bedroom. He had called the night before to check in with Nick after a dinner meeting with Virginia's Democratic Party leadership, and said he was on his way home. Nick had reminded his thirty-six-year-old boss to set his alarm.

"Senator?" John hated when Nick called him that when they were alone, but Nick insisted the people in John's life afford him the respect of his title.

The odd stench permeating the apartment caused a tingle of anxiety to register on the back of Nick's neck. "John?"

He stepped into the bedroom and gasped. Drenched in blood, John sat up in bed, his eyes open but vacant. A knife spiked through his neck held him in place against the headboard. His hands rested in a pool of blood in his lap.

Gagging, the last thing Nick noticed before he bolted to the bathroom to vomit was that something was hanging out of John's mouth.

Once the violent retching finally stopped, Nick stood up on shaky legs, wiped his mouth with the back of his hand, and rested against the vanity, waiting to see if there would be more. His cell phone rang. When he didn't take the call, his pager vibrated. Nick couldn't find the wherewithal to answer, to say the words that would change everything. *The senator is dead. John's been murdered.* He wanted to go back to when he was still in his car, fuming and under the assumption that his biggest problem that day would be what to do about the man-child he worked for who had once again slept through his alarm.

Thoughts of John, dating back to their first meeting in a history class at Harvard freshman year, flashed through Nick's mind, hundreds of snippets spanning a nearly twenty-year friendship. As if to convince himself that his eyes had not deceived him, he leaned forward to glance into the bedroom, wincing at the sight of his best friend—the brother of his heart—stabbed through the neck and covered with blood.

Nick's eyes burned with tears, but he refused to give in to them. Not now. Later maybe, but not now. His phone rang again. This time he reached for it and saw it was Christina, his deputy chief of staff, but didn't take the call. Instead, he dialed 911.

Taking a deep breath to calm his racing heart and making a supreme effort to keep the hysteria out of his voice, he said, "I need to report a murder." He gave the address and stumbled into the living room to wait for the police, all the while trying to get his head around the image of his dead friend, a visual he already knew would haunt him forever.

Twenty long minutes later, two officers arrived, took a quick look in the bedroom and radioed for backup. Nick was certain neither of them recognized the victim.

He felt as if he was being sucked into a riptide, pulled further and further from the safety of shore, until drawing a breath became a laborious effort. He told the cops exactly what happened—his boss failed to show up for work, he came looking for him and found him dead.

"Your boss's name?"

"United States Senator John O'Connor." Nick watched the two young officers go pale in the instant before they made a second more urgent call for backup.

"Another scandal at the Watergate," Nick heard one of them mutter.

His cell phone rang yet again. This time he reached for it.

"Yeah," he said softly.

"Nick!" Christina cried. "Where the *hell* are you guys? Trevor's having a heart attack!" She referred to their communications director, who had back-to-back interviews scheduled for the senator that morning.

"He's dead, Chris."

"Who's dead? What're you talking about?"

"John."

Her soft cry broke his heart. *"No."* That she was desperately in love with John was no secret to Nick. That she was also a consummate professional who would never act on those feelings was one of the many reasons Nick respected her.

"I'm sorry to just blurt it out like that."

"How?" she asked in a small voice.

"Stabbed in his bed."

Her ravaged moan echoed through the phone. "But who… I mean, *why*?"

"The cops are here, but I don't know anything yet. I need you to request a postponement on the vote."

"I can't," she said, adding in a whisper, "I can't think about that right now."

"You have to, Chris. That bill is his legacy. We can't let all his hard work be for nothing. Can you do it? For him?"

"Yes…okay."

"You have to pull yourself together for the staff, but don't tell them yet. Not until his parents are notified."

"Oh, God, his poor parents. You should go, Nick. It'd be better coming from you than cops they don't know."

"I don't know if I can. How do I tell people I love that their son's been murdered?"

"He'd want it to come from you."

"I suppose you're right. I'll see if the cops will let me."

"What're we going to do without him, Nick?" She posed a question he'd been grappling with himself. "I just can't imagine this world, this *life*, without him."

"I can't either," Nick said, knowing it would be a much different life without John O'Connor at the center of it.

"He's really dead?" she asked as if to convince herself it wasn't a cruel joke. "Someone killed him?"

"Yes."

Outside the chief's office suite, Detective Sergeant Sam Holland smoothed her hands over the toffee-colored hair she corralled into a clip for work, pinched some color into cheeks that hadn't seen the light of day in weeks, and adjusted her gray suit jacket over a red scoop-neck top.

Taking a deep breath to calm her nerves and settle her chronically upset stomach, she pushed open the door and stepped inside. Chief Farnsworth's receptionist greeted her with a smile. "Go right in, Sergeant Holland. He's waiting for you."

Great, Sam thought as she left the receptionist with a weak smile. Before she could give in to the urge to turn tail and run, she erased the grimace from her face and went in.

"Sergeant." The chief, a man she'd once called Uncle Joe, stood up and came around the big desk to greet her with a firm handshake. His gray eyes skirted over her with concern and sympathy, both of which were new since "the incident." She despised being the reason for either. "You look well."

"I feel well."

"Glad to hear it." He gestured for her to have a seat. "Coffee?"

"No, thanks."

Pouring himself a cup, he glanced over his shoulder. "I've been worried about you, Sam."

"I'm sorry for causing you worry and for disgracing the department." This was the first chance she'd had to speak directly to him since she returned from a month of administrative leave, during which she'd practiced the sentence over and over. She thought she'd delivered it with convincing sincerity.

"Sam," he sighed as he sat across from her, cradling his mug between big hands. "You've done nothing to disgrace yourself or the department. Everyone makes mistakes."

"Not everyone makes mistakes that result in a dead child, Chief."

He studied her for a long, intense moment as if he was making some sort of decision. "Senator John O'Connor was found murdered in his apartment this morning."

"Jesus," she gasped. "How?"

"I don't have all the details, but from what I've been told so far, it appears he was dismembered and stabbed through the neck. Apparently, his chief of staff found him."

"Nick," she said softly.

"Excuse me?"

"Nick Cappuano is O'Connor's chief of staff."

"You know him?"

"Knew him. Years ago," she added, surprised and unsettled to discover the memory of him still had power over her, that just the sound of his name rolling off her lips could make her heart race.

"I'm assigning the case to you."

Surprised at being thrust so forcefully back into the real work she had craved since her return to duty, she couldn't help but ask, "Why me?"

"Because you need this, and so do I. We both need a win."

The press had been relentless in its criticism of him, of her, of the department, but to hear him acknowledge it made her ache. Her father had come up through the ranks with Farnsworth, which was probably the number one reason why she still had a job. "Is this a test?

Find out who killed the senator and my previous sins are forgiven?"

He put down his coffee cup and leaned forward, elbows resting on knees. "The only person who needs to forgive you, Sam, is you."

Infuriated by the surge of emotion brought on by his softly spoken words, Sam cleared her throat and stood up. "Where does O'Connor live?"

"The Watergate. Two uniforms are already there. Crime scene is on its way." He handed her a slip of paper with the address. "I don't have to tell you that this needs to be handled with the utmost discretion."

He also didn't have to tell her that this was the only chance she'd get at redemption.

"Won't the Feds want in on this?"

"They might, but they don't have jurisdiction, and they know it. They'll be breathing down my neck, though, so report directly to me. I want to know everything ten minutes after you do. I'll smooth it with Stahl," he added, referring to the lieutenant she usually answered to.

Heading for the door, she said, "I won't let you down."

"You never have before."

With her hand resting on the door handle, she turned back to him. "Are you saying that as the chief of police or as my Uncle Joe?"

His face lifted into a small but sincere smile. "Both."

Two

SITTING ON JOHN'S sofa under the watchful eyes of the two policemen, Nick's mind raced with the staggering number of things that needed to be done, details to be seen to, people to call. His cell phone rang relentlessly, but he ignored it after deciding he would talk to no one until he had seen John's parents. Almost twenty years ago they took an instant shine to the hard-luck scholarship student their son brought home from Harvard for a weekend visit and made him part of their family. Nick owed them so much, not the least of which was hearing the news of their son's death from him if possible.

He ran his hand through his hair. "How much longer?"

"Detectives are on their way."

Ten minutes later, Nick heard her before he saw her. A flurry of activity and a burst of energy preceded the detectives' entrance into the apartment. He suppressed a groan. *Wasn't it enough that his friend and boss had been murdered? He had to face* her, *too? Weren't there thousands of District cops? Was she really the only one available?*

Sam came into the apartment, oozing authority and competence. In light of her recent troubles, Nick couldn't believe she had any of either left. "Get some tape across that door," she ordered one of the officers.

"Start a log with a timeline of who got here when. No one comes in or goes out without my okay, got it?"

"Yes, ma'am. The Patrol sergeant is on his way along with Deputy Chief Conklin and Detective Captain Malone."

"Let me know when they get here." Without so much as a glance in his direction, Nick watched her stalk through the apartment and disappear into the bedroom. Following her, a handsome young detective with bed head nodded to Nick.

He heard the murmur of voices from the bedroom and saw a camera flash. They emerged fifteen minutes later, both noticeably paler. For some reason, Nick was gratified to know the detectives working the case weren't so jaded as to be unaffected by what they'd just seen.

"Start a canvass of the building," Sam ordered her partner. "Where the hell is Crime Scene?"

"Hung up at another homicide," one of the other officers replied.

She finally turned to Nick, nothing in her pale blue eyes indicating that she recognized or remembered him. But the fact that she didn't introduce herself or ask for his name told him she knew exactly who he was. "We'll need your prints."

"They're on file," he mumbled. "Congressional background check."

She wrote something in the small notebook she tugged from the back pocket of gray, form-fitting pants. There were years on her gorgeous face that hadn't been there the last time he'd had the opportunity to look closely, and he couldn't tell if her hair was as long as it used to be since it was twisted into a clip. The curvy body and endless legs hadn't changed at all.

"No forced entry," she noted. "Who has a key?"

"Who *doesn't* have a key?"

"I'll need a list. You have a key, I assume."

Nick nodded. "That's how I got in."

"Was he seeing anyone?"

"No one serious, but he had no trouble attracting female companionship." Nick didn't add that John's casual approach to women and sex had been a source of tension between the two men, with Nick fearful that John's social life would one day lead to political trouble. He hadn't imagined it might also lead to murder.

"When was the last time you saw him?"

"When he left the office for a dinner meeting with the Virginia Democrats last night. Around six-thirty or so."

"Spoke to him?"

"Around ten when he said he was on his way home."

"Alone?"

"He didn't say, and I didn't ask."

"Take me through what happened this morning."

He told her about Christina trying to reach John, beginning at seven, and of coming to the apartment expecting to find the senator once again sleeping through his alarm.

"So this has happened before?"

"No, he's never been murdered before."

Her expression was anything but amused. "Do you think this is funny, Mr. Cappuano?"

"Hardly. My best friend is dead, Sergeant. A United States senator has been murdered. There's nothing funny about that."

"Which is why you need to answer the questions and save the droll humor for a more appropriate time."

Chastened, Nick said, "He slept through his alarm and ringing telephones at least once, if not twice, a month."

"Did he drink?"

"Socially, but I rarely saw him drunk."

"Prescription drugs? Sleeping pills?"

Nick shook his head. "He was just a very heavy sleeper."

"And it fell to his chief of staff to wake him up? There wasn't anyone else you could send?"

"The senator valued his privacy. There've been occasions when he wasn't alone, and neither of us felt his love life should be the business of his staff."

"But he didn't care if you knew who he was sleeping with?"

"He knew he could count on my discretion." He looked up, unprepared for the punch to the gut that occurred when his eyes met hers. Her unsettled expression made him wonder if she felt it, too. "His parents need to be notified. I'd like to be the one to tell them."

Sam studied him for a long moment. "I'll arrange it. Where are they?"

"At their farm in Leesburg. It needs to be soon. We're postponing a vote we worked for months to get to. It'll be all over the news that something's up."

"What's the vote for?"

He told her about the landmark immigration bill and John's role as the co-sponsor.

With a curt nod, she walked away.

AN HOUR LATER, Nick was a passenger in an unmarked Metropolitan Police SUV, headed west to Leesburg with

Sam at the wheel. She'd left her partner with a staggering list of instructions and insisted on accompanying Nick to tell John's parents.

"Do you need something to eat?"

He shook his head. No way could he even think about eating—not with the horrific task he had ahead of him. Besides, his stomach hadn't recovered from the earlier bout of vomiting.

"You know, we could still call the Loudoun County Police or the Virginia State Police to handle this," she said for the second time.

"No."

After an awkward silence, she said, "I'm sorry this happened to your friend and that you had to see him that way."

"Thank you."

"Are you going to answer that?" she asked of his relentless cell phone.

"No."

"How about you turn it off then? I can't stand listening to a ringing phone."

Reaching for his belt, he grabbed his cell phone, his emotions still raw after watching John be taken from his apartment in a body bag. Before he shut the cell phone off, he called Christina.

"Hey," she said, her voice heavy with relief and emotion. "I've been trying to reach you."

"Sorry." Pulling his tie loose and releasing his top button, he cast a sideways glance at Sam, whose warm, feminine fragrance had overtaken the small space inside the car. "I was dealing with cops."

"Where are you now?"

"On my way to Leesburg."

"God," Christina sighed. "I don't envy you that. Are you okay?"

"Never better."

"I'm sorry. Dumb question."

"It's okay. Who knows what we're supposed to say or do in this situation. Did you postpone the vote?"

"Yes, but Martin and McDougal are having an apoplexy," she said, meaning John's co-sponsor on the bill and the Democratic majority leader. "They're demanding to know what's going on."

"Hold them off. Another hour. Maybe two. Same thing with the staff. I'll give you the green light as soon as I've told his parents."

"I will. Everyone knows something's up because the Capitol Police posted an officer outside John's office and won't let anyone in there."

"It's because the cops are waiting for a search warrant," Nick told her.

"Why do they need a warrant to search the victim's office?"

"Something about chain of custody with evidence and pacifying the Capitol Police."

"Oh, I see. I was thinking we should have Trevor draft a statement so we're ready."

"That's why I called."

"We'll get on it." She sounded relieved to have something to do.

"Are you okay with telling Trevor? Want me to do it?"

"I think I can do it, but thanks for asking."

"How're you holding up?" he asked.

"I'm in total shock…all that promise and potential

just gone…" She began to weep again. "It's going to hurt like hell when the shock wears off."

"Yeah," he said softly. "No doubt."

"I'm here if you need anything."

"Me, too, but I'm going to shut the phone off for a while. It's been ringing nonstop."

"I'll email the statement to you when we have it done."

"Thanks, Christina. I'll call you later." Nick ended the call and took a look at his recent email messages, hardly surprised by the outpouring of dismay and concern over the postponement of the vote. One was from Senator Martin himself—What the fuck is going on, Cappuano?

Sighing, he turned off the cell phone and dropped it into his coat pocket.

"Was that your girlfriend?" Sam asked, startling him.

"No, my deputy."

"Oh."

Wondering what she was getting at, he added, "We work closely together. We're good friends."

"Why are you being so defensive?"

"What's your *problem*?" he asked.

"I don't have a problem. You're the one with problems."

"So all that great press you've been getting lately hasn't been a problem for you?"

"Why, Nick, I didn't realize you cared."

"I don't."

"Yes, you made that very clear."

He spun halfway around in the seat to stare at her. "*Are you for real?* You're the one who didn't return any of my calls."

She glanced over at him, her face flat with surprise. "What calls?"

After staring at her in disbelief for a long moment, he settled back in his seat and fixed his eyes on the cars sharing the Interstate with them.

A few minutes passed in uneasy silence.

"What calls, Nick?"

"I called you," he said softly. "For days after that night, I tried to reach you."

"I didn't know," she stammered. "No one told me."

"It doesn't matter now. It was a long time ago." But if his reaction to seeing her again after six years of thinking about her was any indication, it *did* matter. It mattered a lot.

Continue reading Sam and Nick's story
in FATAL AFFAIR, available in print and ebook
from Carina Press.

Copyright © 2010 by Marie Sullivan Force

COMING NEXT MONTH FROM

HARLEQUIN®

ROMANTIC suspense

Available October 6, 2015

#1867 SECOND CHANCE COLTON

The Coltons of Oklahoma • by Marie Ferrarella

Detective Ryan Colton didn't know that when he set out to prove his sister's innocence, the forensics expert proving her guilt was the woman he'd loved and lost many years ago. This is one fight they'll never forget...

#1868 THE PROFESSIONAL

Dangerous in Dallas • by Addison Fox

When Violet Richardson is kidnapped by the man who has been terrorizing her from the shadows for weeks, it's up to ex-military man Max Baldwin to rescue and protect her from a heist gone horribly wrong.

#1869 HER MASTER DEFENDER

To Protect and Serve • by Karen Anders

It's hate at first sight between agent Amber Dalton and marine Tristan Michaels while investigating a murder, but soon a horrific evil hunts them through the frigid Sierra Nevada mountains, where they must depend on each other to survive.

#1870 LIAM'S WITNESS PROTECTION

Man on a Mission • by Amelia Autin

Bodyguard Liam Jones must shield eyewitness Cate Mateja while she attempts to testify against a human-trafficking organization. It's only a matter of time before danger—and a lethal attraction—takes over his mission.

YOU CAN FIND MORE INFORMATION ON UPCOMING HARLEQUIN® TITLES, FREE EXCERPTS AND MORE AT WWW.HARLEQUIN.COM.

HRSCNM0915

REQUEST YOUR FREE BOOKS!

2 FREE NOVELS PLUS 2 FREE GIFTS!

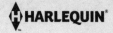

ROMANTIC suspense

Sparked by danger, fueled by passion

YES! Please send me 2 FREE Harlequin® Romantic Suspense novels and my 2 FREE gifts (gifts are worth about $10). After receiving them, if I don't wish to receive any more books, I can return the shipping statement marked "cancel." If I don't cancel, I will receive 4 brand-new novels every month and be billed just $4.74 per book in the U.S. or $5.49 per book in Canada. That's a savings of at least 12% off the cover price! It's quite a bargain! Shipping and handling is just 50¢ per book in the U.S. and 75¢ per book in Canada.* I understand that accepting the 2 free books and gifts places me under no obligation to buy anything. I can always return a shipment and cancel at any time. Even if I never buy another book, the two free books and gifts are mine to keep forever.

240/340 HDN GH3P

Name   (PLEASE PRINT)

Address   Apt. #

City   State/Prov.   Zip/Postal Code

Signature (if under 18, a parent or guardian must sign)

Mail to the **Reader Service**:

IN U.S.A.: P.O. Box 1867, Buffalo, NY 14240-1867
IN CANADA: P.O. Box 609, Fort Erie, Ontario L2A 5X3

Want to try two free books from another line?
Call 1-800-873-8635 or visit www.ReaderService.com.

* Terms and prices subject to change without notice. Prices do not include applicable taxes. Sales tax applicable in N.Y. Canadian residents will be charged applicable taxes. Offer not valid in Quebec. This offer is limited to one order per household. Not valid for current subscribers to Harlequin Romantic Suspense books. All orders subject to credit approval. Credit or debit balances in a customer's account(s) may be offset by any other outstanding balance owed by or to the customer. Please allow 4 to 6 weeks for delivery. Offer available while quantities last.

Your Privacy—The Reader Service is committed to protecting your privacy. Our Privacy Policy is available online at www.ReaderService.com or upon request from the Reader Service.

We make a portion of our mailing list available to reputable third parties that offer products we believe may interest you. If you prefer that we not exchange your name with third parties, or if you wish to clarify or modify your communication preferences, please visit us at www.ReaderService.com/consumerchoice or write to us at Reader Service Preference Service, P.O. Box 9062, Buffalo, NY 14240-9062. Include your complete name and address.

HRS15

SPECIAL EXCERPT FROM

Ⓗ HARLEQUIN®

ROMANTIC suspense

*Can this Colton cowboy save his wife—and his
beloved ranch—when a killer threatens everything
they hold dear?*

Read on for a sneak preview of
PROTECTING THE COLTON BRIDE
by New York Times *bestselling author*
Elle James,
the fourth book in the 2015
COLTONS OF WYOMING *continuity.*

"Why don't we get married?"

Even though she'd known it was coming, it still hit her square in the chest. The air rushed from her lungs and a tsunami of feelings washed over her. A surge of joy made her heart beat so fast she felt faint. She crested that wave and slid into the undertow of reality. "A marriage of convenience?"

"Exactly." Daniel reached for her hands.

When she hid them behind her back, he dropped his arms. "It wouldn't have to be forever. Just long enough to satisfy the stipulations of your grandmother's will and save your horses, and that would help me get past the Kennedy gauntlet. We could leave tomorrow, spend a night in Vegas, find a chapel and it would be over in less than five minutes."

With her heart smarting, Megan forced a shaky smile. "Way to sweep a girl off her feet."

He waved his hand and Halo tossed her head. "If you want, I can make an official announcement in front of my family."

Megan shook her head. "No."

"No, you won't marry me?"

"No." She pushed past him to pace down the center of the barn. "Your plan is insane."

"Do you have a better one?" he asked. "I'm all ears."

The plan was the same as the one she'd been thinking of before Daniel had woken up. Only when she'd dreamed it up, it didn't sound as cold and impersonal as Daniel's proposal. Somewhere in the back of her mind she'd hoped that marriage to Daniel would be something more than one of convenience.

After yesterday's kiss, she wasn't sure she could be around Daniel for long periods of time without wanting another. And another.

Don't miss
PROTECTING THE COLTON BRIDE
by New York Times *bestselling author Elle James,*
available September 2015

www.Harlequin.com

Copyright © 2015 by Harlequin Books S.A.

Limited time offer!

$1.⁰⁰ OFF

Mixing romance and politics can be fatal in the *New York Times* bestselling *Fatal Series* by

MARIE FORCE

Fall for fast-paced political intrigue, gritty suspense and a romance that makes headlines.

Save $1.00 on any one book in The Fatal Series!

carina press™

www.CarinaPress.com
www.TheFatalSeries.com

$1.⁰⁰ OFF
the purchase price of any book in *The Fatal Series* by Marie Force.

Offer valid from September 1, 2015, to October 5, 2015. Redeemable at participating retail outlets. Limit one coupon per purchase. Valid in the USA and Canada only.

52612998

Canadian Retailers: Harlequin Enterprises Limited will pay the face value of this coupon plus 10.25¢ if submitted by customer for this product only. Any other use constitutes fraud. Coupon is nonassignable. Void if taxed, prohibited or restricted by law. Consumer must pay any government taxes. Void if copied. Inmar Promotional Services ("IPS") customers submit coupons and proof of sales to Harlequin Enterprises Limited, P.O. Box 3000, Saint John, NB E2L 4L3, Canada. Non-IPS retailer—for reimbursement submit coupons and proof of sales directly to Harlequin Enterprises Limited, Retail Marketing Department, 225 Duncan Mill Rd., Don Mills, Ontario M3B 3K9, Canada.

5 65373 00076 2   (8100)0 12091

U.S. Retailers: Harlequin Enterprises Limited will pay the face value of this coupon plus 8¢ if submitted by customer for this product only. Any other use constitutes fraud. Coupon is nonassignable. Void if taxed, prohibited or restricted by law. Consumer must pay any government taxes. Void if copied. For reimbursement submit coupons and proof of sales directly to Harlequin Enterprises Limited, P.O. Box 880478, El Paso, TX 88588-0478, U.S.A. Cash value 1/100 cents.

® and ™ are trademarks owned and used by the trademark owner and/or its licensee.

© 2015 Harlequin Enterprises Limited

CARMF00257COUP

Turn your love of reading into rewards you'll love with
Harlequin My Rewards

Join for FREE today at
www.HarlequinMyRewards.com

Earn **FREE BOOKS** of your choice.

Experience **EXCLUSIVE OFFERS** and contests.

Enjoy **BOOK RECOMMENDATIONS**
selected just for you.

PLUS! Sign up now
and get **500** points
right away!

Earn
FREE
REWARDS
HarlequinMyRewards.com
Join
Today!

MYR16R

THE WORLD IS BETTER WITH

Romance

Harlequin has everything from contemporary, passionate and heartwarming to suspenseful and inspirational stories.

Whatever your mood, we have a romance just for you!

Connect with us to find your next great read, special offers and more.

f /HarlequinBooks

🐦 @HarlequinBooks

www.HarlequinBlog.com

www.Harlequin.com/Newsletters

H HARLEQUIN®

A *Romance* FOR EVERY MOOD™

www.Harlequin.com

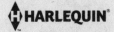

SERIESHALOAD2015